take me i'm yours

A FORBIDDEN ROMANCE

LILI VALENTE

take me i'm yours

By Lili Valente

about the book

He's my ex-boyfriend's father, my dad's former business partner, and probably the most forbidden man on earth...at least as far as I'm concerned.

But when we first meet, Gideon is just a heroic pilot saving three sweet puppies from a kill shelter, and I'm the lucky woman who keeps him safe from the storm one night.

A night that turns into the hottest of my life...

Losing my virginity to a sexy older man who seems to instinctively know how much I love to be called his "good girl," isn't on my summer Bingo card, but I'm so grateful for the memory.

Memories are all I'll ever have of Gideon. Our lives are going in different directions, and I doubt I'll ever see him again.

But Fate has other plans...

Just a month later, I run into Gideon at my ex-boyfriend's fundraising party. Only he isn't there as a donor. He's there as a supportive *parent.*

We realize our scandalous connection and swear to stay away from each other while he's in town on business.

Only we can't seem to keep our hands to ourselves, no matter how hard we try.

Soon, I'm spending my nights in his penthouse, falling deeper under his erotic spell, and perhaps even more dangerously…losing my heart to this magnetic man.

But what happens when the real word comes crashing in all around us? Will the man I love still want to call me His?

To The Guy. Thanks for your sweetness.

A very good girl...

"Good girl..." His deep voice vibrates my ribs as he kisses his way between my breasts, making my nipples tighten into aching points that beg for his touch.

But I don't make a sound. He told me to be quiet until I come, and I'm determined to show him I can play this game.

I can play it better than anyone he's played with before because I've had *so much* practice. In a strange way, it feels like my entire life has been leading up to this moment.

I've always been a "good girl."

When Samantha George pulled the other kids aside in third grade to tell them about S-E-X, I hid under the slide with my hands over my ears. In high school, while the cool girls slipped up to the roof to smoke cigarettes, I headed to the library to squeeze in extra study time.

I've never skipped class, played sick to get out of a social obligation, or paraphrased a source in a paper that wasn't credited in my bibliography. I don't speed, waited until I was twenty-one to have my first glass of wine, and have my holiday cards written a full month in advance every year. I graduated college with a 4.15, made the honor roll every semester, and won multiple "outstanding campus citizen" and "environmental ally" awards along the way.

But no matter how many awards I've won or benchmarks I've hit; I've never felt good *enough*. There was always another rung on the ladder, another goal to achieve, another person working even harder than I was, making me ashamed of myself for thinking I'd achieved anything at all.

There was always my father, standing on the sidelines, looking unimpressed, no matter how hard I tried…

It isn't until this moment, with a near stranger's mouth between my legs, driving me wild as he tells me how sweet I taste and what a good job I'm doing at staying silent that I finally feel like I've made it.

I'm not just a good girl, I'm the *best* girl.

I'm a champion of erotic endurance who comes with a silent scream as the sexiest man I've ever met curls two fingers deep inside me.

"Yes, Sydney," he murmurs. "Fuck, you're so beautiful when you come. So perfect, so wet." He curses again, this time beneath his breath. "I can't wait to be inside you. Can you feel how you're drenching my hand, butterfly?"

I press my lips more tightly together, refusing to do so much as moan until he's given me permission, even if the sight of him rising between my legs, his cock a thick column behind the fabric of his boxer briefs, makes a hundred needy sounds rise in my throat.

"Tell me, baby. You can talk," he says. "Are you ready?"

"Yes," I gasp as I reach for his chest. "Yes, please."

He pulls his boxers down around his thighs, and I get my first good look at his cock. It's long and thicker than any I've seen before, with a plush mushroom top that I find completely...beautiful.

I've never found a penis beautiful before.

Interesting, yes. Amusing? Also yes, thanks to my high school boyfriend's slightly crooked one and a bad case of "first time on third base" jitters.

But this man's body is so much more than interesting and not the slightest bit amusing. When he whispers, "Spread your legs for me. Show me every inch of you," I don't hesitate for a second.

I obey, and he rewards me with a husky, "Good girl," that has me on the verge of coming a second time, even before he slides on the condom and grips the thick base of his cock.

In that moment, I know I'll never think of that phrase the same way again.

And that I *very* much want to be this man's *very* good girl...

one

Sydney Perry-Watson
*A woman about to meet
the most forbidden, off-limits man...*

A few hours earlier...

"**M**y turn! My turn! I get to pick the book this
time." Elaina, my best friend in Sea
Breeze, Maine, plops down on the overstuffed couch beside me in her cozy café.

Instantly, three cats vie for the chance at her lap.

Most of the kitties at Sweet Pussy Cat Café are up
for adoption, but it's hard to imagine any of them will-
ingly leaving Elaina's side. She's not just their mama,
she's their fairy godmother and cat-whisperer extraor-
dinaire.

I swear, the woman speaks feline, a fact she proves by making a soothing sound low in her throat that sends two of the cats scurrying off to play, while the smallest, a black cat named Maybe, leaps onto the couch beside her.

She swoops the tiny beast into her arms and cuddles him close, setting off a surprisingly deep purr that makes the rest of us smile.

"Aw, he's such a lover," Maya coos from the couch across from ours, where she's stroking Pudge, a giant orange tabby who's busy falling asleep on her lap.

"He is." Elaina kisses the top of Maybe's head. "And he gives the best kisses."

"Gah, I want him so badly." Gertie looks up from the floor, where she's teasing two gray kittens with a piece of fluff tied to the end of a stick.

"Too bad your gramps is allergic," Elaina says.

Gertie snorts. "Is he, though? Or is he just a cranky old lobster fisherman who wants to make sure his granddaughter ends up in a toxic relationship with the sea like the rest of the family? I'm tempted to sneak a cat into my room for a week and see what happens."

Maya's eyes go wide. "But what if Gramps goes into anaphylactic shock or something? You know the closest hospital is—"

"Nearly an hour away," we all echo in unison, laughing when Maya's freckled nose wrinkles.

She's the hypochondriac of our friend group, but she comes by it honestly. Every member of her large family has one odd medical condition or another. Nothing too serious, but serious enough that she had to make that hour-long drive to the hospital dozens of times growing up.

She hitches her chin higher. "I was just trying to help."

Gertie squeezes Maya's knee through her flowered skirt. "And we were just kidding. Gramps will be fine. He's not *that* allergic or he wouldn't go over to Aunt Cathy's for Christmas, even with all the cats out in the garage." She sighs. "I'll probably be too tired to try it anyway. He's had me out on the boat at three-forty-five every morning this summer. If we aren't on the water before the Tripp boys, he loses his shit and blasts that horrible Moby Dick audiobook over the loudspeaker all day." She yawns and runs a hand through her wild, sandy blond hair. "I can barely stay awake through dinner, let alone give a new pet the love and attention it needs."

"Well, there's no rush," Elaina says. "Maybe will be here for a while. People tend to shy away from adopting black cats. They think they're unlucky or evil or something."

My jaw drops. "Really?"

She nods. "Really. It took six months for Shadow to be adopted. Same with Nightfall. Not a lot of black cat lovers in the world."

"Wow." I blink, truly shocked. "That's wild. And sad. I guess more people are living in the Dark Ages than I thought."

People like my father, a man who insisted running

marathons was bad for a woman's reproductive system so many times, my mom stopped running before I was born, leading to a diet pill addiction that probably didn't do her reproductive system any favors.

I shake my head and sip my London fog tea with a hint of whiskey.

I'm not going to think about Dad right now. I'm not going to think about any of the stressful people or things waiting for me in New York. I'm on Maine time for another ten days and I intend to enjoy every second of it.

Out here, at the edge of the world, surrounded by seabirds and rare butterflies and friends who have no idea I'm heir to a global real estate empire, I can relax and just...be.

Be with friends.

Be with nature.

Be with the still, peaceful part of myself that's so much wiser than my perfectionist side. The part that knows I'm enough, just the way I am, even if I fail to become the epic girl boss my father is determined to coax out of me before I turn twenty-five.

Silas Atticus Perry-Watson is ready to retire and has allotted one year to teach his daughter everything she needs to know about captaining a worldwide real estate conglomerate and vast charitable trust. Dad figures that since I graduated top of my class, with honors, training me to take over should be a piece of cake.

But the man has had servants cooking for him his entire life. (Before he was a Perry-Watson, he was one of the shipping empire Watsons, with family roots in

New York stretching back to the eighteenth century and the fortune to equal his perfect pedigree.) Dad has no idea how complicated cakes can be. Elaina makes one with seven different rainbow layers that takes half a day to bake, assemble, and ice. (And Elaina has a knack for baking that rivals her way with cats.)

Despite my excellent grades and much-lauded thesis on the benefits of sustainable, heat-resistant construction in a warming world, I have zero experience with running a business in real life. Especially one with tens of thousands of employees and a GDP the size of a small country.

There's an excellent chance I'm about to crash and burn.

Speaking of crashing and burning—or hopefully *not* crashing and burning—I glance at the cuckoo clock above the cat climbing structure on the opposite wall.

Nearly six.

The Pilots for a Paws coordinator said she would call by six if she needed help. She must have found someone else to pick up the pilot in distress. As much as I love book club time, I can't help but feel a little disappointed. I've been a volunteer for the organization for two years, but all I've had the opportunity to give is money. I'm happy to donate, of course, but I'm a hands-on girl. I want to help save puppies with my boots on the ground.

And I wouldn't have minded meeting a heroic pilot who volunteers his time and private plane to save animals from kill shelters. I've sworn off men for at least the next five years—I'm going to be way too busy for dating—but that doesn't mean a girl can't look.

"Speaking of the Dark Ages," Elaina says, stroking a still purring Maybe. "Did I tell you that Mrs. Spiegel is back on the warpath again? She's lobbying the town council to shut me down until I change the café's name to something more 'family friendly.' Ugh."

Gertie rolls her eyes. "God, when is that woman going to give it a rest? You've been open almost three years."

"I know," Elaina says with a baffled shake of her head. "Who knew people would get so upset over the name of a cat café?"

Maya hums. "Um, *I* did? People around here look for things to be outraged about, just to alleviate the boredom. Hazard of small-town life." Her lips quirk up on one side. "And you knew the name sounded dirty, Elaina. No way was that an innocent mistake."

Elaina grins. "Well, of course, I did." She lifts Maybe into the air with her hands beneath his front legs, nuzzling her face into his as she adds in a sweeter voice, "But that's part of the fun, isn't it, Maybe? And you *are* the sweetest pussy in the world, yes, you are."

"That's not what Mark said last night," Gertie mutters beneath her breath, triggering a round of excited squealing that sends Maybe dashing across the shop to play with the other cats.

Even Pudge, Maya's sleepy friend, lifts his big head, blinking annoyed green eyes before melting back onto her thigh with a huff.

"Tell us everything," Elaina demands, leaning her

elbows on her crossed knees, her dark brown eyes bright beneath her black fringe. She looks so cute with her new rockabilly haircut. I'm tempted to try a similar look when I get back to the city, but Dad would have a fit.

Perry-Watsons don't do trendy haircuts.

Perry-Watson's embrace a classic, Upper East Side aesthetic that skews heavily beige and soulless gray. The fact that I have strawberry blond hair instead of something more sedate like sandy blond or respectable brown is already flashy enough as far as my father is concerned.

"But it was your turn, remember?" Gertie grins as she exchanges her toy for a catnip mouse that she tosses across the carpet for the kittens. "You were about to tell us the title you've selected for our September book club enjoyment."

Elaina snorts. "No way. You're not dropping a sex bomb and moving on like nothing happened. Book club business will still be here when we're done hearing about your star-crossed, but clearly hot-and-heavy romance with Mark Tripp." She nods my way. "And Sydney won't be here in September. It would be rude to get her all excited about our next pick and leave her out of the fun."

"She could join us online," Maya says, sympathy flooding her blue gaze as she shifts her focus my way. I've never said a word about how much I'm dreading the return to the city, but Maya's too empathetic for her own good. "Or you could come stay with me that weekend, Syd. You're always welcome at my place. I do have to put the lighthouse back up for rent, though. See if any winter tourists bite."

"Of course, no worries. I get it," I say. "And I'd love to come back for a book club weekend. I doubt I can make it in September, but October might work."

"Oo! Oo! And we could do a scary romance that month in your honor," Gertie says, tossing the mouse again, sending the kittens bouncing across the room like intoxicated jumping beans. "You love spooky stuff as much as Maya and me."

"We could do All the Reasons to Be Afraid by Logan Riley," Maya says, book nerd excitement shining in her eyes. "It's been on my To Be Read list for ages. It's about two teens falling in love while they're on the run from their killer imaginary friends."

"No. No teen romance," Elaina says. "I need sex in my books to make up for the lack of sex in my life." She cuts a sharp glance Gertie's way. "And I need dirt from my friends who have miraculously found a decent guy to date in this one lobster town."

"Okay, okay." Gertie leans back, her hands braced on the carpet. "But there's honestly not that much to tell. We aren't dating. We aren't even having sex. At least not, full on sex… We're just…" She laughs and shrugs. "I don't know what we're doing. But whatever it is, it's doomed. Gramps hates Mark's dad for being a rich seafood overlord who's destroying the mom-and-pop vibe around here, and Mark's dad hates my entire clan. He's convinced my dad is the one who dumped fish guts in his convertible when he was visiting last summer, and Gramps has a 'Tripp

Lobsters Taste Like Oppression' t-shirt he wears to dock meetings."

Elaina sighs. "You're the Romeo and Juliet of the lobster world. Which reminds me..." She collects her mug of spiked cider from the end table, taking a sip. "My book club pick is similarly juicy and star-crossed, but with less fish guts."

"Thank goodness," Maya says.

"There's a new stalker romance out based loosely on Romeo and Juliet," Elaina continues. "But Romeo's a creepy stalker, Juliet's blind, and they're both in college. I'm pretty sure there's a decent amount of bondage and kinky shit, too." Her lips curve into a Cheshire Cat grin. "In any event, I need it in my eye holes, and I want you nerds to fall in love with evil Romeo along with me."

Maya pouts. "But I don't want a man to stalk me. I don't like bad guys."

Elaina clucks her tongue. "Of course, not, Maya-Moo. Neither do I. But there are different rules for book boyfriends."

She's so right.

Take my ex, Adrian, a tortured, rebel-without-a-cause type with brooding brown eyes and a beef with his real estate tycoon father. He would make a great romance novel hero. In real life, however, Adrian's family issues and unrelenting drive to be more successful than his dad left little time to attend to the needs of anyone else...including his girlfriend. He was never there for me, even when I could tell he wanted to be. He was too distracted by his own unresolved issues.

Eaten alive might be a better description...

I can *sort of* identify. My father is a workaholic, too. He stayed late at the office most of my childhood and left me with nannies in the city while he went to The Hamptons every other weekend on alleged "business." But he was there when I really needed him. He never missed an award ceremony or science fair, unlike Adrian's dad, a soulless, money-hungry billionaire who basically disappeared from Adrian's life when he was still in elementary school.

But of course, Bad Dad got away with abandoning his child without the slightest stain on his reputation. Men routinely get away with the kind of behavior that would end a woman—in real life and in novels. Romance heroes can be flawed as hell, but so many heroines are still virgins who run cafés and save animals in their spare time.

Huh…

Elaina would actually be a *great* romance novel heroine, if it weren't for the fact that she's slept with every reasonably attractive man in a fifty-mile radius. She's unabashedly sex-positive.

I'm the uptight virgin, but not even my best friends know about that.

At twenty-four, being inexperienced is starting to feel like something I should keep to myself, just to avoid uncomfortable questions I'm not sure how to answer.

"Book boyfriends are fantasy, not reality," Elaina continues. "Book boyfriends can be psychotic, obsessed, bossy jerks, and it's fine. Hot, even. Some real-life guy tries that shit, and we're going to have a problem."

"Though Mark *was* doing some pretty hot bossy talk

the other day behind the warehouse," Gertie mutters, sending Elaina leaping from the couch to tackle her onto the carpet.

"Spill *all* the details, you evil weasel!" Elaina shouts. "Quit taunting me!"

They grapple amidst the cavorting kittens, Gertie giggling and Elaina cursing, while Maya calls out over the ruckus, "Why do you two always have to get physical? You haven't played rugby in years."

"Because Gertie is a tease," Elaina says, grunting as the taller, more muscular Gertie easily flips her onto her stomach and pins her arms behind her back.

"When are you going to learn, woman?" Gertie asks with a fond shake of her head. "You run a cat café. I haul lobster cages onto a boat six days a week. You are no longer any match for my level of physical fitness."

Elaina grunts and squirms fruitlessly for her freedom. "I'm going to start working out any day now. Yoga starts back up at the YMCA in September."

"Yoga will not be enough," Gertie says flatly. "Yoga girls are no match for lobster girls. That's just science."

"Speaking of lobster, are we still on for the Friends of the Feast lobster boil at the Moose Club next Friday? It's my last weekend before I head back to the city," I say, collecting Maybe from the floor as he returns to our side of the otherwise empty café. He snuggles against my chest, but his gaze remains locked on Gertie and Elaina as he lets out a plaintive meow.

"We're totally going." Elaina grunts, trying to poke Gertie in the back with her ballet flat and failing miserably. "Wouldn't miss it."

"Good. Now stop wrestling. You're upsetting Maybe," I say, laughing as the tiny cat meows in agreement.

"Sorry, Maybe, I gotta show this skinny brat who's boss every once and a while." Gertie rolls off Elaina and hops to her feet. "And I need more spiked cider. Anyone else? I finally have a day off tomorrow. I intend to spend it gently hungover, eating French fries in bed and watching bad horror movies."

"More for me, too." Elaina rocks into a seated position. "I'm not going to open tomorrow, either. Even the most hardcore tourists aren't going to be out petting cats or eating scones in a squall like this one."

"It's really bad, isn't it?" Maya casts a worried glance toward the windows, where the rain is pelting the glass hard enough to blur our view of the world outside. "Are you going to be safe getting home, Sydney? The pedestrian bridge to the lighthouse can get hairy in a bad storm."

I stroke Maybe, comforted by the steady vibration of his ribs against mine. "I'll be fine. I drove so I could take the long way home around the heath. So, I probably shouldn't have any more alcohol."

"How about hot chocolate, then?" Gertie asks. "And sugar cookies? If Elaina isn't opening tomorrow, we shouldn't leave those day-olds in the case."

Elaina perks up. "No, we shouldn't. I also have some white chocolate truffles that won't be good in two days. Let's have a sweet feast, and I'll find a link to that book I was talking about to send to everyone!"

"Sounds great," I say, as my cell begins to blare in my bag.

Really blare.

Like a siren…

My pulse picks up.

I might be getting my boots on the ground, after all…

Maya flinches, her hands flying to cover her ears. "What is that? Is there a weather alert?"

Setting Maybe on the cushions beside me, I bend to paw through my backpack. "No, sorry, it's that charity organization I volunteer for. The one I told you might be calling. I have their ringtone set as a siren, so I won't miss any calls. Just a second." I grab the phone, bringing it to my ear as I rise and head for the windows.

Cell service is sketchy all over Sea Breeze, especially on the south end of downtown, in the shadow of the hills surrounding the bay. But being even a few feet closer to the water usually helps. "Hello, Sydney speaking."

"Sydney, I'm so glad I was able to reach you," Moira, the woman I spoke to earlier, says in a tight voice. "I tried to call a few minutes ago, but it wouldn't go through."

I wince. "I'm so sorry. I'm downtown where service

is bad. I should have given you the landline number for the café."

"No worries. I'm just glad I have you now. That pilot we discussed...there's no chance he's reaching Quebec in this weather. He's going to be landing at the Jonesville Regional Airport, about ten miles from your location. Any chance you'd be able to pick him up and find pet-friendly lodging for the night?"

"Absolutely," I say, my heart beating faster. "I can be there in fifteen or twenty minutes."

"Wonderful. Thank you so much," Moira says, clearly relieved. "He has three pit bull puppies with him. Oh, and maybe look for a place that has availability for two nights, just in case. The storm may not move on as quickly as we hope."

"Of course, I'll start calling bed and breakfasts as soon as we're done here."

"Perfect. Thank you so much, you really are a godsend. The pilot's name is Gideon, by the way," Moira says. "I'll text you his arrival time as soon as I have it. We lost touch with him in the storm, but based on his last known coordinates, it likely won't be long now."

"Got it," I say. "I'll be there."

We end the call and I turn back to the others just as Gertie and Elaina arrive with trays filled with fresh drinks and snacks. "Sorry, guys, but I have to bail. That pilot needs to be picked up, after all."

"And she has to find pet-friendly lodging," Maya says, scrolling through her phone. "I'm checking my contacts for you, Syd. I'll find something and text details as soon as I have a reservation."

I exhale, some of the tension easing from my shoulders. Thank goodness for friends with connections in the rental market. Maya's parents have several vacation homes they rent out to tourists, but they're also close with the various bed and breakfast owners in town.

If anyone can find last-minute, pet-friendly digs, it's Maya.

"Thank you so much." I grab my backpack before starting toward the coat tree by the door. "I'll text when I'm home safe and send pictures of the puppies. The woman on the phone said the pilot is flying three baby pit bulls."

Gertie groans. "No, don't! No pictures. I want a dog even more than I want a cat, and pit bulls are so cute. I love the way they smile when they're happy. And their chonky little bodies."

"Ew, cats rule, dogs drool." Elaina sets her tray down on the coffee table in front of Maya before shooting a serious look my way. "Be careful out there, Syd. The wind is even more intense by the airport. Don't get too close to the runway. No getting crushed by airplanes allowed until we've done our girls' trip to Iceland next December."

"But after that, it's fine," Gertie teases, earning a slap on the arm from Elaina.

"Of course, it's not fine. But I've been saving for that trip for three years!"

"Me, too," Maya says. "I can't wait to go. I want to see the northern lights so bad."

"I want to eat all the smoked salmon and soak in one

of those steamy mineral lakes," Gertie says, easing into my empty spot on the couch.

"I want to seduce a Viking. Maybe two," Elaina says with a wink. "And I hear they have a fabulous penis museum in Reykjavik."

Maya huffs. "You're kidding."

"Scout's honor," she says. "It's supposed to be great."

Leaving the ladies debating what makes a penis museum "great," I shrug into my raincoat and step out into the storm.

I'm instantly slapped by a gust of wind that takes my breath away. Elaina's right. The wind is vicious and likely to be worse on the other side of the heath. Hopefully the pilot has experience flying in nasty weather.

Chin to my chest to shield my face from the worst of the rain, I hurry to my rental car. I have a vintage BMW in the city, but it would never survive the gravel roads and mud pits of rural Maine. I rented a Subaru Forester for the summer, an extravagant expense that ate up almost every dime of my pay from the Maine Wetland Preservation Project.

But this job was never about the money.

I have enough money.

My mother left me a lump sum when she died, and there's still plenty left to see me through until the trust *her* mother left us opens on my twenty-fifth birthday. After that, I'll never have to worry about money again. I'll be a millionaire on my way to being a billionaire, just like my dad and Adrian's asshole father, a fact I was careful to hide from my former boyfriend, once I realized how he loathed trust fund babies.

I knew Adrian would never believe me if I told him that money doesn't solve all your problems. I'm incredibly grateful that I've never had to worry about how to pay for college or make rent after working a low-paying wildlife conservation job every summer since high school, but money creates its own set of issues.

If the future of a billion-dollar company weren't at stake, would my father be so determined to see me take over the reins at Watson Global? If he were a mechanic or a real estate agent, would he care this much about his only child following in his footsteps?

"Probably," I mutter, squinting at the road as the windshield wipers slap furiously back and forth.

My father is an egomaniac. A generous egomaniac who loves me very much, but a maniac, nevertheless.

He insists he needs me on board to keep Watson Global evolving in a way my mother would have been proud of, but that's only part of it. He doesn't simply want to leave behind a thriving, compassionate enterprise. He wants to leave behind a piece of himself, a child sprung from his loins who will rule over the Watson legacy in his stead.

It would have been better if I were a boy, obviously —Dad's the kind of old-fashioned CEO who prefers his boardroom heavy on testosterone—but he's also a practical man. I'm a hard-working woman with a good head on my shoulders who graduated with honors from Boston University. I'm also old enough to start learning the ropes now, which is far preferable to my father to starting over again with a new family and fresh kids, who might not turn out to be boys, either.

Dad's always said he was glad I was born an old soul. He can't handle "ordinary children," with all their noise and mess and lack of self-control. The fact that I might have been an "ordinary" child if I'd sensed "ordinary" was enough to win my father's love, never seems to have crossed his mind. It didn't cross mine until I started reading more about internal family systems in grad school and realized my *external* family system was probably a little messed up.

Sometimes, I wish I hadn't connected those dots.

Sometimes, I wish making Dad proud and being his perfect daughter was still the only thing that mattered to me. In many ways, life was easier back then.

Way easier than pulling into a parking lot where the lines on the pavement are blurred suggestions hidden beneath several inches of standing water...

Thankfully, there aren't many other cars at the airport at six p.m. on a stormy night. It's just me and a dozen other Subarus parked along the cracked, tree-lined pavement in front of the one-room terminal building.

I shut off the engine and turn in my seat, peering through the back glass toward the runway. With the rain coming down this hard, I can't see much except smears of light coming from the various runway beacons and a few grayish white blobs I'm assuming are planes. But I can't tell what kind they are or if any of them are small enough to be a private aircraft. Thanks to the storm clouds, it's far darker than it would usually be at this time on a clear summer evening.

I pull out my cell, but there's no text from Moira and no service.

Looks like the only way I'll be finding out if my pilot has arrived is if I head into the terminal to ask.

Bracing for the onslaught, I jam my phone into the inner, waterproof pocket of my raincoat, grab my keys, and swing out into the storm. I run for the terminal, wincing as my clogs fill with rainwater, making my bare toes go slimy in my shoes.

So slimy, I lose a clog halfway across the parking lot and have to backtrack to fetch it...

I'm standing in the rain, doing my best to squirm my foot into my shoe and cursing myself for not wearing more practical footwear—even if this *was* supposed to be a night in with the girls—when lightning claps through the air. Only there's no flash of light or accompanying rumble of thunder, just a sharp crack followed by a rushing sound that reminds me of sliding into a pile of fall leaves.

Leaves...

I hitch my chin up to see one of the parking lot's large trees on a collision course with my face. Before I can decide which way to jump, a thick arm snatches at my ribs, jerking me back toward my car.

On instinct, I reach for the person holding me and encounter wide, strong shoulders I cling to as we sail through the air. It all happens so fast; I don't have time to dread the impact with the pavement. But if I had, it would have been time wasted.

Somehow, the man spins us in the air as we fall, ensuring his back takes the brunt of the collision. I end up with a tree limb across my legs, leaves in my hair, and what feels like the start of a bruise where my knee crashed into the pavement, but it could have been so much worse.

Hopefully, the same can be said for my rescuer…

"Are you all right?" I ask, batting at the leaves covering my face "Sir? Are you…"

My words trail away as a big hand lifts the thin limb up and away, clearing the space between us. I stare down into kind brown eyes set in the most handsome face I've ever seen. My hero is all perfect angles, a strong jaw, and cheekbones a male model would kill for.

From what I can see (and feel) of his body, he's built like a model, too. Like an underwear model, who spends hours in the gym ensuring each muscle is more perfectly sculpted than the last. Add in shaggy brown hair streaked with gray and a commanding presence that fills the air around him—even when he's flat on his back—and the man should be intimidating as hell.

But those eyes…

They're so kind, so warm and familiar.

It feels like I've met him before, and when he cups my face and asks—"Are you okay? Are you hurt?"—I don't flinch or pull away the way I usually would with a stranger.

I don't even think about it.

I don't think anything except the fact that his fingers feel solid and safe against my cheek, and that I'd like him to keep touching me for a *very* long time.

I've never wanted that.

Not with anyone, not even when things with Adrian

were new and a wink from him across a crowded lecture hall could make my skin flush all over.

I'm so stunned that I don't speak for several long seconds, long enough for the man to repeat himself, "Are you okay?"

Swallowing hard, I nod, but before I can speak, we're attacked.

No, not attacked. It's more like we're mobbed, but sweetly mobbed, by soaking wet, wriggling balls of furry enthusiasm. Three dogs—puppies, it looks like—tumble over us, between us, licking and whimpering as my savior does his best to keep the leaves out of our faces and grab for their collars at the same time.

"No! Down, Bacon," he rumbles as one of the dogs leaps onto my back, flattening me onto his strong chest again. "Sorry," he adds. "I have no idea how they got out of their kennels."

"It's fine," I say, my words ending in a grunt as Bacon leaps off my spine. I take the opportunity to wrench myself into a seated position and reach for the tree limbs. "Here. Let me hold those while you get up."

"Thanks," the man says, cursing as two of the dogs hurl themselves across his thighs. He sighs, humor mixing with the frustration in his voice as he says, "No, Egg and Cheese. Get up. I told you; we'll snuggle when we're somewhere safe and this isn't it."

As if to underscore his words, another cracking sound splits the air as the trunk splinters more at the base.

The dogs on Sexy Stranger's legs launch into startled motion, bolting across the parking lot toward the terminal entrance, where Bacon is wriggling in front of a man in a blue uniform. The man dangles something brown in the air above the dog, sending him into fresh paroxysms of excitement.

"Bacon's about to eat bacon," the man mutters as he comes to stand beside me, smoothing his wet hair away from his face. He casts a quick smile my way, one that's every bit as warm as his eyes and instantly makes the crush I'm developing ten times worse. "I didn't name them. The people at the shelter did. As much as I love a breakfast sandwich, I wouldn't have gone for bacon, egg, and cheese as puppy names."

"Valid," I breathe as my traumatized brain connects the dots. A man with three puppies, three pit bull puppies... What are the chances this gorgeous, heroic human is anyone *but* the pilot I've been sent to collect? "Good way to stay hungry all the time."

"Exactly." His grin widens as he extends his hand. "I'm Gideon. Nice to meet you..."

"Sydney." Yep, he's my guy, all right. My cheeks burn as his fingers close around mine. They're still oddly warm despite the chill in the air and the urge to keep touching him is stronger than ever. "Sydney Watson." I force myself to squeeze his palm once and release it. "Moira with Pilots for a Paws called me a little while ago. I'm here to pick you up and take you to your lodging for the night."

His expression softens with relief. "Thank God. And good thing I kept you from getting crushed."

"Very good," I say, with a nervous laugh. "Thank you for that. I don't know if I would have made it out of the way in time. I thought the sound of the tree falling was lightning at first. By the time I realized what was happening…"

"Yeah. Glad I wasn't too late." His smile dims as he reaches for my cheek again. "You do have a little cut though. Just here."

I fight the urge to lean into his touch. "Really? I can't feel it."

"It's small, and barely bleeding, but you'll want to clean it when you get home."

"Thanks, will do." I tell myself to step away before I do something embarrassing like nuzzle his palm, but I lack the willpower at the moment. "We should get you and the puppies settled." I glance back toward where the three dogs are performing very wiggly "sits" for the man in blue to win pieces of the bacon. "And we should get them back in their kennels before our nice friend over there runs out of treats."

Gideon's hand falls to his side with a sigh. "Agreed. I'll go wrangle the pups. Could you pull your car around to the terminal to load the kennels? I wouldn't usually mind a walk in the rain, but this is a lot of rain, and I tweaked my back a little when we fell."

My forehead furrows. "Oh no, I'm sorry."

"Don't be." His gaze locks with mine in a way that makes the blood rush in my ears. "I'm just a little bruised. Nothing a couple Ibuprofen won't cure. I'm just glad you're all right. After the day I've had, the last thing I needed was to witness a beautiful woman being crushed by a tree."

My cheeks burn from the compliment. "Thanks

again. I'll bring the car around. There should be plenty of room in the trunk for all three kennels, but if not, we can put the seats down in back."

"Great. See you up there," he says before he turns and strides away.

I only watch him go for a second, but it's plenty of time to note that he's every bit as gorgeous from the back as he is from the front. He has an easy, confident gait that reminds me of professional athletes. He walks like a man who's at home in his own skin, a man who has no doubt that he can handle any challenge that comes his way.

If there's anything sexier than that, I can't name it.

I also can't name the feeling buzzing beneath my skin as I hurry back through the rain toward the car. I only know that it's warm and achy and reminds me of how starved I always felt after a long day of classes with no time to grab lunch in between.

It's like I'm hungry.

No, not hungry...another "h" word, one I've never experienced in connection with a man I've only known for five minutes. I'm more of a slow burn kind of girl. I don't contract cases of spontaneous lust, but there's no denying that's what this is. I'm filled with lustful feelings for a complete stranger.

Hell, Gideon could be a serial killer for all I know.

Okay, fine, a man who volunteers his time and private plane to transport animals to no-kill shelters probably isn't a serial killer, but he could be awful in other ways. He could throw his recycling in the normal trash or pick his nose in public or take loud business calls in the coffee shop.

Or, even worse...he could be married. He looks like he's in his late thirties and all the good guys are off the market by then. My New York City girlfriends in their thirties are always complaining about the lack of fish in the dating sea.

The chances that this sweet, handsome, confident, wealthy man—private planes don't come cheap—is single are slim to none. He's likely either married or happily cohabitating with the long-term woman of his dreams.

Letting this crush get any more out of hand would be a serious mistake.

Determined to keep things professional from here on out, I start the car and pull around to the front of the terminal, where Gideon and the nice man in blue have managed to get all but one rambunctious puppy into his kennel.

Bacon, however, still zooms back and forth in front of the entrance, making the doors open and close over and over again as he gambols past, easily avoiding the grasp of both men as he romps through the puddles.

I'm about to step out to help when my cell bleats several times, one right after the other. I reach into my coat pocket, grateful my phone didn't sustain any damage in the fall.

I only have one bar, but it was enough for Maya's texts to make it through—*I'm so sorry, Syd, but there aren't any rooms available. The Knolls B&B is closed for repairs, and the Rose and Bramble doesn't take pets.*

I did have an idea, though! You could let the pilot and the puppies stay at the lighthouse, and you could come to my place for a sleepover. That way you don't have to share the house with a stranger.

Though, if you wanted to stay at your place, you could always make the pilot sleep upstairs in the lantern room. He might not get much rest since it's so loud up there on a rainy night, but he'd be farther away from your room and you'd have more privacy. Anyway! Hope you're safe and let me know what you want to do when you have the chance. I don't mind, either way.

Love you!

"Privacy," I murmur as I glance outside to see Gideon scooping Bacon into his arms, his muscles flexing deliciously under his sweater.

That's the problem, Maya, I think. *I don't want privacy. I want as much time with this man as I can get before he leaves tomorrow.*

But he's married, I remind myself. He has to be married. And even if he isn't, I'm not a one-night-stand kind of girl. If I were, surely, I would have had one by now and would no longer be New England's oldest virgin.

Popping the trunk, I step into the rain, helping Gideon and Bruce, the helpful man in blue, load the kennels into the back. When we're done, Gideon and I shake Bruce's hand, before loading into the car, even damper than we were before.

I push my hood back, shivering as water runs down my neck into the light summer sweater beneath, and decide I might as well break the news now. When I've finished explaining the lodging options—or lack thereof —Gideon nods, his brow furrowed with concern.

But it's not concern for himself or the dogs.

"Is that okay with you?" he asks, his worried gaze fixed on mine. "You're a young woman living alone, and I'm a stranger. Would you feel comfortable having me in your home?"

"You're a stranger who saved my life," I remind him, making his lips twitch.

"Maybe, but I don't want you to feel obligated because of that. Especially if you don't feel safe. I've been vetted by Pilots for a Paws, and I can give you some people to call as references, but I understand if you'd rather I find other accommodations. I have friends in Bucksport. We haven't talked in a while, but—"

"No, not at all," I say, shaking my head. "Bucksport is almost two hours away. You and the puppies are cold and miserable now, and I'm sure the roads are danger-ous." I smile, my stomach fluttering as I add, "I'd be happy for you to stay with me. There's plenty of space. We can get the dogs settled in the rec room, and you can have your pick of guest rooms. There are still two empty, one upstairs and one downstairs."

He studies me for a moment, making my face feel too hot again, but finally nods. "All right. Thank you. We'd be grateful for your hospitality. But you have to let me buy dinner to say thank you. We'll find a nice restaurant that delivers, and you can have your pick of the menu."

I laugh. "Thank you, but the only restaurant that

delivers in Sea Breeze is the pizza place. Though they do make a mean calzone."

Hunger flashes in his eyes. "Sounds delicious."

"It is. We can order as soon as we get back."

"I'd like that, Sydney," he says, the sound of my name on his lips enough to make me melt. "Thank you."

"You're welcome, Gideon," I say, enjoying his name on my lips, too.

Nearly as much as I enjoy glancing down at his left hand and seeing no ring in sight.

three

Phillip "Gideon" Gabaldon

A man having a no good, very bad day,
that has suddenly taken a wonderful turn.

She's too young for me.

Way too young.

On the ground, in the rain, with the dogs climbing all over us and fear she'd been hurt making my heart race, I didn't notice her age at first—only that Sydney was stop-your-heart beautiful—but now...

Well, now, it's obvious that my generous hostess is younger than I am.

Probably *much* younger.

Once we have the dogs dried off and settled in the lighthouse's rec room with water and food, Sydney gives me the tour of her rental. She blushes a little as she opens the door to a bedroom overlooking the water.

"This is my room. Kind of small, but bigger than the dorms, so it feels spacious to me."

Dorms.

Fuck. She can't be more than twenty, twenty-two tops. I'm ancient in comparison, and I've never had any interest in dating younger women.

This wouldn't be dating, anyway. This would be one night, maybe two, and I'd likely never see Sydney again. I can't remember the last time I was in Maine, only that it was so long ago, I was nervous my friends in Bucksport might have forgotten me. And this isn't even a part of Maine that's easy to get to. Sea Breeze is on a peninsula in the middle of nowhere, so close to Canada, I can smell the maple syrup and poutine.

If Sydney and I were to start seeing each other, I'd have to fly in for every date.

As much as I'd love to drop everything for a beautiful woman, I learned the dangers of long-distance relationships the hard way.

You're insane. You're not going to have a relationship with this woman. You're not going to sleep with her, either, even if she is interested. She's a child.

I clear my throat, feeling properly chastised by the inner voice, and ask, "So what are you studying in school?"

She glances back at me as she leads the way farther down the hall. "Oh, I'm not. I'm done. I got my MBA in the spring."

MBA. My ears perk up at the news. She has a graduate degree. Maybe she's older than I thought.

"So, you're twenty-four? Twenty-five?" I hear myself

asking without consciously deciding to go there. But I can play off my curiosity. I flash an easy smile her way. "I have a twenty-two-year-old son. He starts grad school in the fall."

"Oh wow." She hesitates with her hand on the door-knob to the next room. "You... I..." She laughs and shakes her head. "I'm sorry. You don't look old enough to have a twenty-two-year-old."

"Thanks," I say, accustomed to that response by now, though I don't get it as often as I used to. After going part-time at my firm to spend more time outdoors, I'm in the best physical shape of my life, but the gray hair adds a certain gravitas I didn't have in my early thirties. "My high school girlfriend and I weren't as good at birth control as we thought we were."

Sydney makes a sympathetic face. "It's hard to be truly good at anything in high school. Are you two still together?"

"No, we're not." I do my best to keep the words neutral. I've had enough therapy to have moved past the worst of my anger with my ex, but I'll never forgive her for the things she's done. Even if my son and I finally mend our relationship someday, the part his mother played in turning him against me has done so much needless, painful damage. "We were married for five years, but..." I shrug. "We grew into people who didn't have much in common."

Sydney nods thoughtfully. "I can imagine. My parents were married young. By the time I was seven or eight, it was hard to see how they ever fell in love. They were so different."

"Are they still together?" I ask, enjoying that we're jumping into real conversation without wasting time on small talk. I hate small talk.

"No," she says, tightening her grip on the door handle. "My mother passed away when I was thirteen and my father never remarried."

"I'm so sorry."

Her lips curve in a tight smile. "Thanks. It was hard. We didn't even know she had a heart condition until it was too late. But my dad and I got through it." She opens the door and steps inside. "This could be your room if you'd like. It's small, but cozy, and big bonus…" She grins at me over her shoulder. "There aren't any tragic local legends set in this part of the house."

"Tragic local legends? I'm intrigued."

"I'll tell you the tale over dinner," she says. "And you're welcome to sleep on the third floor if you want. The legend *is* tragic, but it's almost two hundred years old, so…"

"Nah, I'll be good here." I motion toward the full bed beneath a window overlooking the churning sea. "I've done enough puppy wrestling today. I don't have the energy for the third floor."

"Good call. It can get loud up there in the rain," she says, her clever eyes dancing in a way that makes me want to kiss her.

But everything this woman does makes me want to kiss her. It's a strange and unsettling state of affairs. I haven't felt this kind of pull toward someone in years.

Maybe…ever.

"I'll leave you to get settled and grab a shower.

There's a bathroom at the end of the hall you can use. I'll use the one by the rec room." She moves toward the door but lingers for a beat. "Calzone still sound good?"

"Yes, but I'm paying. It's the least I can do to thank you for the rescue and putting us up for the night."

She grins. "All right. I'll order a calzone, salad, and extra breadsticks before I shower. Pepperoni and mushroom filling okay with you?"

"Perfect," I say as she leaves, telling myself the fact that we like the same kind of calzone isn't a sign that flirting with her is okay. Everyone likes pepperoni. Mushrooms are a more niche choice, but still fairly common. If I'm looking for signs, this isn't it.

And I *shouldn't* be looking for signs.

I'm on a volunteer mission of mercy. This weekend is supposed to be about me, the dogs, and some time alone in the sky to take a hard look at what I want from the next stage of my life. I'm almost forty. I love my job and the company I've built. I love that I've gone part time and can be out in nature almost every day even more. But it still feels like there's something missing. When I lay down alone at night, I'm haunted by a longing for something I can't quite put my finger on.

But I have a feeling it might have something to do with how much I'm looking forward to sharing dinner with Sydney tonight...

I unpack my small backpack into the empty chest of drawers and grab jeans and a sweater to change into after my shower. The bathroom is as small as the guest rooms, but the water heats up nicely, and I'm so grateful not to be in soggy clothes, I couldn't have enjoyed the shower more if it were in a suite at The Ritz.

When I'm dressed, I head back into the kitchen to find Sydney still in her damp sweater with a lobster on the front, her phone in hand.

"I'm sorry." I move to face her across the small island. "Did I use up all the hot water?"

She shakes her head. "No, not at all. The pizza place is closed because of the storm, so I started calling other places, thinking we could go pick some-thing up, but...everything's closed." She wrinkles her nose my way. "I was just about to try the Thai Mexican fusion place one town over, but their food is an acquired taste, and it's about a twenty-minute drive."

I wave an easy hand. "Don't worry about it. I can whip something up for us here."

Her brows lift. "Are you sure? I don't have much in the fridge or the pantry. I'm leaving in ten days, so I've been trying not to buy too many groceries."

I reach for the fridge handle, pulling it open to see a head of cauliflower, some spinach, and the remnants of a few different cheeses. There are also a couple of apples, oat milk, an old lemon, and a bottle of balsamic salad dressing. "You have rice or pasta?" I ask, pondering the ingredients for a beat before I shut the door.

"Both," she says, motioning toward the cabinet in the corner. "In the lazy Susan, by the sweet potatoes."

"Great." I grin. "I've got dinner covered, then. Go take a shower and warm up. I'll get the rice started."

She shoots me a quizzical look. "Okay. If you're sure."

"I'm sure," I say, laughing as she continues to study me like a virus she's spotted under a microscope. "What? You doubt my cooking skills?"

"I've never known a man who could cook. My father is hopeless in the kitchen, and my guy friends' culinary skills extend to boiling water for ramen noodles."

I huff. "You've been hanging around the wrong men."

"Clearly," she says in a lilting voice that makes me wonder if she feels it, too, this connection, this potential between us. She clears her throat. "Speaking of men, I should check on the furry boys. They're being way too quiet."

"They're probably sleeping," I say. "They had a big day and didn't get much rest on the flight from Georgia. The air pressure change in the plane and all the noise can be scary for animals the first time or two, until they realize what's happening."

Her brow furrows. "I bet. Poor things."

"Yeah, but Atlanta to Quebec is too far to drive. Better to get the trip over with and get them settled in their new home. Hopefully, they won't be as stressed out when we go up tomorrow. Since they've lived through the experience once before."

Sydney glances toward the kitchen windows, her pale blue eyes doubtful. "If you're able to fly tomorrow. Last time I checked, it looked like the storm was going to linger through the end of the day."

I sigh as I follow her gaze toward the rain-smeared

glass. "And I don't want to take off too late or I'll have to worry about finding pet-friendly lodging in Gaspé. The shelter is only open from nine to five."

"You can stay here another night if you need to," she says. "It's no problem."

"Are you sure? The dogs and I won't cramp your style?"

"Not at all. I don't usually work on Saturdays anyway. But even if I wanted to, driving rain and high winds aren't the best conditions for finding butterflies."

"Butterflies?" I smile.

"I'm cataloguing a newly discovered crowberry blue population. We thought they were only found in Washington County, but I've found almost twenty this summer." She laughs. "Doesn't sound like much, but it's very exciting for us wildlife nerds."

"I get it. That is exciting."

She shrugs. "But I can't count butterflies or sea bird nests in the rain. So, I'll have the whole day free to help with the dogs and anything else you need."

"Okay great," I say. "Thanks again."

Anything else I need...

I don't *need* to spend the day in bed with Sydney, discovering if she tastes as wonderful as she smells, but God, I want to. I want it so much that a part of me hopes the weather will take a turn for the better. As much as I enjoy her company, the less time I spend here, the better the chances I'll leave before I do something I'll regret with a woman who's too young for me.

The thought reminds me that she never answered my question about her age.

But I can't very well ask again. Asking once was suspect. Asking twice would be flat-out sketchy. But that's fine. I don't need to know how old she is. Sydney and I can only ever be friends and age doesn't matter when it comes to friendship.

"Friends, just friends," I mutter to myself after she's left to check on the dogs and grab a shower.

I can do this. I can be just friends with a beautiful, generous, clever woman who gets adorably excited about butterflies and who's gotten under my skin in roughly an hour and twenty minutes.

Piece of cake.

I repeat the mantra as I start the rice and set the oven to preheat to roast the cauliflower and potatoes. I'm making decent progress in convincing myself I only feel friendly feelings toward Sydney Watson when she materializes in the doorway leading into the living room in gray sweatpants, a tight black sweatshirt, and giant black-and-gray striped socks. She doesn't have a trace of makeup on, and her hair hangs in damp, strawberry blond waves around her face, but she's easily the sexiest thing I've seen in years.

She looks so cozy. So at home and so...herself. Sydney is clearly comfortable with who she is and confident in her own skin. I didn't see my last girlfriend without makeup until we'd been dating for seven or eight months. But Sydney's a natural beauty.

Likely, she's aware of that and knows she doesn't need makeup to knock a man's socks off.

Or maybe she just thinks of me as a nice older man, a big brother type or—God forbid—a dad. She knows I have a son around her age, after all. She could have emerged in her comfy clothes simply because she doesn't think of me as a man at all. At least, not in *that* way.

"I had to embrace pajamas," she says, her tongue sweeping out to dampen her lips. "All my jeans are dirty and it's way too yucky outside to put on dress pants."

"Dress pants would have been an abomination at a time like this," I agree, ribs tightening when she laughs. God, she's beautiful.

"I knew you'd get it," she says, her gaze dragging down my chest to my hips, lingering below my waistband long enough to make me feel things I shouldn't feel before sweeping back up again. "If you want to join me in the comfy sweatpants life, you're welcome to."

"I may take you up on that after dinner," I say, already knowing I won't.

It would be much harder to hide the hint of an erection I'm sporting in a pair of sweatpants.

I turn back to the stove and give the rice a final stir before removing it from the burner, determined to get myself under control. "Dinner should be ready in about fifteen minutes. Just waiting for the cauliflower and sweet potatoes to finish roasting. I'll sauté the spinach while they're cooling. I'm making vegetarian rice bowls with a lemon balsamic dressing and a cheese and apple plate for dessert."

"Sounds and smells delicious," she says, appearing beside me and reaching for the fridge handle. "Looks like all we need is a glass of wine. Chardonnay okay for you? I have a bottle open from last night."

"Chardonnay is great," I say, even though I know wine isn't a good idea.

But I'll only have one glass. Just enough to make me sleepy, not enough to make cradling Sydney's face in my hands again seem okay.

She closes the fridge and fetches two wineglasses from the cupboard beside the stove, her body so close to mine, I can smell the honeysuckle scent of her shampoo, feel the warmth of her skin. If she were mine, I would pin her against the cabinet, kiss her until she forgets all about pouring the wine, and slip my hand down the front of her sweatpants. I'd give her a proper thank you for picking me up in the middle of a storm and show her how glad I am I was there to keep her safe.

I want to keep this woman safe. From everything.

Even before she told me about losing her mother when she was barely a teen, I could sense sadness beneath her contagious smile, a wound that hasn't completely healed. If Sydney were mine, I'd like to think I could help her with that. That I could care for her enough to make up for the mother who didn't live to love her.

But I can't do any of those things.

And the fact that I'm longing to *care* for this woman as much as I want to touch her isn't rational. Or sane.

I'm making a mental note to call my therapist for an emergency session when I get back to Vermont when Sydney asks, "So is there a Mrs. Gideon? Or a girlfriend back home?"

I shift her way, my heart lurching when I realize

how close she is. Close enough to feel her breath on my neck, to see the hunger in her eyes.

A hunger that has nothing to do with grain bowls or a cheese plate...

A part of me is savagely excited that she wants to know if I'm available. The other part of me warns that this is still a bad idea.

But that second voice is a whisper now.

Maybe by the end of dinner, it will be quiet enough to ignore completely...

four

W *hat is wrong with you?*
      How are you this awkward?
      Pre-teen girls have more game than you do,
Perry-Watson.

The inner voice is right, but I don't care.

I have to know if Gideon is with someone. If he is, it will help me get control of the crazy fantasies that have been tumbling around in my head since we met. (The ones that took an especially vivid turn in the shower…)

And if he's a free man…

Well, then maybe it's okay to trust the hunger in his eyes and the hunger in my bones and the sudden certainty that I'm done waiting for Mr. Right. I'm finally ready for Mr. Right Now. I've never had such an instant, powerful attraction to a man, and the more I think about it, the more certain I am that Gideon would be the perfect choice for my first time.

He's older, wiser, and way more experienced than any of the boys I've fumbled around with in the dark.

He's gorgeous and strong, sexy and kind, and he's already proven he'd risk his life to keep me safe.

If I can't trust a man like that to be my partner in a major life event, who can I trust?

And even if things go horribly awry, he's leaving in a day or two. Moira said he was based out of Burlington, Vermont. I've never been to Burlington, and if needed, I can avoid going there for the rest of my life, ensuring our paths never cross again.

He's perfect.

So perfect, I hold my breath as he studies my face.

After a long beat, he says, "No, there's no Mrs. Gideon. Or girlfriend. What about you?"

I shake my head, willing my face to give no sign of the giddy celebration taking place in my cerebral cortex. I have to play it cool. This man is a *man*, not an inexperienced boy who will be swept off his feet by a sloppy display of puppy love. "No. Not a lot of dating prospects in the marsh with the butterflies and seabirds."

"But you love it here anyway," he says, his voice rumbly in a way that makes the innocent question feel scandalous. Electric.

I smile. "I do. It's so beautiful and peaceful. And I feel like I'm making a difference here. Even if it's a small difference."

"Nothing more important than that."

I cock my head, warmed by his words. "I think so. I'm going to miss it so much when I leave." I glance outside, my chest tightening. "This is my last summer on the marsh. Once I start my real job, I won't have time to do fieldwork."

He makes a sad noise beneath his breath. "That's a shame."

I turn back to find him gazing down at me, a light in his eyes that makes me ache again, but not just to touch him. I *absolutely* want to touch him, but I also want to *know* him, this man who seems so honest and real.

In my high society world back in Manhattan, it seems like everyone is pretending to be something they're not. Pretending to be richer than they are or to have connections to people they've never met. Pretending they didn't have a nose job and would never dream of sleeping with their secretary or their trainer or some other tired cliché.

Even at school, my classmates were seldom what they seemed. Take Adrian. He would tell anyone who stood still long enough that his family and friends meant everything to him, but he regularly dodged his mother's phone calls and had an excuse every time a friend needed help moving across town. I've learned that you can't always take people at their word. Not because they're bad people, per se, but because who we *want* to be isn't always the same as who we truly are.

But with Gideon, I can tell things would be different. With him, I sense that he means what he says, all the way down to the deepest part of his soul.

That hunch is enough to give me the guts to whisper, "I'm glad there's no girlfriend. There's something about you, Gideon."

Recognition flares in his dark eyes, but he doesn't lean closer.

He eases away.

He does it under the pretext of moving the rice to another burner, but I'm sensing it's another kind of heat he's trying to avoid when he murmurs, "There's something about you, too, Sydney. The second I stepped out of the terminal, my eyes went straight to you. And I..." His tongue slips out to wet his lips, sending a shiver of longing through my core. "I couldn't look away."

"I'm glad, and not just because you kept me from getting crushed." I search his profile for clues as to why he's holding back. My gut says he's feeling the connection between us, too, but maybe... "And I'm not looking for anything long-term. In case you were wondering."

He shifts his focus, his gaze sharpening on mine. "Am I that easy to read?"

I shake my head, dizzy from the rush of being so direct with a man for the first time in my life. "No. There's something else that's bothering you, too. Something I can't figure out."

He exhales a rough breath before adding in a softer voice, "You're young, butterfly girl. I'm not sure how young, but I'm betting too young for a man about to turn forty on December thirty-first."

A sudden smile stretches my face. "You're a New Year's Eve baby? Me, too."

His brows lift. "Really?"

I nod. "Yeah. I loved it as a kid. My parents would throw these huge parties for their friends and work colleagues, but I got to invite a few friends, too. We'd have a sleepover and stay up as late as we wanted. There was always amazing food and music, and the entire party sang Happy Birthday to me before they started Auld Lang Syne. It was really special." I shrug, embarrassed by my overzealous trip down memory lane. "Those are some of my best memories from…before."

His forehead furrows. "The parties stopped after your mother died?"

"Yes, but I understood. She was the social one, the planner. And my dad always got me anything I wanted for my birthday. It's amazing I wasn't spoiled rotten."

"There's not a rotten thing about you," Gideon murmurs. "You're…stunning. And sweet. And I want to kiss you, but…"

Air caught in my lungs, I wheeze, "But?"

"You still haven't told me how old you are."

"Oh," I say with a very un-smooth laugh that sounds more like I'm choking. I cough, regaining control before I add, "Sorry. I'm twenty-four."

He winces. "You're only two years older than my son."

I press my lips together for a moment, trying to decide why I don't find that as troubling as he seems to. After a moment, I say, "Well, yes. But you had your son when you were still in high school. My father is way older than I am and I don't… I just…"

I trail off, losing my courage before I reach the end of the thought.

"You just," he prompts, easing closer, until I could rest my forehead on his chest if I leaned in.

Instead, I lift my chin, forcing myself to hold his

gaze. "You don't feel like a father figure to me. Not even a little bit. Do I seem like a kid to you?" I inject a flirty lilt into my next words. "Do you want to give me advice and make sure I eat all my vegetables?"

His lips twitch. "Well, I *am* about to pull roasted cauliflower and sweet potatoes from the oven. But…no, you seem older than my son. Not to sound like an older guy cliché, but you're very grounded. Very mature." He rolls his eyes with a shake of his head. "Fuck, that sounded as gross as I thought it would."

"No, it didn't," I say. "I *am* grounded and mature. I graduated top of my class and have a lot of responsibilities waiting for me once this summer is over. I've known for a long time that big things were going to be expected of me and that I needed to grow up fast." I study him for another beat before digging deep for the last of my big ovary energy. "I'm a full-fledged adult who knows what…and *who* she wants."

His lips part and his eyes blaze with the same hunger burning through my veins. He leans a hand on the fridge behind me and steps in close, making my nervous system light up like the Christmas tree in Rockefeller Center.

But before Gideon can kiss me or chastise me or whatever else he might have had planned; the oven timer goes off, the beeping loud and insistent, enough to break the spell.

A moment later, a soft howl sounds from the rec room, followed by the footsteps of rampaging puppies. Bacon bursts into the kitchen first, woofing as he lifts worried brown eyes to mine.

"Hey, buddy," I say, my voice trembling. Clearing my throat, I add, "We're fine, no worries. It was just the oven."

Cheese, the handsome ginger puppy emits a warble of anguish that makes both Gideon and I laugh, banishing the last of the tension.

"Yes, I'm sure," I assure the dog. "We're fine, and as soon as the sweet potatoes cool down, you can all have a treat."

Egg flops down on the floor, squirming in happiness at the word, exposing the circular orange spot on his mostly white belly.

I kneel down, laughing as I rub his tummy. "Yes, a treat for all the good boys. Now that you're sunny side up, I see why you're named Egg."

Gideon sets the sheet pan on top of the stove and turns to us with a grunt. "You're right. I didn't notice that before. Maybe egg *is* the perfect name for you, buddy."

"Or Sunny." I glance up at him, petting Egg as Bacon and Cheese squirm closer, angling for affection. "If he were mine, that would be one of his nicknames for sure."

Gideon arches a brow. "If you're looking to adopt, I could pull some strings."

I shake my head. "No. Sadly, I won't have time for a dog in my new life. It wouldn't be fair to Sunny. And he's so attached to his brothers. It would be nice if they could find someone willing to take all three of them." I rotate between the three puppies, delivering neck scratches and tummy rubs. "They're such sweethearts."

"Sweethearts who are going to get at least two times bigger before they're finished growing and need regular exercise and playtime. That's a lot of work and a lot of dogs for most people. I'm sure once they're placed in good homes, they'll be happy with their new families."

I stand, moving toward the sink on the other side of the stove, keenly aware of how close Gideon is as I turn on the water to wash my hands. "You're probably right." I glance his way, desperate to return to our previous conversation, but unsure how to make the transition.

Luckily, making eye contact is enough to thicken the air between us all over again.

Gideon runs a hand through his damp hair. "You've made some very good points, Sydney," he says, and I know he isn't talking about the dogs.

I bite my bottom lip, loving the husky way he says my name. "I have," I agree, faking a confidence I don't completely feel.

"But I think we should eat," he says with a half-smile. "A person shouldn't make decisions on an empty stomach." He nods toward the cabinet above me. "Would you mind putting rice in two bowls while I sauté the spinach?"

"Sure," I say, though I would rather we put off dinner until after he's ravaged me against the refrigerator.

Or he could lift me up onto the cabinets so I could wrap my legs around his hips…

My usually PG-13 mind is suddenly alive with X-rated kitchen fantasies.

I don't know what's happening to me, but I have no interest in slamming on the brakes. I'd rather pour fuel on the fire, and I know just the person to ask for advice...

I pull two bowls from the cupboard and quickly spoon rice into the bottom of each, before telling Gideon, "I'll be right back. I promised to send my friends pictures of the dogs. I'll take them to the puppy pads in the garage to go potty, snap a few shots, and be right back."

Gideon nods as he drops pieces of sweet potato into a napkin. "Sounds good. Don't forget their treat."

"Thanks." I accept the napkin before grabbing my cell from the island and tucking it into the pocket of my sweatpants. To the dogs, I add, "Come on, guys. Let's go to the garage and potty. Then you can have a yummy treat."

All three puppies squirm faster, proving they know exactly what a "treat" is, and Egg flops down on his back again, showing his Sunny side. Clearly, he's the submissive one of the bunch, a thought that leads my brain into uncharted territory as I move through the rec room to the entrance to the garage.

I've never been a fan of the whole Dom/sub theme in romance novels—that's more Elaina's thing—but I wouldn't mind it if Gideon wanted to boss me around in bed.

In fact, I think I'd really, *really* enjoy it.

In the garage, I quickly coax all three very good boys into peeing on the puppy pads and reward them with a treat. Then, I throw one of the tennis balls on the shelf in the corner for them, letting them run off some of their puppy energy as I text the girls—

Hey guys. I'm home safe and about to sit down to eat with the pilot, but I'd be a lot happier if he were having ME for dinner...if you know what I mean.

I realize this is totally not my style, but he's so kind and sexy and saved me from getting crushed by a tree at the airport. He's also fifteen years older, but there are zero Dad vibes. I've never been this attracted to a man in my entire life.

I've also never had a one-night stand or seduced a man who's put off by our age gap. (But he almost kissed me before the oven alarm went off, so this is NOT an exercise in futility. He's feeling the energy, too. He just needs a little push, I think.)

So, what do I do ladies?

I need advice, and I need it quick!

*I'm putting my phone on silent while we eat, but I'll be back to check for seduction strategies in forty minutes. Don't let me down. *smiley face**

Oh, and here are a few shots of the puppies. Aren't they adorable?

I send over the pics I took while the boys were sitting pretty to earn their treat and leave the puppies in the garage with a few of the toys Gideon brought with him. It's a cool summer night, but it's warm in the garage and Bacon, Egg, and Cheese will have more fun running around here than being cooped up in their kennels, so they don't devour the couch while we're eating.

Or spend the entire meal begging for scraps.

You *could beg Gideon for scraps. Maybe that's the fastest way to ease his mind. Be completely honest about how desperate you are to have him toss you on a mattress and show you everything you've been missing. Tell him that no strings attached sounds like the perfect first time as far as you're concerned.*

But that would involve telling him that I'm a virgin.

Call me crazy, but that doesn't seem like a good plan. He's already hesitant to bridge our age gap. If he knew there was an experience gap, too, he'd probably insist on sleeping in the garage with the puppies, the better to be as far away from my tempting, too-young-and-virginal body as possible.

"But at least he finds me tempting," I murmur as I plug my cell in to charge at the desk in the living room.

Willing the girls to come through for me with the advice I need to make this a night I'll never forget, I head into the kitchen, starved in more ways than one.

five
GIDEON

The conversation flows easily over dinner, but beneath our discussions of favorite New England camping spots, sexual tension simmers like a pot about to boil over.

My knee brushes hers under the small table, and an electric shock of awareness races across my skin. Her fingers brush mine as we reach for the dressing, and I forget how to inhale. She sweeps her tongue across her full bottom lip and moans in appreciation of our simple meal, and I'm instantly hard beneath my cloth napkin.

I want this woman, want her more than I've wanted anyone or anything in a very long time.

I want to trace the path her tongue just took across her lips, feel the heat of her plush mouth beneath the pad of my thumb. I want to tell her how fucking beautiful she is, how sexy, how much I want to make her feel good. Most of all, I want to ask her what she fantasizes about at night when she slips her hand down the front of these unexpectedly sexy sweatpants.

Does she dream about a man fisting his hand in her hair while he drags his teeth down her throat? Does she long for hours of foreplay, complete with a full-body massage, lingering attention to her breasts, and the kind of focused, devoted oral that leaves her boneless with pleasure?

I can already tell I'll be a fan of anything that makes Sydney's breath catch and heat blaze in her sky-blue eyes.

I want to watch her get turned on, to see her lips part and her breasts rise faster as she nears the edge. I want to hear her call my name and beg to feel me inside her. Then I want to give her everything she's begging for and more.

Fuck, I have to think of something else, anything else, or I'm not going to be able to stand at the end of this meal. I'm so hard not even the thick fabric of my jeans can conceal my erection.

Praying for strength and a return of at least a modicum of self-control, I ask, "So, where to next? Once you're done here?"

She sips her chardonnay. "I'm going back to New York to join my family's business. It's time to put my MBA to work."

I start to reach for my own wine but think better of it. I'm already struggling to think clearly. More than a sip or two of wine would be a mistake. I stab a forkful of rice and cauliflower from the bottom of my bowl, instead. "And what's the family business?"

"Real estate development," she says, making my brows lift.

"Really? I work in the sector, too. My firm's specialty is retrofitting existing structures to be more environmentally friendly, but I do some new construction. If the project is the right fit."

Her eyes widen. "Wow. That was my thesis. I mean, not exactly that, I focused on sustainable building practices with an emphasis on mitigating extreme heat in warming climates, but…yeah." Her brows draw closer as a smile curves her lips. "We have a lot in common."

Like how much we want to sweep all these dishes to the floor and fuck on the table, I think. Aloud, I say, "Let me know if the family gig doesn't work out. I'm always recruiting bright young talent."

Her lids droop to half-mast in a way I'm not sure she realizes is seductive. There's an innocence to her flirtation that's as charming as it is sexy. "How do you know I'm a bright young talent?"

"You said you graduated top of your class, right?"

She lifts a shoulder. "Sure, I performed well in a classroom setting. But I could be a disaster waiting to happen in real life."

"That's what on-the-job training is for. And I can already tell you'll be an asset to any company lucky enough to have you. You're sharp, personable, and have a good heart."

She nibbles at her lip, sending fresh fantasies about what I'd like to do to her mouth flooding through my head. "You really think that's an asset?"

"What do you mean?"

"I mean, my dad's a nice guy, but I wouldn't say he has a good heart. Not when it comes to the company's bottom line. He's from the tough as nails, show-no-weakness school of business." She sighs and sets her fork down beside her bowl. "I'm sure he's going to spend a good chunk of my on-the-job training trying to toughen me up. Bring out my ruthless side."

I arch a brow and reach for my wine, after all, hoping it might slow my racing thoughts. "Do you have a ruthless side?"

She tilts her head thoughtfully, causing her now dry, glossy curls to slide over her shoulder, exposing her neck. "I'm sure I do. Most people do, I think, given the right circumstances. I've just been lucky enough not to have my ruthless side forced to the surface." She spins her wineglass in a slow circle on the table, gazing wistfully at the golden liquid. "But I don't want to be ruthless for a job, *any* job, even one that's my family's legacy."

I'm about to ask her what that legacy is and, more importantly, what she wants *her* legacy to be, when the grandfather clock in the living room starts to chime.

Sydney sits up abruptly. "Is it eight already?" She reaches for the napkin in her lap, drawing it across her mouth before standing to push her chair in. "Excuse me, I have to run upstairs for a minute. I'll be back to help with the dishes."

"Don't worry about it," I assure her, grateful our talks of ruthlessness and legacies have made it possible for me to stand without embarrassing myself. "What do you need to do upstairs? Anything I can help with?"

She hesitates beside me, sending her sweet smell rushing through my head and making the urge to draw her against me almost unbearable. "You want to see? You can come along if you want, but I'll warn you…it's a little weird."

"I'm not afraid of weird." I drop my napkin beside my now-empty bowl.

Sydney's mouth hooks up on one side. "You don't seem like you're afraid of much."

She's right. I'm *not* afraid of much.

So why are you so spooked by the chemistry between you two? I wonder as we head toward the circular staircase in the living room. Is it just a case of not wanting to cross a line with a woman who's so much younger than I am? Or is it something else entirely?

Maybe I'm not afraid of starting something with Sydney; maybe I'm afraid of how hard it will be to stop wanting more of her. I can already tell one or two nights wouldn't be enough. If I feel her under me, around me, coming on my cock, I'm going to need to feel it at least a hundred times.

Two hundred.

And neither of us is in a place for something like that to come easy.

We're both transitioning into new phases of our lives, but those phases couldn't be more different. She's diving into her career full force, and I'm continuing to step away from an active role in mine. She's starting her young adult life, and I'm spitting distance from middle age.

We might both love wildlife and daydream about hiking in Spain, but only one of us can take a month off next summer to do it. As much as I feel drawn to her, I should look for a partner closer to my own age or continue to fly solo.

Solo is good. I've been happily single for nearly two years and haven't had a serious relationship in far longer.

It's been so long that I thought my fantasies about whirlwind passion leading to the kind of close, loving family I couldn't make work the first time around were a thing of my past. I'm old enough now to know that not all dreams come true. That's just life, and it's better to be grateful for what you have than waste time lamenting what you've missed.

But there's something about Sydney that makes me want to throw all that out the window, to believe in miraculous twists of fate and mystical second chances.

So many factors had to align for us to have this night together. Wouldn't it be arrogant to think I know better than a universe that's conspired to connect me with this incredible woman?

At the top of the circular staircase, Sydney reaches out to flick a switch on a lightbox fixed to the railing. All around us, blue lights flicker to life in the floor and ceiling, until the large circular landing glows softly in the darkness.

"Wow." I step out onto the wooden floor and turn slowly, taking in the windows on every side of the old lamp room.

"Right?" Sydney smiles as she crosses her arms over her chest. "Sometimes, on clear nights, I'll bring a sleeping bag up here and sleep on the floor so I can watch the moon rise over the ocean." She points toward another smaller circular staircase to our right. "That leads to the third-floor guest bedroom. It's nice, too, but the windows are smaller. You can't see as much as you can down here."

"It's incredible," I say with a shake of my head. "If this place were mine, I'd be up here all the time."

Sydney hums beneath her breath. "You say that now, but it can get spooky up here. Especially once you know the legend of the woman in white."

I arch a brow her way. "This is the tragic tale you were going to tell me over dinner?"

She nods and launches into the story. "When the Civil War broke out, Maine was one of the first states to send soldiers, including the Sea Breeze lighthouse keeper at the time. He and his wife had just moved into the lighthouse after their honeymoon, but she supported his choice to volunteer. Allegedly, the marriage was already on the rocks. He had a terrible temper and a drinking problem, and she missed her old life in Portland. So, she wasn't too sad to see him go. She promised she would keep the lighthouse going on her own while he was gone, since she was young and in good physical health. But...she didn't know she was pregnant at the time or how long her husband would be away."

"Oh no." My brows pinch together.

She smiles. "You have very expressive eyebrows."

I relax my forehead with a smile. "Sorry. I'm not going to like the end of this story, am I?"

"I told you it was tragic." She crosses to the staircase leading up to the bedroom and plucks a candle in a bronze holder from the fifth step up. "If you don't want to hear the rest, I can skip to the candle-lighting part."

"No, don't skip," I say. "What happened to the pregnant lighthouse keeper?"

Sydney turns back to me, collecting a blue lighter from the holder's wide tray. "She lit the giant lamps for the ships every night, but as her due date grew closer, she knew she had to find someone to take over while she was recovering from childbirth. She put the word out around town and a handsome young man from a village north of Sea Breeze applied. He'd lost his foot in a threshing accident as a child, so he couldn't serve in the military, but he had a prosthetic and was fit enough to take care of the lighthouse."

"And to take care of banging the sexy lighthouse keeper?" I snap my brows together again, extra sharply, and am rewarded by Sydney's laughter.

"Not at first." Her lips hook up in a wry smile. "That didn't start until a few months later, when the baby was older. The handsome young man still lived in the cottage behind the house, but the rumor mill said he spent most nights in the lighthouse keeper's bed. That's where he was, anyway, when her husband came home a few months before the baby's second birthday."

I wince. "Ouch."

"Ouch all around," she agrees, her smile fading as she thumbs the lighter to life and touches it to the candlewick. "The husband beat the young man to death with a cast-iron skillet. His wife ran out of the house with the baby, but only made it to the edge of town before her husband caught up with her and tried to kill her, too."

"Jesus," I say, shaking my head.

"She was saved by some fishermen who were out late at the pub and her husband went to prison, but she was never quite right after that. People said she talked about her lover like he'd gone out to sea and would be back any day. That's when she started lighting two lights every night. The lamp for the boats in the harbor and a single candle as a sign to the young man that her love still burned bright." She crosses to a table by the glass overlooking the water and sets the candle on top. "As soon as Maya told me that story a few years ago, I started lighting a candle every night, too. It just seemed right."

She turns back to me with a shrug. "It probably seems silly, but I thought maybe the lighthouse keeper would like that. Wherever she is. She vanished a few years after her son went to college in Portland and was never seen again."

I fix my attention on her face, glowing a soft blue in the ambient light. "You're a romantic."

She shrugs again. "Maybe. I don't really know for sure. Haven't had much experience with romance."

"I find that hard to believe."

"Believe it," she says, her hands flopping at her sides.

"Were the boys at your college blind?"

"Um, no." She exhales a laugh. "They could see just fine. They just had trouble showing up. My last boyfriend stood me up four times before we broke up," she says, but without any heat in her tone. She's clearly over the douchebag. "Then, I tried dating apps for a while." She rolls her eyes. "By the time my third blind date stood me up, too, I decided it wasn't worth the effort."

I shake my head. "What's wrong with people?"

"Not people. Boys." She lifts her arms, fingers spread wide in surrender. "I'm not a man-hater, I promise, but none of my girlfriends stand people up like that. They call two hours in advance and back out of plans with a nice lie because they want to stay home in their sweatpants like civilized people."

"Boys," I murmur. "Maybe that's your problem."

She tips her head to one side. "Should I try girls instead?"

"If you swing that way, absolutely. Women are the superior half of the species. No doubt."

"I don't swing that way," she says, warmth in her gaze. "But I like that you think that. I can tell you mean it."

"I do." I take a step closer. "Maybe you just need a man instead of a boy."

She lifts her chin, holding my gaze as I continue to close the distance between us. "I'm trying, but so far, the only man I've liked told me I was too young for him. What's a girl supposed to do?"

Before I can respond, the lights in the room flicker and die, plunging us into darkness.

six

Gideon reaches out, wrapping an arm around my waist and drawing me protectively against him in the flickering candlelight, sending a zap of awareness tingling across my skin.

"Don't worry," I assure him. "This happens all the time during storms. The lights usually come on again in an hour or so."

"I'm not worried," he says, his voice husky. "At least, not about that…"

I mold my hands to his chest, relishing the solid feel of him beneath his sweater. "Good. I'm…" I swallow before continuing in a breathier voice, "I'm not worried either. About anything."

"I can't offer you more than tonight," he says as his hand slides lower, settling at the small of my back, just above the swell of my ass. "And you're the type of woman who deserves a hell of a lot more than that, Sydney. I wish I could be the man who shows up for you, on time, every time."

"I'd like that," I say, the ache between my legs so intense, it's almost painful. I've never wanted anyone the way I want this man, and I intend to have him, even if it is only for a night. "But I understand. I'm okay with one night, though I've never..." I swallow, then wet my suddenly dry lips. "I've never had a one-night thing before."

"I would be honored to be your first," he murmurs seconds before his lips touch mine.

His words make me think of other "firsts" he should probably know about, but his kiss soon banishes thought from my mind entirely. For the first time in ages, I'm out of my brain and in my body, lost in the way his tongue sweeps against mine, the way his hands roam over my curves, setting fire to every place he touches. The way he rasps my name like a prayer as his hand slips up and under my sweatshirt, cupping my bare breast in his hand.

"No bra." He curses beneath his breath. "Fuck, Sydney."

"Not a fan of bras," I say, moaning as he rolls my nipple between his fingers. "Really not a fan of them now. I love your hands on me."

"I want more than my hands on you," he says, making my breath catch as he leverages one thick thigh between my legs, giving me something firm and delicious to rock against as he continues to play with my nipples. "I want to spread you out on the floor and devour your wet pussy with my mouth."

"How do you know I'm wet?" I ask, gasping as his

free hand dives down the front of my sweatpants and panties, slipping between my slick folds with a confidence that makes my knees even weaker.

"I know you're wet because I know you feel the same thing I feel," he says, pushing two fingers inside me as his thumb circles my clit. "That you felt it the second we touched. Chemistry like this doesn't happen every day. Not to me, anyway."

"Me, either," I say, clinging to his shoulders as he swiftly drives me to the brink of the first non-self-administered orgasm I've experienced since my junior year of undergrad. Adrian and I never made it past the fully clothed make-out stage, and I was too busy to date before that.

No, not too busy, I admit to myself as Gideon's lips wage gentle war with mine. I just didn't understand what all the fuss was about. Yes, the making out was great, but I had so many other things I wanted to accomplish and goals I was determined to achieve. Finding someone to mess around with wasn't a priority for me.

I had no idea desire could feel like this, like a giant wave bearing down on the shore or a fire hot enough to burn down the world. It's inescapable, wild, and a little scary, but fear is no match for the things Gideon's voice does to me as he whispers, "Come for me, butterfly girl. Come on my fingers before I fuck you with my mouth. I can't wait to taste you, to have this wet pussy gushing all over my tongue."

"Gideon," I cry out, my head falling back as an

orgasm unlike anything I've felt before slams through me. I come so hard that time seems to skip. I lose myself in ripples of thick, sticky pleasure, only realizing I'm on the floor when I hear Gideon say, "Lift your hips, baby. I need this off you. I need to see you."

My lashes flutter, bringing the ceiling of the lamp room into focus. I glance down to see Gideon hovering over me, his fingers curled over the top of my sweatpants. My shirt vanished somewhere between standing and lying down. My breasts are bare, and my hard nipples stand at attention in the cool room. Once Gideon strips my pants and underwear down my legs, I'll be completely exposed, while he remains fully clothed.

I shake my head. "You first. I want to see you, too."

"Anything you want," he says, holding my gaze as he rips off his sweater, revealing his spectacular chest. His muscles are toned in a natural way that speaks to hours spent living an active life, not pumping iron in a stuffy gym, and dusted with the perfect amount of dark hair. He's beautifully masculine, and I'm already a huge fan of naked Gideon, even before he reaches for the button at the top of his jeans. "I mean it," he adds. "Anything you want. I don't have any hard limits."

Hard limits? I know that's a sex thing, but I'm not sure what separates a hard limit from a soft limit, and have no idea what my personal limits might be. I don't have enough experience to know what I like or don't like.

But I'm still sufficiently in my right mind to know

better than to tell him that. Instead, I let my gaze drag down to the front of his jeans as he pushes them down his thighs, revealing gray boxer briefs and an erection thick enough to send fresh heat pooling onto the cotton panel of my panties.

"I don't have any hard limits, either, I don't think," I say, biting my lip. "I just want to please you."

He arches a curious brow as he stands, shedding his jeans completely. "You like to please your lover?"

"Yes," I whisper, deciding the part about me never having had a lover before can wait.

"Then here's something you can do for me, beautiful." He kneels between my legs again, reaching for the top of my pants. "You can be quiet as a mouse while I eat your pussy. No talking, no moaning, not so much as an audible sigh. Think you can do that? No sounds from that sweet mouth until you're coming all over mine?"

I nod and he smiles a wicked grin I haven't seen on his face before.

But I like it.

I like it a lot.

"Good." He bends to kiss my bare belly before murmuring against my skin, "Your mileage may vary, but I think limitations can make an orgasm even more intense. Now lift your hips." I do and he whispers, "Good girl."

A sound rips from my throat, a needy moan I didn't realize I had inside me.

Gideon looks up, recognition I don't quite understand flaring in his dark eyes. "Noted, good girl. Now silent as a mouse. I need to focus on making you come so hard you forget your own name."

And good Lord, the man knows how to focus.

Before I know what's happening, I'm at the mercy of his talented mouth, clutching at his hair, his shoulders, shamelessly grinding into his tongue as he does things to me no one ever has before. And yes, I've heard that oral sex is incredible, but I always thought I'd be too shy to enjoy it, that the knowledge that all my less-sexy private parts are out for show and tell along with the sexy ones would have me in my head about the whole thing.

But I'm nowhere near my head as I come on Gideon's swirling tongue as his fingers thrust and curl inside me. I'm a creature of flesh and feeling, but a creature who doesn't forget to play by her new rules.

Gideon's right, the fact that I refuse to make a sound ramps up the intensity of my orgasm until I'm writhing on the floor. And hearing him call me his "good girl," again, after I come?

Well, that gives me feelings I'm not sure what to do with. I only know that I truly feel "good," truly *enough* for the first time in so long.

As I watch Gideon roll on a condom from his wallet and lean forward between my spread legs, I feel like I'm exactly where I'm supposed to be, doing exactly what I'm supposed to be doing. There's no need to strive or push harder or try to be the most perfect version of myself.

The me reflected in his eyes is already perfect.

But she might not be for long, the inner voice suddenly pipes up, *not if you let him go in blind like this.*

The inner voice is right. I don't want Gideon to think any less of me, and that means being honest.

Now. Before it's too late.

I reach up, putting a firm hand on his chest, "Wait. There's something I should tell you first."

seven

I freeze, going still, though every cell in my body is screaming for me to push forward. The head of my cock is already nestled between her legs. I can feel her heat through the condom and smell her arousal in the air.

I've never wanted to be inside a woman as badly as I want to be inside Sydney right now. But if she says wait, I wait.

I never want to give her a reason to doubt that she can trust me.

"What is it, what's wrong?" I ask, my voice ragged, but the rest of me holding strong.

"I just…" She pulls in a breath, swallows, then adds in a rush of breath, "I wanted you to know that it's my first time."

For a moment, I think she must mean her first time with an older man or her first time in a long time. Maybe her first time this summer? But the worry etched into her features isn't that kind of worry.

It's an "I'm in uncharted territory here" kind of worry.

I sit back on my heels, my breath rushing out as my erection begins to soften.

Sydney props up onto her elbows, shooting me a stricken look. "No, please. I don't want you to stop. I really don't. I just thought you should know. I wanted to be honest with you."

"I'm glad you were." My cock flags further as I imagine how easy it would have been to hurt her, simply because I didn't realize how careful I needed to be. "But this changes things, Sydney. I told you I can't promise more than one night and—"

"I know." She sits up fully, pressing her hand to my chest, just the feel of her fingers on my skin enough to send fresh desire surging between my legs. "And I'm okay with that, I promise. What I'm not okay with is stopping." Her eyes widen, pleading with mine. "I want you so much, Gideon. I want you inside me more than I've ever wanted anything."

I arch a brow, and she bites her lip. "Okay," she amends, "maybe not more than *anything*, but more than anything I can remember right now." Her fingers trail down my chest, skimming over my abs, making my balls ache. "I trust you, and I'm so attracted to you, and I…" Her lips curve into a soft smile. "I kind of love the idea that this is just one night. One magical night, that I'll never forget…"

"You're sure?" My breath catches as her curious fingers reach my stomach, coming within inches of where I'm fully hard for her again.

"I'm sure," she whispers, a teasing light in her eyes. "I'm not scared of your big bad cock, I promise. I can handle it."

"I bet you can handle anything you set your mind to," I say, floored again by how self-possessed she is. This woman may be inexperienced, but she knows her own mind.

And she certainly knows how to drive a man crazy...

Her fingers are at the base of my cock now, squeezing me gently, making my head spin. "Good. Because right now, my mind is set on kissing you again." Her lips part as she adds in a whisper that goes straight to my already throbbing dick, "And fucking you in the candlelight."

I curse, bringing a smile to her face. "Is that a yes?" she asks.

"Lay back," I say, my voice rough. "Tell me the moment you want me to stop and we'll stop."

"I don't want to stop," she says, her arms twining around my neck as I guide her back onto the smooth boards and settle between her legs once more.

I've never had sex with a virgin. Even as a teenager. Angela had already been with someone before we started dating. It was my first time, but it wasn't hers.

But I'm an excellent communicator and I like to think an attuned, connected lover. Hopefully, I'll be able to sense if things are getting uncomfortable for Sydney. And if I don't, I trust her to tell me.

Still, I can't help adding, "Let me know if there's any pain, okay. We can go as slow as you want."

"I'm so wet, it's not going to hurt," she says, her eyes

widening as I begin to press the head of my cock inside her. Her voice is breathier as she adds, "Wow, that's…" Her hands tremble on my back as I sink in another inch, then another, pushing gently through where she's so damned tight. "Oh my God. Wow."

"Back off?" I ask, pausing where I am, with half of my cock in paradise and the other half aching to join it.

"No," she says, a look of wonder in her eyes. "It feels amazing. So much different than I thought, but…so good. Wow."

"Agreed," I murmur, pleasure zipping up my spine as her body pulses around me, gripping every inch of me lucky enough to be inside her. I sink in a little more, summoning a moan from deep in her chest as I reach a zone of increased resistance.

"God, Gideon." Her fingernails claw at the flesh between my shoulders. "It's so good. I think I'm in love with your cock."

I smile, pretty sure I feel the same about her pussy. "Let's see if you feel the same way when I'm all the way in, butterfly. Take a breath for me and relax a little if you can?"

"Only if you kiss me first," she whispers.

"Anytime," I say, my tongue dancing with hers as I brush my thumb over her nipple, rubbing and teasing as her breath comes faster. Slowly, carefully, I push deeper, deeper, until I'm almost completely seated in the heaven between her legs.

"A little more, sweetness," I whisper against her lips. "Relax and let me in, butterfly. Let's see if you can take the rest of me."

"Yes, I want all of you," she says, but instinctively tenses as I try to shift forward. For a moment, I think we may have gone as far as we can tonight, but then she takes a deep breath. As she exhales, her inner walls relax the slightest bit.

"That's it, that's my good girl," I say, my jaw clenching as she hums in pleasure at the words.

Fuck, this woman... Not only is she beautiful and sexy as hell, but she clearly craves praise every bit as much as I love to give it.

"That's right, baby, you're doing so well," I whisper, doubling down. "Just relax and let go. Yes, Sydney, that's it, take every inch of me. Fuck, butterfly, do you feel how wet you're getting for me? How much your pussy wants everything I have to give you?"

"Yes," she moans, clinging to my shoulders. "Yes, Gideon."

"I'm almost there. Almost..." I ease forward that final inch, until I'm buried balls deep. "That's it, baby. That's my good girl."

Her breath emerges as a turned-on sob. "It feels like I have another heart beating inside of me, between my hips. Deep inside. Pulsing all around you."

"Is that a good thing?"

"It's incredible," she says, her legs wrapping slowly, carefully around my hips. She shifts beneath me, exploring the way we're connected with an innocence that makes sweat break on my upper lip. She's so damned tight, I can feel every ripple of her muscle and tissue, even through the condom. "It stings a little bit, but mostly it's…" She sighs and shifts again, making the urge to thrust inside her almost too much to resist.

But I don't want to rush a second of this. I want her to have all the time she needs to process everything she's feeling.

"I get it," she continues. "I finally understand why Elaina loves the spicy parts in romance novels so much. Sex really *is* amazing."

I kiss her forehead, grinning against her warm skin. "Oh, we haven't even gotten started yet, sweetheart." I pull back, gazing down at her in the glow of the candlelight. "It's going to get so much better, I promise."

"Yeah?" A hint of worry creases her forehead. "I don't know if I can come again. It's not you, I just… I can't usually get there more than once a night. And I've already come twice, so…"

"Who told you that?"

She blinks. "Well, no one, I just…" Her cheeks flush. "I mean, my vibrator is top-notch, but once the train has reached the station once, that's always been it."

"Huh, well…I'm not worried, and you shouldn't be, either. We'll get you there, no doubt in my mind."

She arches a wry brow. "Cocky, much?"

"Just confident." I shift my hips back before gliding slowly inside her again, holding her gaze as I fill her. "I love the way your mouth falls open when I'm turning you on. Now wrap your arms around me and hold on, butterfly. I'm going to make you scream."

She shudders, but when I crush my lips to hers, her arms lock around my chest without hesitation. A beat later, her legs tighten around my hips, forcing me even deeper inside her on my next thrust.

I fist my hand in her hair, groaning as our kiss grows hotter, deeper, and my sweet girl begins to lift into my cock with increasing confidence.

My girl...

I wish she could be mine. I wish it more with every thrust of my hips, with every hungry whimper that escapes her throat, with every gasp as I bend to suck her nipple into my mouth.

But we've agreed—all we have is tonight.

So, I'll just have to make the most of it.

With that in mind, I wedge my hands between her gorgeous ass and the floor, squeezing tight as I shift the angle of her hips, ensuring I'm grinding against her clit with every thrust.

"Oh God." Her nails dig into my shoulders as I continue to lick and suck at her nipples and ride her slow, but deep. "Oh God, Gideon. I think I'm... I think—"

She comes with a sharp cry, the release so intense I can feel her inner walls clutching around my cock.

And that's when my control begins to slip.

"Yes, fuck, yes, Sydney," I rumble as I piston faster, driving into her wet, throbbing heat, chasing after her toward the edge. "That's my good girl, keep coming for me, baby. Keep coming all over my cock while I—"

I come with a cry loud enough to set the dogs to barking downstairs, my dick jerking inside Sydney as she holds me tight.

The waves last for what feels like forever...but

unfortunately, the dogs' barking lasts even longer.

"I should go calm them down," I say when we've caught our breath, brushing her hair from her sweat damp forehead. "I'm sorry."

"Don't be sorry," she says, her eyes still glassy from her orgasm. I'm about to say "I told you we'd get you there," when she adds, "Just be in my bedroom in ten minutes or less. I need you again, Gideon. Already." She bites her bottom lip before asking, "Is that okay?"

"It's more than okay," I say, my cock already perking up inside the condom again. "It's fucking perfect, and so are you. Grab a condom from my bag in the guest room on your way. They're in my toiletry bag. I only had one in my wallet." I kiss her forehead. "I'll go to your room as soon as I get the dogs settled."

"Will do," she says, moaning as I pull out, gripping the bottom of the condom to hold it in place. "I definitely need you inside me again. At least one more time."

One more time…

I already know it's not going to be enough, but I'm not going to think about that now. I'll stay focused on making this a night Sydney will never forget, not even if she has a dozen lovers before she eventually settles down.

Not wanting to think about Sydney with anyone else, either, I tug my phone from my discarded jeans and tap the flashlight button to light my way down the stairs. Then, I grab my clothes and start down to the dogs still naked, determined to be back inside my butterfly as soon as humanly possible.

eight
SYDNEY

I dress quickly before grabbing the candle for light and hurrying down the stairs into Gideon's room. I can hear the rumble of his deep voice from the garage as he comforts the dogs, and it's enough to make my hands shake as I drag open the zipper on his toiletry bag.

I'm like an addict, already trembling for her next fix.

I never imagined I'd be this way. I'm not the kind of person who enjoys losing control or altered states of consciousness.

I never have more than a glass or two of wine at dinner and avoid adrenaline-rush-inducing activities at all costs. I don't drive fast or ride my bike through the city streets (I stick to the park, where I'm less likely to be run over). I've never tried drugs of any kind, including marijuana, even though my college dorm smelled of weed most of the time. Hell, I don't even allow myself more than one cup of coffee. No matter how much I love a little buzz, I know too much caffeine is bad for me.

But right now, I don't care if having sex all night with Gideon is bad for me. I don't care if I wake up tomorrow sore or sad or beating myself up for letting myself become obsessed with a man I hardly know.

I'll worry about tomorrow, tomorrow.

Tonight is for discovering all the things I can feel when a gorgeous man's naked body is tangled up with mine.

I set the candle on my bureau and the box of condoms by the bed. By the time I turn back to the door, wondering if I should go brush my hair or make some other effort to tidy myself, Gideon is in the hall outside my room.

He's in the hall, and he's still naked.

"Way too many clothes, woman," he says, shutting off his light and setting his phone on the bureau. "Come here and let me help you out with that."

I step in and his lips are instantly on mine, reawakening the fire he stoked to life inside me. Soon, I'm clinging shamelessly to his shoulders, his strong arms, moaning and kissing him at the same time as he magically makes my clothes vanish. Once again, I don't remember a break in the kissing or him pulling my sweatshirt over my head, but suddenly I'm naked except for my panties and Gideon is drawing me down onto the bed on top of him.

I gasp as my knees settle onto the mattress on either side of his hips and his erection presses between my legs. I'm a little sore, but he still feels incredible. I rock against him, shivering as waves of awareness flow from my clit to every well-loved inch of my body.

Not love, sex. It's just sex, the inner voice reminds me, but I shove her bliss-killing words away.

No, it's not love, but it's not just sex, either. The way Gideon looks at me as he cups my breasts in his hands, dragging his tongue over my nipples until I'm panting and dying to feel him inside me again, makes me feel more beautiful than I have in my entire life.

He makes me feel like a goddess, like the best "good girl" in the world.

Just thinking about his voice in my ear, praising me for taking every inch of his cock, is nearly enough to make me come again.

I've read enough Elaina-chosen romances to know this dynamic is closer to kinky than "normal," but I don't care. Everything I've done with Gideon has felt so right. Kinky or not, I want more of it, more of *him*, more of how safe and wild I feel when he's telling me how to please him.

"I want you so much," I whisper as he finally abandons my breasts to cradle my face in his hands again. "Please. Now?"

"Absolutely, butterfly." But he doesn't shift to move on top of me. He just lays back, his hands behind his head. "Get a condom and roll it on me."

I swallow. "I...I'm not sure I know how."

"That's okay," he murmurs, his gaze roaming over my body with appreciation as I sit perched on top of him. "I'll help you if you need it. Just get one out of the foil and we can go from there. You're going to set the pace this time. We can go as slow or as fast as you want."

I reach over, plucking a condom from the box and opening it up. The foil tears easily, but once I've discarded it on the table, I'm not sure what to do next. The condom is slipperier than I thought it would be and hard to hold onto. I nearly drop it on Gideon's belly as I'm turning it over, trying to sort out which side to place over his cock.

"Here," he says, his hands joining mine. "See the well, right there? That's there to catch my come, so it goes like this." He helps me fit the right side of the condom to the head of his cock before drawing his hands away again. "Now, just hold it in place there while you roll it down with your other hand." I do as I'm told and he murmurs, "Good girl," instantly making my nipples harder.

"Is it weird that I like that so much?" I ask, my breath already coming faster, even before he grips the sides of my hips, tugging my pussy against the base of his erection.

"No, it's perfect. You're perfect." He reaches down, rubbing a thumb over my clit through my panties, making me moan. "So how do you want me, perfect girl? Like this, with you on top? Or do you want to be under me again? Or maybe something else entirely? My cock is at your disposal."

"I think like this," I say, shimmying quickly out of my panties before straddling him again. I look down at his cock, simultaneously turned on and intimidated. He's not a small man in any sense of the word. It was all I could manage to take every inch of him when I was lying beneath him, focused purely on relaxing.

Will I be able to manage him this way?

"Brace your hands on my chest and take it slow," he says. "If it feels like too much, just tell me and we can find an easier position. You're so tight, and I'm sure you're sore. It's okay if this angle is too intense right now."

But it's not okay, because "right now" is all we have. If I want to know what it feels like to ride this beautiful man while he lies eager beneath me, it has to happen tonight.

"I think I can handle it," I say, sounding far more confident than I feel.

But I know all about faking it until I make it. It's what I did for years after my mother's sudden death, pretending I knew how to live without her, until it became true. I'll do the same when I return home to New York and start my new life as my dad's protégé.

The thought of working for my notoriously hard-to-please father is way scarier than anything that might happen in this bedroom tonight.

Worst case scenario, I can't comfortably manage Gideon this way and we go back to the missionary position. The missionary position may be boring to some, but everything is still so new to me.

New and so exciting my voice is breathy as I add, "And who knows? Maybe I'll find out I like intense things."

Gideon grips my hips as I reach between us, positioning him at my entrance. "No pressure, either way," he murmurs, his words thick with the same hunger humming through my veins. "Fuck, you're so beautiful like this." His features tighten as I begin to sink down on top of him. "God, baby, you're still so tight."

"Does it hurt you?" I ask, pausing with just the tip of him inside me.

His lips twitch. "No, it feels incredible. But it's also why I only lasted about ten minutes last time."

I smile. "Was it only ten minutes? It felt like longer. In a good way." I sink lower, holding his gaze as I take his thickness into where I'm still so tender. There's a degree of pain, there's no denying that, but there's pleasure, too. I'm so sensitive, the friction is intense. So intense, I'm on the edge of another release by the time I'm halfway down his shaft.

"Gideon," I pant, my arms shaking on his chest as his fingers dig deeper into my hips.

"We can stop, baby," he says. "I can help lift you off. Don't hurt yourself."

"I'm not hurting," I say, breath coming faster. "I'm close." I bite my lip, moaning as my body ripples around his cock and slickness leaks down my thigh.

He curses. "Then come, sweetness. Come on your cock."

I shake my head. "Not yet. Not until I have all of you…inside me." I sink lower, the slight shift setting sparklers to spinning in my belly.

I feel like one of those cartoon animals about to be shot out of a cannon. And then Gideon starts rubbing his thumbs over my nipples again and I detonate so fast,

I barely have time to slam my hips down before the most intense orgasm of my life rips through me.

I'm not sure what I say at first, but by the time I become aware of the words spilling out of my mouth, I'm embarrassed to realize it's mostly a mixture of "god, oh god, oh Gideon, oh god," on repeat as I grind against him. I don't remember shifting positions, but my lips are suddenly on his neck and my body is draped in a smothering half-moon over his chest, but he doesn't seem to mind.

"That's it, Sydney," he says, his big hand on my ass, helping me rock back and forth. "I love feeling you come on me. It's so good, baby."

I pull back, holding his gaze as my breath rushes out. "Wow. They just... They keep getting better. I don't think I can handle it if they get any more intense."

He smiles, that wicked grin I love every bit as much as his kind one. "How about we find out?"

He grips me tight, making me giggle as he flips us over with his erection still locked deep inside me. And then he starts to move, taking me with long, languid thrusts that make me feel like I'm spinning through a pink, sunset sky. He tells me how sexy I am, how beautiful, how much he wants me to come for him again, all while his hands roam over my skin, setting little fires everywhere he touches.

"Fuck, Syd, you destroy me," he says as he moves faster and I cling to him like the hopeless addict I've become. "I'm going to come. I'm so close." He reaches between us, finding my clit with his fingers as he continues to thrust inside me. "Come with me, sweetness, come on your cock again."

I arch into his fingers, crying out as my fourth orgasm of the night rips through me. Gideon's rhythm grows faster, then wild, erratic, until he thrusts forward with a groan. This time, I can feel him pulsing inside me and it makes my entire body shiver, drawing out my own release until I'm a boneless puddle.

I'm so spent, all I can do is whimper when Gideon whispers, "Good girl. I knew you could come for me again."

It isn't until nearly ten minutes later, after Gideon's pulled out, disposed of the condom, washed up in the bathroom, and made his way back to my door that I finally summon the strength to lift an arm and beg, "Water, please? I would get it myself but I've been sexed into a coma."

Gideon laughs from the doorway, a deep laugh that makes me tingle again. "You're chatty for a woman in a coma."

"Not really," I say, sighing. "That's it. Those are all the words I have."

He laughs again. "Hold on, butterfly. We'll bring you back to life. Be right back." He reappears a few moments later with water, a glass of wine, plates, napkins, and the cheese and apple board we neglected to have for dessert.

We spread the food out on the bed and dig in. Halfway through our treat, the lights come back on, but we shut them off again, enjoying our candlelit picnic.

When I'm full of food, water, and wine, Gideon

cleans the mess and returns to hover in the doorway, "Do you need to be carried to the bathroom to get ready for bed?" he asks. "If you do, it's a service I'm happy to provide. When I sex a woman into a coma, I like to take full responsibility until she's back on her feet."

I wrinkle my nose. "I don't like to think of you sexing other women into comas."

"Me, either," he says softly. "If another man did this to you, I'd be tempted to *punch* him into a coma."

I smile. "No, you wouldn't. You're a good egg, I can tell."

"Thank you, Miss Watson," he says with an affection that makes my chest ache. "Right back at you. Thank you for one of the best nights of my life."

"Same," I whisper, feeling a little guilty for lying to Gideon about who I am, even if it's only a lie of omission. I suddenly want to tell him that I'm a Perry-Watson and that the job waiting for me at my "family company" is so massive, it's terrifying. I want to talk through all my feelings and fears and hear what I'm sure would be Gideon's very thoughtful advice.

But then he's beside the bed, scooping me into his arms, and I forget about everything but how good it feels to be close to him.

I rest my cheek on his chest on the way to the bathroom, soaking in every second of my first princess carry. I've never had any fantasies about being swept up in a strong man's arms, but I know I'll have them now.

I'm going to fantasize about everything that happened tonight for a very long time.

Maybe the rest of my life...

nine

I've never been so sad to wake up to the sun streaming through a window.

But today isn't a day for hiking or climbing or getting outside to enjoy the end of summer. Today is the day I say goodbye to Sydney.

Maybe forever.

With conditions fine for flying, there's no excuse to stay another night, and the shelter is expecting the puppies.

The puppies...

I glance at the clock on Sydney's small dresser on the other side of the room. It's only six-fifteen. The dogs can wait a little longer to be taken out, and if they really need to use the bathroom, the puppy pads are still in the garage.

There's time to say a proper goodbye, to show Sydney how much I'm going to miss her.

Ignoring the sadness twisting in my chest, I wrap my

arm tighter around her sleeping body, pulling her back tighter to my front.

She emits a sleepy moan and wiggles her ass closer to my cock. I'm already hard, but if I weren't, that's all it would take to get me there—just a wiggle of this woman's incomparable ass and the knowledge that she isn't wearing panties.

I could be inside her in two seconds…if I were the type of man to start something without express consent. After all, just because she couldn't get enough of me last night doesn't mean she feels the same way this morning.

But that doesn't mean I can't tease her awake…

I lift her thigh up far enough to leverage mine beneath it, giving me space between her legs to play. I reach down, gripping my cock and guiding it to the piece of heaven I wish I never had to leave.

When I feel how wet she already is, I nearly lose it and slide inside her. But I need a condom and Sydney's pretty eyes open first. I clench my jaw, limiting my sexy "good morning," to rubbing the tip of my cock gently back and forth over her clit until she shifts restlessly against me, her breath coming faster.

A few moments later, she's awake, her shoulders tensing against my chest before she relaxes with a happy sigh. "Not a dream," she murmurs sleepily, spreading her thighs wider. "You weren't a dream."

"Not even a little bit." I leave my cock pulsing against her clit as I skim my hand up to play with her sensitive nipples.

She moans, arching into my touch. "God, how do

you do that? I never loved that before. Now, I can't get enough."

I smile against her back before pressing a kiss to her shoulder. "How does the rest of you feel this morning. Sore?"

"Yes," she says, "but I want you too much to care."

"We don't have to have penetrative sex," I assure her, even though I desperately want to. But I want all her memories of her first time, of *me*, to be perfect far more. "I can make you come on my mouth again."

She shakes her head slightly, her chest rising and falling faster as I continue to play with her breasts. "No. I want you inside me. I want it so badly." She reaches back, dragging her nails over my bare ass and pulling me closer, making my heavy balls ache. "From behind."

"There's no need to rush," I say, trailing my hand from her breasts to between her legs, teasing two fingers over her clit. "I believe in foreplay."

"I know you do," she says, her voice sultry as she moves her hand between our tangled legs to grip the end of my cock. "But I've been dreaming about you all night. I'm ready. I promise." She strokes what she can reach of my shaft, making me ache to feel her slick heat tight around me from base to tip. "But if you need more time, I can take point on foreplay. I hear men like to have women suck their balls. Is this true?"

"I'd love your mouth around my balls," I tell her, reaching for a condom on the bedside table. "But right now, I think we're on the same page."

"You don't want to wait?" she asks, her breath

catching as I pull away from her long enough to slide the protection on.

"Not another second." I grip her knee, guiding her leg fully up and over my thigh. I start to reach down to position myself, but her hand is already gripping my shaft, guiding my erection down over her clit to the wet heat between her legs. "Yes, baby, put me in you."

She makes a hungry sound low in her throat as she fits me to her entrance and shifts her hips back slightly, instinctively knowing how to line our bodies up to fit. I sink inside her, biting the inside of my cheek as I fight to go slowly, to give her time to work through any lingering soreness.

She murmurs her approval as she grips my ass again. "Yes, just like that. God, Gideon, your cock is my favorite thing ever. Even the hint of pain feels good."

"So good," I echo, threading my fingers through hers. I nuzzle my face into the nape of her neck, inhaling the sweet scent of her hair as I continue to shift slowly forward, burying myself in her sweetness, inch by blissful inch.

When I'm fully seated, I hold still, murmuring into her ear, "How's that, butterfly?"

"Perfect," she says, her voice tight. "I think I could come right now, Gideon. I'm so sensitive, it feels…so intense."

"Then come, sweetness." The thought of her pussy gripping me is enough to bring me perilously close to the edge. "I think we've established, I can always make you come again."

"I don't want to," she says. "Not yet. I want to wait."

She hesitates a beat before adding in a softer voice, "I want you to *make* me wait. To make me wait because you want me to."

Holy fuck, this woman...

This goddess.

"I love how you ask for what you want," I say, kissing her shoulder again before sweeping her hair away from her neck with my other hand. I kiss her throat, rumbling my approval against her soft skin. "But now it's time to do what you're told. I'm going to fuck you and play with your tits and tease this pretty little clit, but you're not going to come until I tell you to. Do you understand?"

She nods, shivering against me. "Yes, but..."

"But what?" I squeeze the inside of her thigh.

"What happens if I can't... If I can't stop myself?"

"Then you won't be told what a good girl you are," I say, smoothing my palm up her leg to cup her sex. I rub the heel of my palm against her clit as I draw back and glide into her again, making her moan. "And I know you want to be my good girl. Don't you?"

"Yes," she says with a rush of breath as her hands thrust back, tangling in my hair as I rock my palm into her again. "Yes, Gideon. I want that."

"You want all your orgasms to belong to me?"

She makes a sound of such primal pleasure, I know we've tapped into something deep, something that she's maybe never thought about, at least not consciously. "Yes," she whispers as I fist my other hand in her hair, tugging her head back, bringing her lips within kissing range. "I want all of them to belong to you."

Ignoring the voice of reason in my head, noting that owning her orgasms might be hard to manage when we're living hundreds of miles away from each other, I promise, "Then they will. From now on, they're mine. You're mine." Her breath catches, giving me no choice but to ask, "Would you like that? To be mine? Mine to worship and fuck and shower with all the praise you're craving?"

She only whimpers in response, but the next time I rock forward, she pushes backward, taking me deeper, and I decide that's answer enough.

Rolling her onto the mattress beneath me on her stomach, I brace my hands on either side of her shoulders and knee her thighs wider apart. "Then that's how it will be, Sydney. Next time you're on your belly in your bed with your fingers or your vibrator between your legs, you're going to call me. You're going to get me on the phone and wait until I tell you it's okay for my pussy to come."

"Yes, yes," she chants as I rock into her with deeper thrusts.

"Would you let me watch you?" I wedge my hand between her hips and the mattress, finding her clit again. "Would you put me on FaceTime so I could see you when you come?"

"You're a bad man in bed," she says, her breath coming faster. "I love that about you. I love it so much."

And I love the "L" word on her sweet lips, but I'm smart enough to keep that to myself.

Instead, I say, "I'm not bad, I'm just not afraid to be what you need, sweetheart. There's nothing bad or wrong about this. This wet pussy gripping my cock so tight I know she's about to come is the rightest thing in the fucking world. God, Sydney, you're so close. I can feel you, baby, but you'd better not come. Not yet."

"Please," she begs. "Please, it feels like I'm dying. Like I'm going to die if I don't give in."

"Don't," I order her, hoping I'm not pushing her too far. "Wait for me, butterfly. I'll count you down. Ten…"

I pump faster, deeper, sweat breaking out between my shoulders as she claws the mattress with her nails.

"Nine, eight…"

I grind the heel of my hand into her clit, making her cry out and tense beneath me.

"Not yet, baby, not yet," I whisper as she begins to tremble. "Seven, six…" I slam into her, nearly losing it as she bucks back against my cock, taking everything I have to give her. "Five, four…"

"Gideon, oh, Gideon, please. I'm so close, I—"

"Three…"

She whimpers and her breath comes in swift, sharp pants.

"Two…" I bite her shoulder as I push all the way inside her one last time, groaning, "One," as my cock starts to pulse inside her, my release so intense my vision blurs.

She comes with a keening sound that makes me wish I could keep fucking her forever. I never want to leave this bed, this woman, this sweet little pussy that grips me so tight.

"Good girl," I whisper into her hair as her breath finally starts to slow.

She shivers and sighs. "Good man," she whispers, but she sounds…sad.

I pull back, guiding her hair out of her face, troubled to see her eyes shining. "What's wrong? Was I too rough? Did I hurt you?" I pull out, quickly disposing of the condom in the wastebasket in the corner but returning to the bed to pull Sydney into my arms.

She snuggles into my chest, hugging me tight, easing my worry. "No, it was perfect. So perfect."

"But," I prompt after a beat.

"But as much as I want my orgasms to belong to you, as much as I want to see you again…" She lifts her head, gazing down at me with a wisdom far beyond her years. "I can't do this right now, Gideon. I'm already terrified that I'm going to crash and burn at my new job. If I'm thinking about hurrying home to FaceTime you in bed or daydreaming about the next time we get to be together, my focus won't be where it needs to be. I honestly don't think I can juggle both an all-encompassing job and aching for someone I'll only be able to see once or twice a month, at best."

She's right. I know she is, but it doesn't make it hurt any less. "I understand. I've tried long-distance a couple times. It's really hard, even when you're not going through a major life change at the same time."

Her lips turn down. "Yeah. So…you're not disappointed in me?"

I cup her face, my chest aching for her, this woman who clearly doesn't realize how precious she is. "I'm disappointed, but not in you. Never in you. You're incredible, butterfly. You're sexy and smart and kind and so damned beautiful, inside and out. You're going to do incredible things with your life. And the man who gets to be yours for longer than a night is going to be one lucky fucker."

Tears shine in her eyes. "Thanks. And same. I hope you find someone wonderful." Her lips curve. "And that I never see her face, or I'll probably hate her a little."

I smile. "So, I take it we won't be following each other on social media?"

"I think leaving it here is probably best," she says. "A clean break and a beautiful memory I will always treasure. Truly. I couldn't have asked for a better first time."

"Is it wrong that a tiny part of me hopes I've ruined you for lesser men?"

Her eyes glitter. "Not at all. I don't want a lesser man. I want one as wonderful as you or nothing at all."

She's going to be okay. Better than okay. And so will I.

I keep telling myself that as we take the dogs out for a run in the damp grass, wipe them down, and feed them their breakfast. As she reads some of the "how to seduce an older man texts" her friends sent last night while she was already doing just fine in that department upstairs. As we grab bacon, egg, and cheese sandwiches from a deli in town in honor of the puppies and Sydney drives me to the airport.

And as I hug her goodbye one last time outside the terminal.

But I'd be lying if I said walking away from her wasn't one of the hardest things I've ever done.

It's brutal, and as I touch down in Burlington ten

hours later, after successfully delivering the dogs to their new temporary home, I'm still wondering if I've made a mistake.

And if Sydney is thinking of me tonight as much as I'm thinking of her.

ten

New York City
One month later...

The only thing worse than living in the same apartment building as your ex-boyfriend?

Living in the same building as your ex, while your roommate is dating *his* roommate and best friend.

Noelle usually goes down to Ben and Adrian's place to hang out, but there are times when that just isn't possible.

"I'm sorry," my bestie since fifth grade says, tying her pink-and-blond-streaked hair into a high ponytail as she hurries into the kitchen. "The foot stink is just too powerful. It smells like moldy cheese left to rot in a boys' locker room. I can taste it." She shudders. "In my mouth."

I smile from the couch, where I'm camped out with my laptop, as usual, taking work home with me for what feels like the hundredth day in a row even though I've been employed for less than a month. "That's usually where a person tastes things."

"I'm sorry," she says again. "Truly. I tried to get them to call their cleaner in for an emergency sesh or at least tackle some of the laundry, but you know how they are. If work isn't artistic or going to look good on social media, they aren't going to do it."

"But that's part of what you love about Ben." I sigh, fluttering my eyelashes as I mimic Noelle's swoony "I love Ben" voice, "He's a sensitive poet painter genius with a heart too tender for this world."

Her green eyes narrow and her bottom lip pokes out as she fills the electric kettle. "He is. And he's painting a giant portrait of my eye that's the most beautiful thing I've ever seen, Syd. How could I force him away from that for something as mundane as cleaning his room or washing his socks? Sock stink comes and goes, but being a painter's muse makes you immortal."

"And you deserve to be immortal," I say. "I'm honestly fine with them coming over to have coffee before you leave for the party. If they get too obnoxious, I'll go to my room."

She grins, her dimple popping. "You're the best. Have I told you how much I love you lately?"

I roll my eyes. "Stop. You don't have to kiss up to me. I get it." I sigh, forcing my gaze back to my screen. "And Adrian doesn't have anything on these spreadsheets. I'd rather listen to him be pretentious about his stupid app than wade through another profit and loss statement."

Noelle sticks out her tongue. "Yuck. Paperwork. I hate paperwork. I'm so glad I majored in making tiny hats for hamsters instead."

I laugh.

"It's not funny," she says, pouting again. "I have a fashion design degree from one of the top schools in the country. I should be making fabulous gowns for the Met Gala. Or at least B movie red carpet events. Not hamster hats."

"And coats and scarves and teensy tiny shoes with curled toes." I put my finger and thumb a few millimeters apart and stare at her through the space. "Those are my favorite."

She blows air through her lips, then smiles. "Yeah, me. too. They're fucking adorable, and I'm making bank, so I'm not going to complain. I'm just going to be grateful that I have all my orders filled for the week and a fabulous party to look forward to. You really should come. I'm sure Adrian wouldn't mind."

"Ugh. No." I make a gagging sound. "I can't believe I ever thought his DJ performance artist persona was interesting."

Noelle shrugs. "He's a hot tortured artist. I get why you were feeling the vibe. And deep down, he's really sweet. He just needs therapy and to fall madly in love with someone who refuses to put up with his bullshit."

I hum my reluctant agreement. Adrian *is* a nice guy, but lately, he's been getting on my last nerve. But I sense that's more about me than my ex. Every time I look at him, all I can think about is what an idiot I was for wasting five months of my life with an insecure kid, when I could have been with a man like Gideon.

Gideon...

I instantly push thoughts of the man to the back of my mind, the way I have since returning home. I'm not moving to Burlington, and we both agreed a long-distance relationship would be too hard to manage right now. And I was right when I assumed I'd be too busy to date. I'm so busy, I barely have time to eat, and I haven't been on a run in over a week.

It's best that Gideon is just a memory now...a memory I'll replay later, after Noelle has left for the party, and I'm alone in the apartment with the coastal New England-scented candle that reminds me of him and my vibrator.

"Do you want coffee?" Noelle asks as she gathers mugs from the cabinet.

"Sure, thanks. It's going to be another late night at the paperwork factory."

"Then I'll use the big coffee carafe, so you'll have extra to warm up later." She fetches our extra-large pour-over coffeepot from above the stove.

It was a housewarming gift from my dad. He wanted me to move in with him on the Upper East Side—our apartment has two stories and Dad's away at our vacation home in The Hamptons most weekends—but he understood when I insisted on rooming with Noelle. He wants me to remain close with my friends and make time for socializing.

Or so he says...

The company-wide audit he's insisting I perform to "get familiar with the corporate structure" says otherwise. He wants my final report by next Friday, but I've only begun to wade through all the documentation. Our corporation has so many subsidiaries, charitable arms, and shell companies for the limited liability ventures that it's like trying to untangle a wad of necklaces that have been jostling around in a drawer since 1996.

But it's my wad to untangle, so I'd better keep at it. The fact that my boss is also my father doesn't make the thought of failing his first test any less stressful.

I'm about to dive back into the profit and loss statement from Harbor Home, our charity offering sanctuary to victims of domestic violence, when there's a sharp knock on the door.

Noelle squeals and races across the room, making me smile. She and Ben have only been dating for four months and are still in the wildly-in-love phase. It's adorable, and I'm so happy for her, even if Ben does come with a moderately annoying sidekick.

"Come in, come in, coffee's almost done," Noelle says, greeting Ben with a kiss on the cheek and a smitten grin. "Missed you."

"Missed you, too," Ben says in that soft, thoughtful way of his. As he steps inside, he lifts a hand. "Hey, Sydney."

"Hey," I say, but my greeting is drowned out by Adrian's snarky, "You saw each other three hours ago, relax," as he swaggers inside behind his friend.

I snort as I see what Mr. Moderately Annoying is

wearing tonight. "I think you could fit another entire person in those pants."

Adrian grins, his dark eyes dancing as he does a spin, making the shiny black fabric of his pants flare out even further. "You like? That designer who makes those puppet purses that blew up last spring made them for me."

"They're…big," I say tactfully.

"And shiny," Noelle adds, making Adrian frown.

"And cool," he insists. "Tell them, Ben."

"I thought they were a skirt at first," Ben says, following Noelle into the kitchen to pour hot water over the freshly ground beans. "That would have been cool."

Adrian sighs. "I'm surrounded by people with no fashion vision."

"Hey, I'm a designer," Noelle says. "I have vision. I just don't think a giant pair of culottes made in parachute fabric is particularly visionary. Your butt is way too cute to cover up like that." She sniffs and lifts her pert nose higher in the air. "If I were your designer, I'd play to your assets."

"Aw, thanks." Adrian winks at Noelle. "You're a doll." He glances my way. "What do you think, Syd? Is my butt too cute to hide? I know I'm the most annoying ex-boyfriend ever and don't deserve a second of your attention, but my butt is pretty okay, right?"

I roll my eyes but can't help smiling. He's ridiculous, but beneath the bravado, he's also painfully insecure. It's something I've only realized lately, but it's given me more compassion for my ex.

"I would go with your faux leather pants," I say, studying his short-sleeved hoodie, a mishmash of black fabrics that looks like a junior high school kid made it on their at-home sewing machine, but probably cost a thousand dollars at some Soho designer's pop-up shop. "The white ones. They'll look better with your shirt."

"Agreed," Noelle says. "There are so many nice textures in that shirt, but you need a pop of something brighter to help bring them out."

"Cool," Adrian says. "I'll change on our way out." He crosses the room and plops down next to me on the couch. "As soon as I convince Sydney to come and play with us."

"Sorry, can't," I say, my gaze fixed on my screen. "I have too much work."

"It's Friday night," Adrian says.

"And I only have until next Friday night to finish," I insist. "My dad threw me straight into the deep end."

Adrian grunts, his tone markedly less cheery as he says, "Let's not talk about dads. Mine is driving me fucking nuts. He insisted on coming to the fundraiser tonight to 'support me,' even though I told him it wasn't a big deal. Now I'll have to worry about babysitting him while I'm trying to woo investors."

I make a sympathetic sound. "Sorry. But sounds like he's trying to be there for you at least. That's good, right?"

Adrian groans dramatically as he sinks lower into the couch cushions. "Fuck, I don't know. Maybe, but I wish he'd picked another time. There's so much on the line, and I'm already going to be off my game." He turns his head my way, adding in a pained voice, "Gigi broke up with me last night."

I arch a brow, wondering why he's surprised—Gigi is a social climber who's cheated on him twice since they started dating. But he looks truly upset about it. "I'm sorry," I say. "That's hard."

"It is," he agrees. "And it looks bad. What kind of loser can't come up with a plus-one for his own event?"

"I'm sure you could find one if you tried," I say, glancing toward where Noelle and Ben are canoodling in the kitchen as they add cream and sugar to their coffees. "Have you asked Noelle if any of her friends from fashion school are free? A lot of them are your type. They have that starving model with giant anime eyes aesthetic you love."

He makes a dismissive sound. "That's not always my type." He smiles before adding in a silkier voice, "Sometimes I like a natural beauty with wavy strawberry blond hair and a heart of gold."

I cut a sharp look his way. "No."

"Oh, come on, Syd," he says, his grin widening. "It could be fun. You like dancing."

"No," I insist again, shaking my head.

"Yes, you do. And you wouldn't have to hang out with me the whole night. Just do the red carpet and look interested when I talk to the journalists covering the event. As soon as we head inside, we can go our separate ways."

"What part of 'no' don't you understand?" I ask. "The Nuh or the Oh?"

"And we can make it clear it isn't a date," he barrels

on as if he hasn't heard me, which he probably hasn't. Once Adrian starts after something he wants, his listening skills go out the window. "I'll tell the reporters we're there as friends. Just two old college buddies hanging out and hoping to make a difference for the starving artists of the world. Don't you want to help indie artists make the kind of money they deserve? To help traditionally marginalized people reach a world-wide, art-collecting audience and maybe kick a few old dead guys out of The Met while we're at it?"

I sigh, but I can feel myself weakening. "Yes, of course, I do." His app, aimed at connecting collectors with indie artists overlooked by snobby galleries and museums, is actually a good one.

No matter how cheesy he's been while promoting it...

The thought reminds me of how little control I have over my eye-rolling when listening to Adrian pretend to be a humble genius. "But I can't," I insist. "I'm busy and tired and even if I weren't, I have nothing to wear to a club."

"It's not a club," he says. "It's a swanky hotel event space and a night of music-infused performance art. There are going to be dancers, live painting, interactive theater... There will be so much going on, no one will notice a random nature girl wearing a cotton sundress."

"Forget that. I have a smoking hot, black satin mini and stilettos you can wear, Syd," Noelle pipes up from the kitchen. "Show off those long, sexy legs. Remind you there's more to life than work and capitalism." She bats her fake lashes. "Spend some time with your bestie, who didn't get to hang out with you at all this summer, and needs more Sydney in her life?"

Ben nods, his emotional blue eyes finding mine. "She really missed you. A lot."

I glance at Adrian, who folds his fingers together in a pleading fist and mouths, "Please?" then back to Noelle who is still giving me major puppy dog eyes.

Finally, I exhale and snap my laptop closed. "Okay, fine, but I'm going to need you all to promise to carry me home if I get blisters. I haven't worn high heels in so long, I'll probably be limping before midnight."

Noelle cheers, Ben looks slightly less emotional, and Adrian leans over to pull me in for a hug. "Thank you, Syd. Seriously. I owe you one." He leans back, a vulnerable smile curving his lips as he adds, "I'm glad we're still friends."

Softening, I say, "Me, too."

And honestly...I am.

He might be a doofus, but he can't help it. It's who he's always been.

It's my fault that I used to see him with rosy, crush-colored glasses. I'm beginning to realize that's a habit of mine. I want to see the best in people so badly that I ignore the red flags. Sometimes, I even ignore the rainbow ones, like with my first boyfriend in high school.

Skip is now out of the closet and running a specialty dog biscuit boutique in Provincetown, Massachusetts with his boyfriend. And Adrian is...Adrian, as superficial and image-conscious as ever, but with an honest longing to do good. If he could go about it in a less pretentious, performative way, he'd be well on his way to being an impressive human being.

But pretension seems like a necessary evil in the art world. It makes the stuffy, business path I've chosen seem easy in comparison. Yes, I have to be professional and put together at the office, but I don't have to act impressed by a fifteen-foot painting of white smears with a red dot in the middle.

"Then we need to get you dressed, baby," Noelle says, bouncing up and down as she claps her hands. "Come on. I'll slip into my dress and then get you fancied up and marvelous in thirty minutes or less."

"Make it twenty," Adrian says, glancing at his smart watch. "I want to be sure I have time to get inside the venue and meditate before it gets too crowded. I need to be centered to deal with influencers and journalists and gossip hounds asking why Gigi was photographed going down on a soccer player at a bar last night."

I wince as I stand, laptop in hand. "Ouch."

He sighs. "Big ouch." He groans and flops back against the couch cushions. "And my dad's going to want to have a *meaningful* talk at some point, can't forget that. Dad's always thirsty for a meaningful talk, even when it's not the time or the place, and there's nothing to talk about."

"There, there, drink your coffee and think focused thoughts," Noelle says, snagging my wrist on her way past the couch and drawing me toward her room. "You're going to look so hot," she whispers as she closes the door behind us. "I bet you'll meet a fantastic older man while we're out tonight who will help you forget all about Mr. Pilots Puppies."

I haven't told Noelle Gideon's real name. I used a nickname, hoping it might lessen the pain of missing him, but it hasn't. Whether he's Mr. Pilots Puppies or Gideon, the thought of him still sends a stabbing sensation through my chest.

"I don't know," I say, forcing a laugh. "All the women at the office say dating in the city is a waste of time unless you have a matchmaker and do a background check that includes a sweep of the dark web. Apparently, the dating waters are full of sharks, giant squid, and ocean-killing islands of plastic debris."

Noelle's features pinch toward the middle of her face. "I'm not sure what that means, but I disagree. There are wonderful people everywhere." She bobs her shoulders. "And horrible ones. But tonight, we're going to draw the good ones to us like moths to a flame, I can just feel it. Now, let's get you dressed."

She reaches into her jam-packed closet and pulls out a black silk camisole dress with a dropped waist, 1920's style. It has a lace panel across the chest, seed pearl decorations, and a skirt that ends in tiny pleats. On the hanger, it looks sweet and old-fashioned.

But once I slip it over my head…

"Woah." My eyes go wide as I glance at my reflection in the mirror in the corner of her room.

"Right?" She beams. "You're a sexy little snack in that dress. You're going to have your pick of hot older men. You do still like older men, right?"

"I don't know," I murmur, stunned at how much

larger my breasts look with a bit of side boob showing near the dress's spaghetti straps. "I think I just liked Mr. Pilots Puppies. It wouldn't have mattered if he were twenty-five or fifty-five."

"Aw, that's sweet," Noelle says, before pushing on in a no-nonsense tone, "But fifty-five would have been gross. Thirty-nine is perfect. He's old enough to know what he wants, but not too old to keep up with you. If I ever break up with Ben, I'm only dating older guys. They're just so much more dependable and predictable, you know? And I bet most of them don't worry about running out of money to go out for a slice of pizza by the end of the month."

I catch her gaze in the mirror. "But you don't care. You'd rather starve with Ben than eat at a five-star restaurant with anyone else."

Her smile stretches into a mile-wide grin. "You're so right. He's the sweetest and the sexiest and I love him to bits and pieces."

"I'm happy for you guys. You give me hope that love isn't dead, after all."

She frowns and *pishes* at me with a flap of her hand. "Well, of course it isn't. You'll find your Ben. It's just a matter of time. It could happen at any moment, even when you least expect it."

She could be right, I guess, but I'm certainly not expecting anything tonight. The party will be full of Adrian's pretentious friends, artistic people who pity my sad, business life, and models hired to stand around looking bored and fabulous.

Oh, and Adrian's dad, who will probably be a jerk

and make me feel sorry for Adrian, giving him the leverage he'll need to force me to stay at this party far later than I'll want to.

When Noelle's done arranging my hair in a pretty spill of curls and I've allowed her to do my eyes and lips —though I refuse blush on the grounds that it makes me feel like a clown, no matter how tastefully it's applied—I catch her elbow on the way to her bedroom door.

"Hey," I say, when she turns back to me. "Can we have a safe word? Like, something I say if I need to leave the party before Adrian's ready, and I don't want to deal with a big negotiation about it?"

She nods. "Absolutely. Just say the word, and I'll call you a car and make sure you're in it. Ben and I are staying sober tonight. He never drinks at art world events. He wants people to take him seriously as an artist, not think of him as a kid who likes to party."

"Smart. And thank you," I say, approving of Ben's maturity. Noelle's lucky to have found him, and Adrian's lucky to have a best friend with such a good head on his shoulders.

I start to move past Noelle when she pokes my arm. "So?"

"So what?"

"So, what's your safe word? You never said."

"Oh." I laugh and shake my head. "It's good I'm getting out. Clearly, all the corporate research is wrecking my brain." I pull in a breath, searching for a good word. "How about…bacon, egg, and cheese," I say, thinking fondly of the puppies and hoping they've found homes with people who love them. "I'll say I'm hungry for one and you put me in a cab. Deal?"

"Deal, baby. I got you," she says, looping her thin arm around my waist. "But don't head out too soon. The real party doesn't even start until midnight, and we're going to have a blast. I feel it in my bones."

She's so sure of herself that I catch some of her excitement. But I have no clue just how "exciting" tonight is going to turn out to be.

eleven

GIDEON

New York City. She's like an old girlfriend I haven't seen in years.

I watch the skyline grow closer beneath the small commercial jet with a belly full of mixed emotions.

As a kid growing up on Long Island, I couldn't wait to turn eighteen and move to Manhattan. I wanted to be where everything was happening, all the time. As much as I loved being out on a trail or at a campsite, I loved the fevered heartbeat of the city even more.

There was always something to do or someone interesting to see.

And Columbia was there—Columbia, my father's alma mater and one of the best real estate law programs in the country. When I was younger, the plan was to become a lawyer and help my father grow his real estate empire in the posh seaside communities of New York and New Jersey.

Then Angela got pregnant during our sophomore year of high school, and everything changed.

I still ended up going to Columbia for undergrad and law school—with the help of my parents, who moved to an apartment in the city near our student family housing to help care for Adrian while Angela and I were in class—but by the time I graduated with my law degree, my parents were barely speaking to me. My mother never forgave me for letting Angela take Adrian with her on the road while I finished up my final year of law school.

She was afraid that Angela wouldn't bring him back, and that I'd have a hard time proving I deserved custody when I hadn't put up a fight to keep my child with me in the city, but I didn't believe her. I believed Angela when she said she loved me, but that she desperately needed to make her dream of being a professional dancer come true. I believed her when she insisted that Adrian would be devastated if he couldn't see his mother for eight months, and that they'd be back before I knew it.

Honestly, I didn't see how I could say no.

She'd given up so much to have our son. When her fundamentalist parents found out that she was pregnant at sixteen, they disowned her. She had to move in with a friend and then with my family, once Adrian was born and we were officially engaged.

She also lost her summer dance scholarship with the New York City ballet and never got back on toe shoes again. Pregnancy did something to her feet, she said, that made the wooden boxes of the shoes too painful. She'd done her best to make it in the modern dance world, while taking business classes at NYU and caring for Adrian. But in four years of devoting every spare moment to classes, free performances, and networking at dance world parties, she had yet to land a paying gig.

The offer to tour with a small company who'd found funds to hire a nanny for the three dancers with children too young to leave at home, was a once in a lifetime opportunity. And Adrian was only five and such a mama's boy. We had fun going to the playgrounds in Central Park when I had an afternoon off from class or hitting the zoo with my parents on weekends, but Angela was his world.

As much as it would break my heart to only see him on video calls and the few weekends that I would be free to fly out and meet them on the road, I knew it was what was best for my son. My wife.

My family.

I had no idea Angela already had a divorce lawyer on retainer, or that she would file as soon as she'd been away six months, the minimum amount of time her lawyer advised she would need to prove my lack of paternal involvement in Adrian's life.

My parents helped me hire a lawyer to plead my case, but Angela's attorney was a beast, and she had months of advance planning working in her favor. The judge ruled that Angela should maintain sole physical custody, we would share joint legal custody, and I would be granted one weekend of visitation per month —provided I could make it to wherever Angela was living or touring at the time, and five weeks during Adrian's summer vacation.

From the get-go, Angela made the visitations as difficult as possible. Arranging to be in Alaska for a dance festival on one of my first court-appointed weekends and calling Adrian every night in tears the first summer he stayed with me in New York. By the end of the first week, the kid was so upset, I stopped taking Angela's calls, which she used as leverage to claim I was denying her access to Adrian and causing our son psychological distress.

Cue another court battle and more money poured down the drain while my happy, easy-going son grew more withdrawn and emotionally fragile.

By the time he was eight, Adrian rolled his eyes at everything I said. By eleven, he told me I was a deadbeat dad on a regular basis, something he'd obviously heard from his mother. By his freshman year of high school, he appealed the court to stop our summer visits, and...they did.

Since then, he's been willing to take my money for a car for his sixteenth birthday, a senior trip to Barcelona, and college tuition, but acts like having a civil conversation with me is unspeakably grueling.

Now he's dropped out of grad school at NYU to DJ and launch some art app. But he expects me to keep paying rent on his apartment, even though he's a grown man capable of accomplishing great things—as long as it's something he wants to accomplish, not boring things like supporting himself financially.

I can't help drawing a parallel between Adrian and focused, mature, hard-working Sydney.

Sexy. You forgot sexy. What do you think Adrian would

say if he knew you've spent the better part of the past month fantasizing about fucking a woman a couple years older than he is?

I fetch my suitcase from the baggage claim and push the thought away as I head out to find the company car.

I don't let myself think about Sydney. Not during the day, anyway. Thoughts of the one who got away are reserved for late nights with a glass of scotch and memories of how perfect it felt to wake up with her body close to mine.

I find the car waiting at the curb. Smith, my father's old driver, who I hired to work for me full time when Dad retired to Florida, greets me with a hug.

"Hey there, Gid," he says, with a tight squeeze. He's nearly sixty but built like a barrel-chested bulldog and capable of tossing bags into trunks without breaking a sweat. "How's life in the sticks?"

"Good," I say as we part amidst affectionate slaps on each other's arms. "Nice and boring, just the way I like it."

Smith laughs. "Not me, man. I couldn't take it. Gotta have my city life and city food. Which reminds me, Betsy sent a sandwich, since you won't have time for dinner before the party. It's in the backseat. Just sit back, snack, relax, and I'll get you there as fast as the traffic'll let me."

I nod and let him take the handle of my rolling bag. "Thanks. Sounds perfect."

I don't have a personal assistant on staff in Burlington anymore, but for short, always jam-packed city visits, it's nice to have someone making sure things run smoothly. Betsy works for Mitch McMillan, my head guy at the New York branch of G.P.G. Green, but keeps me on schedule and up to speed when I'm in the city.

She's still at the top of her game, a fact proven by the gourmet Italian sub from my favorite Manhattan deli waiting for me on the leather seat inside.

The traffic out of LaGuardia Airport in Queens is typically awful, so I raise the privacy screen in the town car between Smith and myself and tap Betsy's contact button.

"Welcome to New York, Mr. Gabaldon," she answers in her hint of a Southern drawl. "Hope you had a smooth flight."

"It was perfect, and this sandwich is even better. Thank you so much. And won't you please think about calling me Gideon?"

"I'd rather not, sir," she says cheerfully. "My mama and daddy would whip my backside if they knew I was disrespecting my boss like that. Just wasn't raised to first name the people I work for."

"All right. But if you ever decide you're ready to ease up on the formality, know that I'm on board."

"Thank you so much, sir, I'll keep that in mind. Would you like your briefing on company matters now or tomorrow morning, before your breakfast meeting with Mr. McMillan?"

"Now would be great," I say, glancing out the window at the veritable parking lot on the freeway. "Traffic is bad. I have plenty of time."

"Perfect, sir," she says, before proceeding to fill me in

on a couple permitting issues that could use some massaging with my contacts at city hall and minor HR issues that seem to be well in hand.

"I'll reach out to my city hall contacts on Monday, before my flight in the afternoon," I say. "Anything else?"

"Yes, actually," she says. "Mr. McMillan plans to give you a comprehensive overview of the situation tomorrow, but I know you don't like surprises. Especially bad ones, so I thought I should give you a heads-up. It's about the Coney Island project."

I sigh. This project has been one headache after another—from permit issues to zoning confusion to doing battle with the district over an additional parking structure for the office building we're transforming into full-time living spaces—but I keep reminding myself that it will be worth it in the end.

New York has had an affordable housing crisis for years. These units will help with that, while creating an eco-friendly building that won't add to pollution or the city's carbon footprint. The grocery store on the ground floor will provide fresh fruits and vegetables to an area that's on the verge of becoming a food desert and a childcare center will make things easy for commuting parents.

It's going to be a great win for this community...if we can ever get it finished.

"The contractor is still pushing back on leaving the two lowest levels empty," Betsy says. "He thinks at least part of the parking could be shifted there, freeing up the money he needs to update the windows in all the units."

"I'm assuming Mitch and the team managing the project reminded him that storm surges happen all the time down there these days?"

"Yes, Mr. McMillan did," Betsy says, "but the contractor says it's the only way for him to stay on budget. He mentioned that any resident cars parked down there would be insured, so he didn't think it would be a big deal if there were a surge and people had to file a claim or two."

"A claim or two?" I echo with a humorless laugh. "Last time the building flooded, there was water up to the ceiling on the first floor. That's why we're using polished concrete in the retail spaces, to make cleaning up after another event quick and painless. If there were cars parked in the subterranean areas, every one of them would have been totaled."

"I know," Betsy says. "And insurance companies never pay what a car is really worth. It's a bad idea, but he's threatening to quit over it and we're already over budget and behind on this project without needing to find another contractor. Mr. McMillan thinks he can make him see reason when he visits the site on Wednesday, but this might need the Gabaldon touch."

I smile. "Are you calling Mitch a hard-ass?"

"Of course not, sir," she says. "I have the greatest respect for Mr. McMillan's talents, but he's loud and looks angry, even when he's not. You, on the other hand, look calm, even when you're not."

"Are you calling me boring, Betsy?" I tease, surprised when she says, "A little bit, sir. I mean, you do live in Vermont. But you're boring in a good way, in a way that could help smooth this situation over without changes to the plans or the contractor."

I hum beneath my breath, mentally flipping through my calendar. "All right. Pencil me in for the meeting on Wednesday, and I'll look into changing my return flight. I don't think there's anything going on at the Burlington office that can't wait until the following week."

"I've already looked at flights, sir," Betsy says. "I can get you on a five-p.m. flight Wednesday evening. Would you like me to book that for you?"

"Yes, please," I say, relaxing back against the seat and reaching for my sandwich. "You're the best, Betsy. You're going to be running this company someday. Mark my words."

"Oh, I plan on it, sir," she says, surprising me again. "I believe in what G.P.G. Green is doing so much. I want to be a part of the team for the long haul."

"I'd like that, too," I say, signing off with a tight feeling in my chest.

Another impressive young woman kicking ass in her career, while my son refuses to get a job or pay his own bills. I would wonder if it's a male vs. female thing, but dozens of highly motivated young men from the UVM business school apply to be interns at my company every year.

It's not young men in general; it's *my* young man, in particular.

In my gut, I know the way Angela raised Adrian—to reject my love and my presence, while still feeling entitled to unfettered access to my resources—is a big part of that. But plenty of kids have problematic mothers and grow up to be amazing people.

Sydney didn't even have a mom past the age of thirteen…

I unwrap my sandwich and take a massive bite, focusing on the explosion of tangy banana peppers, high-quality salami, and freshly sliced provolone cheese.

I will *not* think of Sydney, and I certainly won't call her while I'm here.

Yes, I'm going to be in town longer than I expected, but it's still only five nights. Then I'll be back in Burlington for the rest of the year. My life is there, hers is here, and our immediate futures aren't any more compatible than they were a month ago.

The New York office practically runs itself. The staff in Burlington still needs me there at least three days a week. Besides, I couldn't stomach traffic like this every day. Or the noise or the frenetic pace or all the ghosts that haunt me in the Big Apple.

The ghost of toddler Adrian grinning at me from the swings in Central Park, of our family getting rainbows painted on our faces at the Brooklyn Pride Parade, of Angela and I dancing to music from our cell phones in our tiny living room after the baby went to bed… For a few years there, I thought Angela and I might be able to make it work. That we would beat the odds and our teenage love would last forever.

But nothing lasts forever.

Which is as comforting as it is sad.

I may not have had the kind of marriage I dreamt

about, but I can still have a decent relationship with my son, maybe even a close one.

Adrian's old enough for us to have an honest conversation about our past and how to move forward with love for each other. Hell, he's past old enough. We should have had a real talk years ago, once he was eighteen and no longer living under his mother's roof.

I'm willing to do the majority of the work to make things better, I just need him to put away the grudge Angela saddled him with and start fresh. I know if he'd only let me in, just a little bit, I could prove to him that I'm not such a bad guy.

Am I perfect? Not even close. But I love my son and it hurts to see him moving through life with so much resentment for no good reason.

When Smith finally fights his way into Manhattan and onto the narrow streets of the East Village, where delivery trucks block every other street, despite the fact that it's nearly nine o'clock, the first sign of Adrian's event is a giant smiling cat projected on the brick exterior of the Inheritance Hotel. I decide to take it as a good omen. He loved my parents' cat when he was little. We used to have so much fun playing with Banksy before dinner there on Sundays.

We have good memories together and I know we can make more, if he'll only give me the chance...

"I'll drop your bags off at your apartment and make sure you have coffee, fruit, and donuts for the morning," Smith says, as we queue up behind the other cars dropping guests at the party.

"You don't have to do that. Just leave the bag with the doorman and head home. It's already late."

Smith shakes his head and grunts. "Nope. Not going to do it. If we're ever going to convince you to come home, we have to make sure it feels like it when you're here."

Smiling, I say, "Thanks, Smith. I appreciate you."

I *do* appreciate him, far too much to tell him that the city doesn't feel like home to me anymore. It hasn't for a long time, not since my wife took my son away and my life toppled like a house of cards.

"Here goes nothing," I mutter, running a self-conscious hand through my hair.

I'm wearing an edgy—for me—combo of a burnt orange dress shirt, navy suit pants, and a matching vest, but I'm sure I'll still look out of place. The people emerging from the cars at the head of the line look terrifyingly trendy.

Just another reason to stay in Vermont. If there's a place that cares less about fashion and appearances, I have yet to find it. I love that about my adopted state. I'm of the opinion that clothes should be comfortable, durable, and classic enough to stay in fashion for at least a decade. The less time I have to spend shopping or thinking about what to wear, the better.

"You'll be fine," Smith says. "Just find the snacks. That's where the rest of the old people who don't care about shaking their ass on the dance floor will be."

I catch his gaze in the rearview mirror with a frown. "I'm not that old. Not yet."

Smith laughs. "Mr. Gideon, you're a fossil compared

to these kids. I just saw that teen singer my grand-daughter loves walk in a minute ago. Just make an appearance, let Adrian know you're proud, and I can be back to pick you up in an hour if you want."

"I'll order a car," I say, cutting him off when he tries to protest. "I insist, Smith. Go home, bring Marian some donuts, too, and have a nice weekend. I won't need you tomorrow. Mitch is coming over to my place for a meeting, and we're going to stick close to Union Square after."

He grunts. "All right. If you're sure."

"I'm sure." I smile as I pull in a breath and grab my small cross-body bag from the floor. If I'm lucky, I'll have time to sneak into the restroom and freshen up before I join the party. I should have run a comb and some product through my hair at the airport, but I didn't want to keep Smith waiting. "See you on Monday," I say. "Have a great weekend."

"You, too," he says as I swing out of the car.

Instantly, the heads of the reporters covering the red carpet swivel toward me, only to swivel away again just as quickly. It's obvious at first glance that I'm not part of the in crowd, which is fine by me.

Great, even. No one's going to care if I bypass the red carpet and head straight to the main entrance to the hotel farther down the block.

I'm heading that way—planning to find a washroom, drop my bag with the coat check, and go looking for Adrian—when I hear my son's laugh. I know it's him right away. Adrian tries so hard to play it cool, but when he laughs—really laughs—it's high-pitched and goofy and wonderful. It reminds me of when he was a toddler and I'd tickle him until he couldn't breathe. His laugh is still exactly the same, just deeper.

I spin toward the sound, a smile on my face.

As soon as my gaze lands on Adrian, the smile falls away—fast.

Because Adrian isn't alone. He's with a beautiful woman in a tiny black dress, his hand resting at the small of her back as he beams at the reporter holding a microphone to his face.

The beautiful woman is gut-punching-ly familiar.

It's Sydney.

Adrian is here with *Sydney.*

My throat squeezes so tight I can barely breathe, my heart slams faster, and my thoughts race in circles, determined to find another explanation as to why Adrian has his arm looped around Sydney's waist. But then my son leans in, pressing an enthusiastic kiss to Sydney's cheek, making her laugh and banishing the last shadow of a doubt.

Adrian is *dating* Sydney, *my* Sydney.

And I'm going to fucking throw up.

twelve

SYDNEY

As soon as Adrian waves goodbye to the reporter and we start down the final stretch of red carpet toward the ballroom entrance, the smile drops from my face.

"That's it, buddy," I hiss beneath my breath. "No more touchy-feely and no more sloppy kisses. We're here as friends, remember?"

"I always sloppy kiss my friends." He's still grinning, clearly pleased with how the red-carpet interviews went. "I save the quality kissing for women I'm trying to get into bed."

I roll my eyes and mime gagging.

"Oh, come on," he says. "I was a good kisser. Admit it, you liked kissing me. Not enough to fuck me, but you liked it. I could tell."

"Behave," I say, pinching his arm below the sleeve of his shirt. "Or I'm out of here. I'm here as a favor to a *friend* not to rehash our brief romantic entanglement."

"You're so old-fashioned sometimes. 'Romantic entanglement.' That's cute."

"Yeah, well I'm cute." I sniff. "That's been established. I'm also nice. Don't make me regret it."

He gives my hand a squeeze. "You *are* nice, and I appreciate you. Try to have fun tonight, okay? And come see me at the booth if you need anything. I'll be busy once I start spinning, but I can always take a break. You know, if you need a dance lesson or someone to show you how to do a Jell-O shot."

I narrow my eyes as he opens the heavy door leading into the space. "And you can come get me if you need someone to take your ego down a peg or two. Sound good?"

"Sounds great." He grins and lifts a hand to someone on the other side of the ballroom as we step inside.

I'm amazed he can see anything. The room is dark, lit only by deep blue lights swirling behind the transparent dome that serves as the ceiling. The effect is beautiful—like we're under a dark, ever-changing night sky—but it's hard to make out faces. Add in the stands of fake trees arranged throughout the space and white fog hugging the ground, adding to the "midnight in an eerie forest" vibe, and I can already tell it will be easier to hide at this party than see and be seen.

Thank God.

I can't wait to ditch Adrian and dive into the snacks. I realized I forgot to eat dinner on the way over, and I'm suddenly starving. I definitely need something in my stomach before I have a drink, or I'll fall asleep under a fake tree way before midnight.

"Are you okay to find Noelle and Ben on your own?" Adrian asks, his eyes scanning back and forth across the crowd, calculating his next move. "I want to get a little networking in before I head to the booth."

"Absolutely," I say, though I haven't spotted a sign of Noelle or Ben, both of whom were able to traverse the red carpet much faster than the host of the party.

But I'll find them. Noelle's dress is bright, bubblegum pink. Surely, even in a shadowy forest, I'll be able to spot a color that aggressive.

I clap a hand on Adrian's back between his shoulders. "Good luck and don't be nervous. You're in your element and you're going to do an amazing job."

The real Adrian peeks out from behind his social mask for a beat, gratitude in his eyes. "Thanks, Syd. Have a great time. You deserve it."

"Thanks," I say, moving away, only to turn back when he adds in a louder voice, "And if you meet someone cool, don't be afraid to shoot your shot, woman. You look hot as fuck tonight."

I blush and awkwardly flip him off before making my escape, weaving my way quickly through the still sparse crowd toward the smell of grilled meat. I know Adrian meant well, but I hate having attention drawn to me in public.

I'm not shy, necessarily, I simply prefer *not* to be the center of attention.

I'd rather slip into a gathering unnoticed, with ample time to linger in the periphery, observing the social dynamics of the players before making my move. Socializing in large groups of strangers doesn't come naturally to me. I'm more of a one-on-one girl. Or three or four people if we're all close friends. Like the book club with my Maine girls.

An ache spreads through my chest, reminding me that I need to call Maya and tell her I won't be able to make it up to Sea Breeze for the October book club meeting, after all. Work is just too hairy. I can still join them via video call, of course, but it won't be the same.

But that's life. Being an adult means making hard choices, and I've made mine. No more Maine until my vacation next summer and no more working for peanuts for wildlife conservation groups.

This is my real life, my grown-up life, and I'll be happy I made these sacrifices someday, when I know everything there is to know about Watson Global and Dad passes the leadership torch into my capable hands. I'll be able to do so much more good for the world as CEO of an international conglomerate making billions than as a poor wildlife worker documenting the nesting habits of seabirds and shouting into the void about how urgently we need to protect animals from climate change.

A lot of people can observe seabirds, only *I* can take on this particular challenge. I'm not simply heir to a fortune, but to power on a global scale. I can't afford to take that lightly. If I don't prove to Dad that I can fill his shoes in the next year, he'll find someone else to do it.

Someone who probably won't care about using Watson Global's influence for good as much as I do...

Instantly, I decide it's going to be a one-drink night. No Jell-O shots, no second glass of wine or signature cocktail. I'll eat, have *one* drink, dance with Noelle and Ben for a while, and head home at midnight. If I'm in bed by one, I'll still be able to get up and hit the books hard by eight or nine tomorrow morning.

Collecting a small white plate from the end of the most whimsical buffet I've ever seen—the ten-foot-long wooden table is filled with flowers and wooden fairy sculptures as well as three different kinds of tacos, fruit, grilled vegetables, and various snack food on sticks—I load up and head to one of the vine-draped high-top tables. There are no seats, but that's fine. I'm not sure I'd be able to sit down in this dress, anyway, at least not without showing my ass.

Noelle is three inches shorter than I am and far more daring in her clothing choices. But she was right about this dress—it makes my legs look like they're a mile long, a fact that isn't going unnoticed by the other guests.

I catch a man checking out my legs while his date is in line for candy from the candy buffet on the other side of the tables and a fashionable woman touches my elbow on her way by, whispering, "You have the most fabulous legs I've ever seen. You should model."

I blush and stammer, "Thank you, but I'm way too awkward."

She smiles, her amber eyes mesmerizing in her dark skin. "I was too when I first started. We all fake it until we make it, love. I can connect you with my coach if you want. He's fabulous."

I shake my head. "Thank you so much, but I don't have time for anything outside of work right now. I just started a new job and…" I trail off with a shrug, proving my awkwardness.

The woman's amazing eyes warm as she nods. "Of course, but take my card anyway." She sets a pale blue business card on the table without breaking eye contact. "You can call me if you find some free time and want to have some fun. We don't have to talk shop. I'm Zara."

"Oh, okay, Sydney. So nice to meet you, Zara," I stammer as she glides away with the grace of a ballerina jungle cat.

"Woah," a familiar voice murmurs behind me. "You just got hit on by a supermodel. How does *that* feel?"

I turn to see Noelle sipping a drink as pink as her dress, her eyes wide over the rim of the frosted glass. "Um, pretty amazing actually," I whisper. "Really makes me wish I were gay."

We giggle and she says, "Girl, every day. Every damned day. I love Ben but women are so beautiful and so much less gross. I've never been to a woman's house that smelled like moldy cheese socks."

I arch a brow. "No, but your makeup table is repulsive, and you always leave a wad of pink hair in the shower."

She props a fist on her hip. "I do not." I grunt and she grins. "Okay, fine, I do. But it's okay. A little grossness is cute. Like a goblin wearing lipstick." She points to her drink. "That's the name of this, by the way. Lipstick on the rocks. It's fantastic. Like roses and grapefruit had a baby and rolled it in sugar. No alcohol but it tastes like there's a hint of gin. You should get one."

"I will," I say, wiping my fingers and dropping my

napkin on my now-empty plate. I feel much better now that I have something in my stomach. "Where's the bar?"

She points to our left. "There are a few, but the mocktail bar is that way. Over by the living A Midsummer Night's Dream sculpture. Lots of nearly naked people, painted different metallic colors, writhing around, you can't miss it. I'll wait here. Ben's getting tacos."

"Okay, be right back," I say, heading out of the seating area and into a darker section of woods, where couples are swaying together to the ambient music. Adrian hasn't started spinning yet, so the beat isn't too loud, but it's nice. The string instruments and light drums add to the enchanted vibe.

Whoever Adrian hired to bring his vision to life, they did a fantastic job.

Making a mental note to tell him later, I start toward the living sculpture, which is as arresting as Noelle said it would be. I'm so drawn in by the slow-motion embrace between a bearded man I'm guessing is the fairy king from Shakespeare's play and a curvy woman wearing nothing but leaves strategically placed on her silver-frosted body that I almost don't notice the man in the orange shirt and impeccably fitted suit pants.

I would have missed him entirely, if it weren't for the fact that he's moving fast, charging through the ballroom like he's late for a flight, the only rushed person in a room full of relaxed partygoers.

I don't get a good look at his face—only a brief glimpse of his profile before he's past me—but I know it's Gideon. I just *know* it, the way I know that the sky is blue, tacos are tasty, and that I'm no longer headed to the mocktail bar.

I'm following Gideon, wherever the night might lead.

My talk with Adrian went about as well as I expected.

Which is to say it didn't "go" at all.

The second I approached him by the bar, surrounded by three women in the tiniest shorts I've ever seen—shorts that made me feel old for being shocked by how much of their asses were out for show and tell—I knew coming here was a mistake.

Trying to approach Adrian before he approached me was an even bigger one.

But I couldn't wait. I had to find out if he and Sydney were—*are*—together, and I tried to be discreet.

I smiled through the sullen introductions to his friends, whose names I forgot instantly, and casually asked if I could "borrow him for a minute," like we were colleagues who needed to discuss business, not family. Most twenty-two-year-olds have outgrown being embarrassed by their parents, but it goes so much deeper than embarrassment with Adrian.

That's at least partly my fault. I should have tried harder, sooner to mend the rift between us.

So, I tried my best to be patient as he clapped me on the back and said, "I'll find you after the show, Phil. If you're still around. Otherwise, we can catch up another time."

Phil. Phil is my father's name. Yes, it reads Phillip Gideon Gabaldon II on my birth certificate, but I've been Gideon since the day I was born. Only strangers and Adrian call me Phil. Strangers because they don't know any better; Adrian because he has a knack for knowing how to get under my skin.

It makes me wonder what he'd say if he knew I'd slept with Sydney before he did. My guess is he would either be horrified and end things immediately or thrilled to have something to rub in my face.

But of course, I can't say anything.

I won't.

I wouldn't do that to my son...or to Sydney. If she has feelings for Adrian, if they're involved, it's not my place to get between them, no matter how much it hurts to imagine them together.

Or how certain I am that my son doesn't deserve her.

Maybe someday Adrian will grow into a person who can stand on equal footing with a woman like Sydney, but right now he's miles behind her in almost every way, including maturity and compassion. A fact he proves when I ask—almost beg—a second time for a few words, and he tells me, "Shoot me a text, and I'll get back to you when I have the chance."

A text.

A fucking *text*, after I rearranged my business trip to coincide with his launch, paid for half the catering, and put in a good word with the hotel owner, an old friend of mine, to get Adrian an excellent deal on the event space.

As I charge back through the party, I'm angrier than I can remember being in years, but not at Adrian.

I'm angry with Angela for poisoning my son's mind against me, and I'm angry with myself. I've enabled this behavior. I've been so afraid that Adrian would cut the final cord between us that I've allowed him to treat me in ways I wouldn't tolerate from anyone else on earth. I've helped teach him that it's okay to be cruel.

But that stops now.

Whether he likes it or not, we *will* be having a talk while I'm here, and I'm going to make it clear the status quo needs to change. Now. He doesn't have to fake affection he clearly doesn't feel for me, but from now on, respect and a certain degree of civility will be mandatory.

I'm also going to find out if things are serious between him and Sydney while we're chatting and make it abundantly clear that he'd better treat her like a queen.

Great idea, the raw voice in my head seethes, *Maybe he'll treat her so well, she'll end up at your table next time Adrian agrees to let you host Thanksgiving. Or, better yet, she might be your daughter-in-law and mother of your grandbabies someday.*

The thought sends acid surging up the back of my throat.

On my way past an art installation composed of half-nude people painted metallic colors, writhing together on a slowly rotating podium, I grab a glass of champagne from a waiter's tray. So far, I've seen five bars, a beer hall manned by actors dressed as hobbit-type creatures, and dozens of waiters offering champagne and Jell-O shots. Adrian's done his best to ensure no one leaves this party sober.

Well, except me.

I can't stay and risk running into Sydney. I'll down this champagne on my way out, head to my apartment building, and hit the treadmill at the twenty-four-hour gym. Maybe I'll do a few weight circuits, too. I skipped leg day this morning to tie up some loose ends at the office before my flight, and my only chance of getting a decent night's sleep is to physically exhaust myself.

Otherwise, I'll be up all night, rehearsing what I need to say to my son and fantasizing about all the things I can never say to Sydney.

Things like…

I can't get you out of my head, no matter how hard I try.

And…

I feel like I've been missing you so much longer than a month.

And…

Don't date him, butterfly. Date me.

Fuck. I'm so fucked.

I down the last half of my champagne in one long swallow, set the empty glass on the edge of the mocktail bar, and quickly move toward the guard manning the exit on this side of the ballroom.

He lifts his chin as I approach. "Hello, sir. Just want to let you know there's no reentry through this door. If you want to come back inside, you'll have to go around to the main entrance and show your invite to a staff member again."

I nod. "Thanks, but I won't be coming back. I've had enough."

He looks surprised, but nods and presses the bar on the metal door, revealing the alley behind the hotel. "Have a good night, sir. The best place to catch a cab this time of night is over on Avenue C."

I thank him and head out into the warm September evening, but I have no intention of calling a cab. A brisk walk to Union Square will ensure Smith has ample time to deliver my bags and donuts and head home to his wife. I don't want to risk arriving while he's still there and having to answer uncomfortable questions about why I left the party after less than half an hour.

I'm nearly to the end of the surprisingly clean alley, when a woman's voice calls out behind me, "Gideon, wait!"

Time slows and my heart lurches in my chest.

I know that voice. I would know it anywhere, even if I hadn't heard it in years.

Looks like I haven't managed to escape without being noticed, after all. Now, I'm going to have to answer some very hard questions. Or come up with some very quick, very slick lies.

But as I turn to see Sydney walking toward me,

looking like something out of a movie in her vintage dress and makeup that brings out every perfect curve of her face, I know I could never lie to her. She's too good, too kind.

And too obviously happy to see me.

She smiles, and it's like the sun coming out from behind a cloud and a knife stabbed deep in my heart at the same time. Because this is it. This is the end, no matter how much I wish it could be something more.

She slows as she gets closer, her smile fading. "Hey." She crosses her arms, making the hint of cleavage at the top of the dress even sexier. The woman is stunning, even in sweatpants. In a dress that skims her curves and shows off the elegant lines of her body, she's a cardiac event waiting to happen. "Leaving so early?"

I clear my throat and nod. "Yeah. It isn't really my scene."

"Mine, either," she says. "I'm here with friends."

Friends. My brain latches on to the word with almost pathetic excitement. Maybe Adrian and Sydney are just friends.

Friends who kiss and touch each other a lot in public...

"Well, don't let me keep you," I say, forcing a tight smile. "If you have a previous engagement."

She frowns. "What's wrong?"

I shake my head, but can't force the word—"nothing" —from my lips. That would be a lie, and I've already realized I can't lie to her.

She steps closer, studying my expression. "I saw you

in there. You couldn't get out of the party fast enough. Did something happen?"

I saw my son kissing you and almost lost my goddamned mind. Then I tried to talk to Adrian and realized I'm a failure as a father and it might be too late to keep my kid from growing up to be a real prick.

Aloud, I say, "I can't talk about it."

"Why?" she asks, her gaze softening. "You seem like the type who can talk about anything. If you're in the right company." She waits, continuing to search my face in the loaded silence before adding in a softer voice, "But if I'm not the right company..."

"You're the best company," I say, the words out before I can stop them. "The past month, I... All I've wanted to do was talk to you."

She arches a brow, heat and shyness mixing in her gaze. "Really? *All* you wanted to do was talk?"

Damn...

This woman.

She undoes me with just a word, a look.

I shake my head, my voice rougher as I say, "No. Not just talk, but there are...things."

She nods. "Things. Huh. Sounds serious."

My lips curve despite the pain I know is coming. For both of us. "Yeah. It is."

"Tell me more about these things."

I weigh my options. Best case scenario, I've misunderstood this whole thing and she and Adrian are just friends. Worst case, she's been intimate with my son and is going to be as shocked and upset about that as I am.

Either way, this isn't a conversation to have in an alley.

"You want to grab some diner food?" I ask. "I know a place a few blocks away. We could have pancakes or scrambles and—"

"Yes. Just let me text my friend Noelle and tell her I'm leaving," she says, her eyes lighting up in a way that makes me want to kiss her.

But I can't. Not now. Maybe not ever.

But at least I get to talk to her, and considering what we have to talk about, the fact that I'm still excited about that says something.

I'm not sure what, but…definitely something.

"You call this a diner?" I mutter beneath my breath as we follow the hostess to a corner booth in what may be the cutest restaurant I've ever seen.

Gideon glances my way. "They serve pancakes."

"They're also serving adorable," I say, glancing around. "I feel like I'm in a fairy tale."

Tucked away on a side street in Alphabet City, Why Not Pie is decorated like the interior of a Bavarian cottage. Dark exposed timber stands out against the cream-colored walls, vintage ads in bright colors serve as wallpaper, and the wooden booths are filled with needlepoint pillows.

Once we're seated, I pluck a pillow from beside me and hold it up for Gideon's inspection. "It's a T-Rex. In a teacup. Therefore, a *Tea* Rex. Color me delighted."

He grins. "Pretty punny."

"My favorite." I set it beside me and pat the dapper T-Rex on the head before turning back to Gideon.

Anxiety prickles across my skin at the tension still clear on his face. "Should we order? Or should you tell me whatever you're going to tell me first? If it's bad enough, I might have to leave, and I don't want to order and dash."

"You can dash whenever you want," he says. "This is on me. I'll stay and cover the bill."

My stomach cramps. "That wasn't comforting."

He sighs and opens his menu. "The lemon souffle pancakes are my favorite, but the scrambles are excellent, as well. And the pie. I'm not much of a pie person, but if you are, they're top-notch."

"I had tacos at the party, so I think I'll try the pancakes. I'm up for sharing some if you're not super hungry."

He sighs again. "I can't tell if I'm hungry. My stomach is in knots."

"Same," I say, nibbling on my bottom lip. "We should share."

He glances up, holding my gaze as he murmurs, "Sounds good."

But it doesn't. Nothing sounds good right now. I just want to know what's going on. Being in the dark is killing me.

As soon as our waitress—a pink-cheeked woman in a green dirndl dress with flowers embroidered across the chest—takes our order for two coffees and a plate of the lemon souffle pancakes to share, I collect my fork from my cloth napkin and point it at Gideon's chest. "Spill. What's going on? I have to know. Now."

He eyes the fork. "I've never been held at fork-point before. Should I be worried?"

"Not as long as you didn't do something horrible," I say, my worst fear bursting from my lips before I can stop it. "You're married, aren't you? You're married and your wife was at that party and that's why you were running out of there as fast as you could. Before you both ran into me, and you had to explain how we know each other."

He frowns. "Why would you think that?"

"You weren't surprised to see me," I say in a softer voice. "When you turned around in the alley. You weren't surprised. You already knew I was there."

He threads his fingers together on top of the table. "I did. But I'm not married, and I wasn't there with anyone. Everything I told you in Maine was true. I promise."

I set the fork back on my napkin and drop my hands to my lap so Gideon can't see me wring them as I add, "Then what's wrong? You look like someone died."

He winces. "Not someone, but maybe some*thing*." He shakes his head. "I know we said seeing each other again was too complicated, but I can't stop thinking about you. I guess some part of me thought... Hoped..."

"That we'd see each other again," I whisper, my heart soaring when he nods. "Me, too. I know long-distance relationships are horrible, but...I've never felt this way about someone before, Gideon."

Before I can work up the gumption to suggest dating might be worth trying, he stuns me into silence by asking, "Even with Adrian?"

I blink, my jaw dropping.

Mercifully, the waitress arrives with our coffees and two glasses of water, giving me a moment to pull myself together before I ask, "How? How did you know I dated Adrian?"

"Dated?" he asks, his gaze guarded "Past tense? Because it didn't look very past tense when you two were together on the red carpet."

Suddenly, it all makes sense. What he saw, what he must have thought. And of course, he knows Adrian in some way. He was at Adrian's party.

I exhale, relief making my voice breathy as I say, "Oh God, yes. Totally past tense. We dated in college but broke up months before I left for Maine. I wasn't even supposed to be at the party, but Adrian's girlfriend broke up with him last night and he needed a last-minute replacement. His best friend is dating my best friend, so he was over at my place with them and asked if I'd be his plus-one. I said yes, but only as a favor to a friend."

"So, that kiss…" Gideon trails off, but some of the stress finally leaves his jaw.

"He was just messing with me," I say. "Teasing. He doesn't want to be anything more than friends again, and neither do I. He's a good guy, deep down, but Adrian is…" I hesitate, not wanting to speak too plainly until I know the nature of Gideon and Adrian's relationship. "He can be a lot. And not always the most thoughtful person. By the time we broke up, it was pretty clear that we didn't have much in common."

"I can imagine," Gideon mutters.

My brow furrows. "How do you know him?"

He pulls in a breath, but our waitress appears again at that exact moment, setting a plate of steaming, lemon-and-sugar-scented pancakes between us. "Here you go. A stack of lemon souffle pancakes. Can I get you two anything else? Would you like another plate? Extra napkins?"

"No, we're fine," Gideon says, before glancing my way. "I mean, I'm okay with eating off the same plate if you are."

"Yes, that's fine." I twitch my lips in the server's direction but abandon my attempt at a smile as soon as she turns away. "So?"

"Let's eat first," he says, collecting his fork and knife and laying his napkin on his lap. "I want you to try these. They really are fantastic. The secret to the perfect bite is to get some of the pancake, some of the gooey lemon stuff, some whipped cream, and a hint of powdered sugar, all in the same bite."

I start to insist that I'm not hungry, but then I catch another whiff of the pancakes and my mouth starts to water. "It does smell really good."

"Tastes even better." He finishes compiling the perfect bite and reaches across the table, offering it to me.

I open my mouth, gaze locked with his as he sets it on my tongue. I close my lips around it, thinking about other things I'd like to close my lips around. Then the explosion of lemon and vanilla hits my taste buds and I moan, my lashes fluttering as I swallow.

"Wow." My tongue slips out to collect the powdered

sugar from my bottom lip. I moan again and reach for my coffee, taking a slow sip, relishing the way the slightly bitter liquid somehow makes the sweetness of the pancake even more delicious.

Gideon curses beneath his breath. "Stop."

I lift innocent eyes to his. "Stop what?"

"I'm already hard beneath the table," he says in a voice too soft for any of the couples around us to hear.

Instantly, my nipples begin to ache, and my panties are damper than they were before. "Oh no," I whisper, catching a bit of whipped cream on the tip of my fork. "Was it something I did?" I swipe my tongue across the whipped cream, licking it off the fork tines with delicate attention, heat dumping into my bloodstream as Gideon's jaw clenches and hunger fills his eyes.

"I want to take you back to my apartment," he says, "and tease you until you beg me to fuck you."

Holy Moses.

This man...

He's as sexy as I remember and he makes me feel more beautiful, more desired than I ever have before. Whatever his problem is with Adrian, I know we can put it behind us. Adrian's a part of my past. He's just a friend now. And honestly, he's a friend I would be fine seeing *less* of if he isn't Gideon's favorite person.

I'm not about to abandon my real ride-or-dies for a man, but Adrian is...problematic, and I have enough problems right now. Trying to live up to my father's expectations and prove to everyone at Watson Global that I'm not some undeserving nepo baby, has had me on edge since the day I arrived back in New York.

Noelle was right—I need to let off some steam and do something just for fun. Just because it feels good. But I don't want to do that at some pretentious party.

I'd much rather let off steam with Gideon, back at his apartment.

The apartment I had no idea he had...

"Why didn't you tell me you have a place in New York?" I ask.

"I knew it would complicate things," he says without missing a beat. "I have a place in the city, and I stay there when I come into town on business, but I'm only here a few times a year and never for more than a week at a time. My life isn't in New York anymore. It hasn't been for a long time. And when I did live here, things were...hard." He glances down at his hands. "I'm much better suited to a smaller city, where it's easy to get outside and hike or climb year-round. It would be hard to give that up, even for the chance at a relationship that made perfect sense."

I nod, my hope shriveling on the vine. "And we... wouldn't make perfect sense?"

He glances up, his gaze troubled again. "You're just so—"

"Young," I cut in, some part of me wanting to keep the word out of his mouth. His gorgeous, sexy mouth I would so much rather be kissing than discussing all the reasons trying to date would be a bad idea. "I know. I *am* young. At least on paper, but..." I sigh and stab another bite of pancake with a little too much force. "Lately, I feel like I'm a hundred years old. All I do is work and no matter how much I work, it never seems to be enough. I never get to relax, and nothing is easy. I don't fit in, no matter where I am. At the office, I'm the youngest person in management and everyone treats me like a dumb kid who's been given too much responsibility. And in my normal life, my friends think I'm a stuffy workaholic who's gotten old and boring before her time. I just want… I…"

I stuff the bite into my mouth and chew as I think. When I swallow, I add, "I just want to be judged on who I am and what I bring to a relationship, any relationship, without my age complicating things all the time."

He nods. "That's a fair ask."

I arch a challenging brow. "Does that mean you're done being hung up on my age? That's behind us now?"

He makes a rumbling sound low in his chest that makes me wish we were naked. But everything about Gideon makes me wish we were naked, from the way he chews to the way he sips his coffee to the way his eyes penetrate me ten different ways as he mutters, "It's not that simple."

"Why?"

"Age isn't the only barrier here, Sydney," he says.

"I know distance is an issue, but—"

"It's not the distance, either," he cuts in, setting his fork down and giving me one hundred percent of his considerable focus. "If it were just the distance and you were okay with seeing each other every other weekend, I'd fly down twice a month. No problem."

My pulse flutters in my throat. "You would?"

"I would," he says. "I didn't make that offer in Maine because I thought… Well, I thought it would be easier to move on. But time apart hasn't made it any easier to stop thinking of you. If anything, it's made it harder."

I press my lips together, fighting a giddy smile. No matter how happy his words make me, now isn't the time for smiling. He's made that obvious with the hint of doom in his voice.

I pull in a breath, keeping my glee to myself as I say, "It's been the same for me. I think about you all the time. And every other weekend would be a great place to start. I'm so busy with work, I don't have a lot of free time, anyway." I take in his increasingly troubled expression and add, "But that obviously doesn't work for you for some reason that you're...refusing to share?"

"I'm not refusing to share," he says. "I'm just dreading it."

I give a sharp shake of my head. "Why? Seriously, Gideon, it can't be that bad. Adrian can be a handful sometimes, but he's a nice guy who wants to leave a positive mark on the world. Whatever he did to upset you, I'm sure we can figure out a way to make it right. Or we can just avoid him. It wouldn't be that hard."

"It would be hard for me," he says, his doom voice in full effect. My eyes widen, but before I can demand that he spill whatever he's holding back, he adds, "He's my son."

fifteen

GIDEON

Sydney's eyes go wide and the blood drains from her face, leaving her looking like a pale, beautiful, slightly repulsed ghost.

I give her a moment to digest the news, taking a sip of my coffee and setting the mug down near the edge of the table as our server walks by carrying a fresh pot.

"Refill for you too, sweetheart?" the woman asks as she tops me off, glancing Sydney's way.

Sydney gives a numb shake of her head before croaking, "No, thank you."

The server casts a curious glance my way—probably wondering what I did to put my dinner date into a semi-catatonic state—before nodding. "All right, let me know if you two need anything else."

As soon as she's out of earshot, I murmur, "If you want to leave, I understand. Like I said, I'll take care of this."

"I don't want to leave, I just..." She blinks faster.

"I..." Her eyes finally focus fully on mine. "Adrian is your *son?*"

I nod.

"Not your stepson. Your *actual* son."

"Yes, my actual, biological son, the one my ex and I had when we were teenagers."

Sydney leans back against the pillows on her side of the booth, clearly still in shock. "But you're so nice." Her gaze sharpens on my face as she considers me anew. "You *are* nice, aren't you? The saving puppies and the planet and being thoughtful and generous and saying sweet things isn't an act?"

I exhale, having a pretty good idea where this is coming from. "Not to my knowledge, but... Let me guess, Adrian said I was a deadbeat?"

She huffs and mutters, "Something like that."

I clear my throat, ashamed of the story I have to tell. But it's the truth, and Sydney deserves the truth.

"My relationship with his mother ended badly." I briefly describe the way Angela left, manipulating me into agreeing to let her leave the city with Adrian, then using it against me. "The ploy worked, she was granted full physical custody, and she did her best to sabotage our visitations when he was little. It was always a nightmare, no matter how hard I tried. By the time Adrian was in high school, he didn't want to spend summers with me anymore. He filed a motion with the court, citing parental estrangement, and...that was it. We only saw each other a few days a year after that, when I could convince him to come with me to my parents' house for Thanksgiving or spend a few days hiking in Colorado.

But we always fought when were together, and I can't pretend our relationship has been anything but strained."

She studies me quietly, her expression giving nothing away. "Was there a fight tonight? When you told him about us?"

"I didn't tell him."

"Why not?"

I sigh. "He wouldn't talk to me. Said he didn't have time."

Sydney rolls her eyes and mumbles something I can't make out.

"But he said I could text him," I continue, "and he'd get back to me when he had a second. That's when I decided I'd had enough of the party."

"I'm sorry," she says. "He can be such a dick. But usually only when he's hurting or feeling insecure. He mentioned that you were coming before we left my place. He seemed stressed about it. He played it off as irritation, but I think maybe he just doesn't know how to behave with you now that you're both adults."

I arch a brow and her lips curve gently.

"Well, *you're* an adult," she amends. "He's still working on it. But he's trying, he really is."

"You think so?"

She nods. "I do. He isn't a bad man, Gideon, and neither are you. It just sounds like there's been a lot of miscommunication and outside interference between the two of you. But there has to be a way to make things better."

"I hope so," I say, regret making my chest ache as I

add, "Though the fact that I left the party with his ex-girlfriend might complicate things."

Her lips peel away from her teeth in a grimace. "Oh God. Yeah. And the fact that you and I… That we…" She clears her throat and reaches for her coffee, only to set it back down again with a sharp exhale. "I wish I'd asked for more coffee. Or a whiskey on the rocks, extra whiskey."

I push my mug across the table. "Take mine."

"Thanks." She reaches for the coffee, her fingers lingering on mine for an electric moment before I pull away. "He's going to be pissed," she adds as she wraps both hands around the warm mug. "Or embarrassed or whatever feeling causes men to be mad that a woman decided to get naked with someone else. As you know, Adrian and I were never…intimate. And that was kind of a big deal for him." She brings the coffee to her lips. "He actually made a joke about it tonight."

My brows shoot up.

"I told him not to kiss me again or I was going to leave," she says. "I reminded him that I was there as a friend, not his date. But he just laughed and made a joke about it being a sloppy friend kiss, not a real kiss. He said he was pretty sure I liked his real kisses, even if I didn't like them enough to…you know."

I want to punch him. My own son. It's not a good look, but what the actual fuck? How on earth did he decide that was an acceptable thing to say to a friend who was doing him a favor?

"I'm sorry," I say.

She frowns. "Why?"

"I raised a douchebag."

She laughs. "He's not a douchebag."

I grunt, and she smiles.

"Fine, he can veer into douchebag territory every once and a while," she admits. "But it never lasts long. And it doesn't sound like you had a whole lot of influence over the way he was raised." She takes another sip of my coffee before setting it on the table and pushing it toward me. "In any event, I don't blame you for Adrian's occasionally less-than-charming behavior."

"Keep it," I say, nodding at the mug. "That whiskey you mentioned is sounding like a better idea right now."

"Then let's go."

"Go?"

She nods over her shoulder. "There's a barber shop speakeasy not far from here. You enter through a secret door in one of the mirrors. Ever been?"

I shake my head, already knowing I can't take this to a second location. If I'm going to have a shot of getting past this awkward situation with Adrian, Sydney has to stay in my past.

No matter how much it hurts.

It's time I ripped the bandage off and stopped prolonging the torture. "I can't see you again, Sydney. In any capacity. Tonight, or any other night."

She flinches, as if the words physically wound her, making me feel worse than I do already.

"I'm so sorry," I add, my voice rough. "You have no idea how much I wish things were different. When we first sat down, I thought..." I sigh. "I don't know what I thought. I was so happy to see you again, I wasn't thinking straight. But the more we circle this, the more I see that continuing to see you in any capacity would destroy my chances of mending my relationship with my son."

She swallows, averting her gaze as she nods. "I understand."

"Telling him we were together once, before either of us realized the two of you used to date, will be bad enough. If I have to tell him I kept seeing you after, or that I was *still* seeing you..."

"He'd hate you even more," she says, confirming my suspicion that Adrian's been more open about his feelings about his shitty father than she initially let on. "You're probably right, but I..." Her tongue slips out to wet her lips. "I..."

"Tell me," I encourage after a moment. "Please. You can say anything to me. You won't hurt my feelings. And if you do, I deserve it for letting you down."

Her eyes fly to mine, cold fire flickering in the crystal blue. "You haven't let me down. And you didn't let Adrian down. You did the best you could, under some pretty shitty circumstances, and someday, he's going to realize that." She rolls her eyes. "Or not. But that isn't your work to do; it's his. He's an adult and it's time people started treating him like one. It's time his mother stopped paying his bills, Ben quit networking for him for free, and Noelle stopped cleaning up his toxic kitchen when she spends the night at their place."

My brows pinch together. "Angela pays his bills?"

"That's what he said." She shrugs. "That his mom paid his college tuition and some of the party expenses for the fundraiser tonight. Even though she wanted him to use the money for grad school and is angry that he dropped out at the last minute." Before I can respond, she adds, "Though he *didn't* drop out at the last minute. He dropped out in the spring but kept it from his mom long enough to get the deposit for the fall semester, which he used for the down payment on the apartment with Ben and a bunch of designer clothes. He's definitely using his mother, too, if that makes you feel any better. She's dumped hundreds of thousands of dollars into his education and he still lies to her and only takes her calls about half the time."

Willing my jaw to unclench, I manage to force out, "Angela didn't pay for those things."

"Then who..." She trails off as her eyes go wide. "Oh."

"Yeah."

"I'm sorry," she says in a softer voice. "I can't pretend to know what it feels like to be in your position, but... I know my father wouldn't continue to subsidize my life if I weren't respectful and honest with him. Relationships have to change and evolve over time. Even relationships between parents and their kids."

I sigh. "Yeah, I was having similar thoughts as I was leaving the party. But I can't cut him off like this. 'Hey, son, I slept with your ex, and I'll no longer be sending you a dime.' He'd never talk to me again."

"You're probably right, but..." She smears a bit of the condensation under her water glass across the sealed wood table before lifting her gaze to mine. "You don't have to tell him. About us."

My brows shoot up my forehead.

"It's our private business," she continues. "It has nothing to do with him. Adrian and I weren't that close, and it doesn't sound like the two of you are, either. I don't owe him any explanations, and it's not like we did this on purpose." She lifts one bare shoulder. "We could pretend it never happened. You can trust me not to say anything. I don't want to hurt you or Adrian."

Her sweet offer hurts nearly as much as the thought of never seeing her again. It's just another sign that she's the kind of woman I've been looking for, someone as beautiful on the inside as she is on the outside. "I can't ask you to compromise your integrity for me. Or Adrian."

"I wouldn't be," she says without hesitation. "I wouldn't be lying. I'd be maintaining a personal boundary between me and a man I used to date, a man who isn't entitled to information about who I'm intimate with now or at any point in the future." She reaches for her small evening bag on the cushion beside her. "I'm honestly not even sure how much longer Adrian and I will be friends. Our lives are moving in very different directions. But even if we end up best man and maid of honor at Noelle and Ben's wedding, I'll never say a word about what happened between us. You can trust me."

"I do trust you," I say. "You're a good person, Sydney. I knew that the second I met you."

"I feel the same way. Maybe in another life…" She smiles sadly. "It was good to meet you, Gideon. Thanks for the memories. And the pancakes." She starts to slide out of the booth, but I reach out to touch the back of her hand.

"Let me call you a car. It's late."

She shakes her head but doesn't pull away. "Thanks, but I'm fine. I grew up here, remember? I'm a city girl from way back. I'll catch a cab heading uptown and be safe and sound way before midnight." She turns her hand over, giving my fingers a quick squeeze. "But thank you for being so thoughtful. Take care, Gideon. I wish you all good things."

Before I can respond, she's up and out of the booth, blowing me a quick kiss before she starts through the crowded restaurant toward the door. As she walks away, heads swivel to watch her go, this gorgeous woman in black, but she doesn't notice. She has no idea how stunning she is, how special and...unforgettable.

She's going to haunt me, but this is for the best.

As I motion for the check and wait for our server to run my card, I repeat the list of reasons why Sydney and I were doomed from the start in my head over and over again.

She's too young, our lives are incompatible, she's my son's ex-girlfriend.

She's too young, our lives are incompatible, she's my son's ex-girlfriend...

When I step outside, I change the last part of the mantra to—*she's had my tongue **and** Adrian's tongue in her mouth*—just to make the truth even more brutal.

I need brutality right now. If I'm not ruthless with myself, there's a chance I might end up chasing after her.

The thought is enough to make me turn right toward Avenue C instead of starting back toward Union Square. I'm not going to chase her, but I *am* going to make sure she's made it safely into a cab. She has a few minutes' head start, but there aren't as many cabs in this part of the city as there used to be, even on a Friday night. She'll likely still be trying to flag one down—or waiting for a car if she decided to call one instead—and I don't feel right about heading for the apartment until I know she's okay.

I don't intend to make contact again. I'll just keep a discreet eye on her from a distance until she's on her way.

That's the plan, and I have every intention of sticking to it.

Then I reach the end of the block and hear soft sobs coming from around the corner. Immediately, I know it's Sydney.

I hurry around the brick building, take one look at her slumped against the side of it, her eyes red and puffy, and the plan is out the window.

I step in, pulling her into my arms, crushing her small body to my chest.

My relief is visceral. It floods through me, loosening the tension in my shoulders and freeing a sob trapped in my throat. I wrap my arms around Gideon and hold on tight, pressing my face to his chest, feeling safe for the first time since I left Maine.

I was born and raised in this city.

If anyone should feel safe here, it's me.

But I don't. And not just because hate crimes are on the rise and the subways are grosser—and less dependable—than they've been in my lifetime. It's the job, my friends, my torn-between-two-worlds existence, and the certainty that I've made a wrong turn somewhere.

Most likely on the morning I dropped Gideon off at the airport without insisting on meeting him in Vermont as soon as humanly possible.

Gideon clearly made certain assumptions about me, but if we decided to give this a shot, he wouldn't have to be the one to fly to meet me all the time. I'm a busy woman, yes, but I'm also a wealthy one. I have the disposable income to purchase a flight to Vermont whenever I want.

Hell, I have the money to buy a home in Burlington, if it came to that, and in a year or two, I should have the ability to work from home at least one or two days a week.

We could make this work; I really believe that.

If only I'd never dated Adrian. If only I'd met his dark eyes across that crowded lecture hall and looked away. I should have. I was a graduate student and his teaching assistant. He should have remained a name on my attendance list. That's it.

But that wasn't it, and I meant what I said to Gideon. I want him to mend things with his son. I can tell how important it is to him. He wouldn't be the man I'm starting to fall for if it wasn't.

Which means we're still doomed and all my boo-hooing is accomplishing is making this harder for both of us.

I try to pull away, but Gideon's arms tighten around me. "It's okay. I've got you," he says, running a warm hand up to curl around the back of my neck.

"I didn't mean for you to see me like this," I mutter as I relax against his chest again, grateful for a few more stolen moments.

"I know."

"I was just so sad," I say, my voice wobbling again. "I've never felt this way before. I know we barely know each other, and I'm probably being ridiculous, but it's like…"

"I feel it, too," he says.

I sniff, then hold my breath. "You do?"

"I do." He pulls back, tipping his head down until his nose is a whisper away from mine. "And smart or not, I don't want to be alone right now. And I really don't want you to be alone." His lips drift closer to mine, making my heart slam against my ribs. "Come home with me?"

"Yes," I whisper, lifting my chin.

"We can talk more," he says, pulling back far enough to take his mouth out of easy reach. But he eases my disappointment as he adds, "And I have a spare room if you want to stay over."

"I want to stay over," I say without thinking. When my brain has a second to catch up with my mouth, I amend, "I'll just have to text my friend again. I'll tell her I decided to stay at my dad's place uptown and work from there tomorrow."

"Sounds good." He pulls his phone from his back pocket. "I'll call a car."

"I'll text Noelle," I say, unzipping my small purse. By the time I'm done, the car is pulling up at the curb.

I look up, surprised. "That was fast."

"We got lucky," Gideon says. "The driver was right around the corner." He reaches for the back door, holding it open. "Ready?"

I nod. I have no idea what we're going to talk about at his place, or if he really intends for me to stay in the guest room, but I'm not worried. I'm just grateful to have been granted a reprieve from a forever goodbye.

I don't want to say goodbye to this man, especially not for forever.

Not when it feels so right to slide into the backseat of a car with him and thread my fingers through his.

The car pulls through Union Square, past the four-story bookstore on Seventeenth Street, where I spent countless hours studying in high school.

Starting our sophomore year, Noelle took classes at the art institute not far from here. We'd take the subway down after our snobby prep school let out at three, and I'd study in the bookstore café while Noelle learned to draft patterns and bring her designs to life. Then, she'd come find me and see if I was ready to grab dinner.

If I wasn't done with my homework yet, she'd make a game of finding the filthiest sex scenes on the romance shelves. She'd carry them back to my table, cradling them like priceless, filthy treasures, and read them aloud to me in a hushed whisper during study breaks.

We'd giggle until we had tears streaming down our faces and the people at the tables around us shot us dirty looks.

Noelle was still a virgin at that point, too. She was on a scholarship to our prep school and spent most of her time studying to keep her grades up, and I was just...me, the girl who was mildly terrified by the thought of being naked with another person.

Back then, we were positive that at least half the

kinky stuff the characters were getting up to in the bedroom was pure fiction.

Now, I would happily reenact every steamy scene I read with the man seated beside me, and I'm pretty sure neither one of us would be laughing.

"This is me," Gideon says when the driver pulls over at the next corner. As he pays for the ride, I lean over, peering up at the white stone skyscraper. Impressive marble pillars on the first two levels give way to more subtle decorative elements as it stretches upward, but it's a luxury building, no doubt about it.

Gideon has clearly done very well for himself. With him, I wouldn't feel compelled to hide the fact that I have money, too. Or, that my *family* has money that is now under my control.

No matter how hard I've worked to get good grades or be the best conservationist in rural Maine, I can't help feeling like I don't deserve credit for the things I've accomplished. After all, it was so much easier for me than people whose parents didn't have the resources mine did. It's like I started the race two laps ahead of everyone else and that's certainly nothing to be proud of.

The issue is already top of mind when we move into the lobby, past the friendly doorman at the front desk, and into the elevator, where Gideon presses the P for penthouse.

Penthouse. Gabaldon...

My brain connects the dots, remembering where I've heard the name before. Edward and Annabelle Gabaldon are friends of my father's, an older couple who own a summer home not far from ours in The Hamptons. I think they're in mining. Platinum or something.

Before I realize my lips are moving, I hear myself asking, "What did you say your parents' names were again?"

He shoots me an amused look. "I didn't. But if you're trying to place them in the high society scene, don't bother. We aren't those Gabaldons. I grew up on Long Island. My dad did well for himself in his business, but not old money well. And he had a chip on his shoulder about snobby city people. He and my mother retired to Tampa a few years ago and couldn't be happier."

"Sorry, I didn't mean to pry," I say, my cheeks heating. My mother is probably rolling over in her grave. She taught me young that it was gauche to discuss money. As far as she was concerned, people who talked about money clearly didn't have enough of it.

Gideon smiles as the elevator slows. "There's no need to apologize. You aren't the first person to ask. And truth be told, we probably *are* related to those Gabaldons in one way or another, but too far up the family tree to bridge the gap between the Upper East Side and Long Island." The car stops and the doors slide smoothly open. Gideon extends an arm, motioning for me to precede him down the short hallway to the only apartment on the floor.

The ornate gold P on the door reminds me of my father's place. Though Dad's "P" is larger and more ornate. The font choice reflects the posh Georgian building I called home as a child.

My friends were always so jealous. Many of them had bigger homes and more opulent bedrooms, but the architecture and private rooftop garden set our place apart. My father also had a small indoor pool installed downstairs in what used to be the bowling alley when I was six. After that, no one turned down my sleepover invitations, even if I was one of the shier girls in class and always looked like I'd just run inside after rolling in the grass, no matter how hard my mother worked to make me look like a little lady.

It crosses my mind that my mother would probably approve of Gideon. Yes, he's older, but he's wealthy. He might not have the pedigree she would have preferred, but being a billionaire forgives a multitude of sins. And our family has the pedigree part covered. If Gideon were with me, previously closed doors would open for him.

But I already know he wouldn't care. Gideon couldn't care less about accessing the private clubs and secret societies of the uber rich. He just wants to do good work, make a positive difference in the world, and spend as much time hiking and rock climbing as possible.

And reconnect with his son, the inner voice reminds me as Gideon opens the door, leading the way into a gorgeous open-concept space filled with plants and softly burbling water features.

Adrian. It all keeps coming back to Adrian. No matter how comfortable I feel with Gideon, and how much I want to be with him, the reality of this complicated, delicate situation isn't going away.

"Sparkling water?" Gideon asks in the kitchen, opening a pale wood panel that conceals the fridge from view. "Juice? Beer? Whiskey on the rocks?"

Leaning on the lovely white marble island with the delicate gray veins running throughout, I say, "Whiskey on the rocks. But only if you'll have some with me."

"Trying to get me drunk and lower my inhibitions?" He glances at me over his shoulder, the fridge still open, showcasing almost nothing inside except drinks, fruit, and a small container of half-and-half. Clearly, he wasn't lying when he said he doesn't spend much time here.

I shrug, my pulse picking up again as I say, "Maybe. Is that bad?"

"Not at all," he says, his expression sobering as he closes the door and reaches for a bourbon tumbler from an artistic display of glasses near the sink. "You don't have anything to feel bad about. None of this is your fault or your responsibility. This is my mess." He sighs as he slides open a drawer below the fridge, revealing the freezer. It's even more empty than the fridge, barren aside from an ice maker full of perfectly formed cubes.

Gideon plops two in the glass before sliding the drawer closed and turning to face me. "Whiskey preference? I have a nice Hakushu single malt from my last hiking trip in Japan."

I arch a wry brow. "You drink whiskey on your hikes?"

He smiles one of his wicked smiles, and my stomach flips. Damn, I've missed that grin. I've missed this man. Even with the specters of Adrian and our doomed relationship haunting the evening, I still feel so comfortable and welcome in his home.

"No, after," he says. "Nothing like a giant steak and a glass of whiskey after a five-day hike over a mountain."

I hum jealously. "Sounds amazing. I've never done more than a weekend trip. School was too intense to get away for longer than that and I didn't want to let the butterflies and seabirds down in the summers."

"What about when you were younger? Did your dad ever take you hiking?"

I snort out a laugh. "If only you knew how funny that was."

"He's not an outdoorsman?"

"That's putting it mildly. He won't even go golfing without bug spray and extra shoes to put on as soon as he steps off the green. Nature is too messy and unpredictable for my father. We did museums and fancy restaurants when I was a kid, not hikes or playgrounds."

Sadness creeps into Gideon's voice as he says, "Adrian used to love the Central Park playgrounds when he was a kid. We'd go to a different one every time. Some of my best memories with him are there."

I reach over, pushing the glass of ice closer to his side of the island. "I think you need whiskey more than I do. And I told you, I don't want to drink alone."

His gaze locks on mine, making my blood rush faster. "If I have a drink with you, I'm going to kiss you. And if I kiss you, I'm not going to want to stop."

My nipples poke shamelessly against the silky fabric of my dress in response to his words, giving me an idea.

"That would be terrible," I murmur as I lean forward.

The neck of my borrowed gown falls forward, baring more of my already scantily covered breasts. Gideon's focus drops to my chest, heat flaring in his eyes that fills me with a dizzying mixture of longing and guilt.

I shouldn't be teasing him, flirting with him. But the more I think about everything Adrian has said about his father over the past year, the less I feel he deserves the right to stand between us. Yes, it sounds like he was manipulated by his mother, but he's not a child anymore. He's old enough to know better than to treat a man who's clearly eager for a meaningful relationship with his son like an irritating inconvenience.

Or an ATM.

It honestly disgusts me.

I hold on to that feeling, letting it banish my guilt as I trace my clavicle with one finger. "Really terrible," I repeat. I catch one spaghetti strap on my manicured nail and guide it down over my shoulder until my right breast is completely bare to his gaze.

Gideon hisses in a breath, his jaw clenching. "One night. I know that's what we said before, but I really can't let this go any further. I wish I could, but..."

"One night," I echo, my panties already soaked. Right now, I'd say yes if he offered me five minutes. I'm pathetic when it comes to this man, so desperate for his touch that before I know it, I'm drawing my dress over my head and dropping it to the glossy wood floor. When I'm in nothing but my panties and the kitten-soft thigh-high stockings I'm so grateful I let Noelle talk me into, I take a step back from the island and nod to my left. "I assume the bedroom's that way?"

"Fuck the bedroom," he mutters.

A beat later, he's sliding up and over the island in one smooth motion that reminds me how much I love the way he moves. His confidence, his control, the way his strong muscles flex beneath his clothes—everything about him turns me into a puddle of boneless desire.

seventeen

I pull her against me, urging her thighs up and around my waist.

She obeys my unspoken direction without hesitation, twining her arms around my neck as our mouths collide. I kiss her hard, one hand braced under her ass, the other fisted in the hair at the nape of her neck, so starved for her, I can't hold back.

Sydney matches my intensity, groaning against my lips as our tongues dance and her breath comes faster. "I thought I was exaggerating it in my memory," she says between kisses as I carry her across the living room toward the master bedroom. "I kept telling myself it wasn't as hot as I remembered. That there was no way you could make me feel like I'm going to explode with just a kiss."

"But it's not," I rasp, squeezing her bottom tighter as we reach the bed. "And you do the same thing to me, butterfly. I need to be inside you. We'll go slow the second time. Are you wet for me, or should I get the lube?"

"I'm so wet," she whispers, her nails raking down my chest as I set her on her feet, making my cock jerk in my pants. "I've been wet since you touched my hand at the coffee shop. See?" She takes my hand, guiding it down the front of her silky little panties.

I slide over her small patch of hair to her sex and nearly melt into a puddle at her feet. "Fuck, baby," I say, driving my fingers into her dripping heat, balls dragging between my legs when she cries out and spreads her thighs, welcoming my invasion. "I love feeling how much you want me."

"Need you," she corrects, tearing at the buttons on my vest before moving on to my belt buckle. "I need you so much, Gideon. A vibrator isn't the same. I can't come the way I do when I'm with you."

"You've been touching yourself?" I ask as I help her dispose of my clothes.

"All the time," she says, her heated gaze lifting to mine as she shoves my pants down around my thighs. "And I always think of you. Of the way you made me feel wild and safe at the same time."

"You're always safe with me, baby," I promise her, before adding in my "be a good girl" voice, "Now get out of those panties and get on the bed. Leave the stockings on. I want to fuck you with them on."

She obeys with a breathy sigh of excitement that ricochets through my chest. This is how it should be with a lover—hot and easy, filthy and sweet. Even before I roll on a condom and join her on the bed, guiding her knees up and out so we can both watch me fill her, inch by inch, I know this won't be the last time. Not tonight, and probably not tomorrow, either.

It's too perfect with her. *She's* too perfect.

She wraps her legs around my hips, crying out as I slide the last inch in to fill her, her hands trembling as they skim down my back. "Yes. God, Gideon. I've missed you like a part of me."

"Every damned day," I agree, kissing my way down her throat as I pull back and glide home again. "I kept wishing we'd had more time. There are so many other ways I wanted to give you pleasure."

"Like on top again?" she asks, a hint of shyness in her voice. "I really liked on top last time."

Before the last word is out of her mouth, I've rolled us both over on the mattress, making her breath rush out with a laugh as I settle her on top of me. But the laugh quickly becomes a moan as I cup her breasts in my hands, licking and sucking her tight nipples.

"Oh God, yes," she says, her hips starting to move—slow and uncertain at first but gaining confidence as I squeeze her ass and assure her, "Whatever feels good for you, butterfly. Ride me however you want. I'm happy to be along for the ride."

"You still feel bigger this way," she says, bracing her hands on my chest and shifting back a bit. "Longer." Her lips part as she sighs, "I can feel you...everywhere."

"Not everywhere," I whisper, sliding my hand between our writhing bodies. "Not yet."

Gathering some of the slickness from her body on my fingers, I ease one back to tease the puckered ring of her ass as she moves. Surprising me, she barely hesitates a beat before leaning forward to grant me easier access.

"You want my finger in your ass, butterfly?" I ask, welcoming the kiss she crushes to my lips with a moan.

"I want everything with you, baby," she says, her words drawing me closer to the edge than her tight pussy.

Because I want everything with her, too. Absolutely everything.

And I like the term of endearment on her lips. I like it so much I almost abandon the plan to show her how nice a little ass play can be. But then she whispers, "Do it. I'm not scared. I trust you," and I have no choice but to ease my middle finger gently into her ring.

She sucks in a breath, shuddering as she adjusts, but she doesn't stop riding me. If anything, her rhythm grows more urgent, her nails digging into my shoulders as she grinds on my cock.

"Yes," she says a few beats later, her breath coming in harsh gasps. "Yes, Gideon. God, I'm going to come. I'm going to come so hard. So hard. Oh God. God!"

She falls apart on my chest and I follow her with a guttural cry of triumph, though I've done absolutely nothing to be proud of. I shouldn't have fucked my son's ex-girlfriend tonight. I shouldn't have done it once, and I sure as hell shouldn't do it again.

But as soon as I've washed my hands, fetched Sydney water, and rejoined her in bed, I'm already sporting a semi again.

All it takes is a brush of her fingers over my cock as she whispers, "I can't decide if I like on top or behind better. Maybe you can remind me what behind feels like?" and I'm rock hard and ready to go.

I stay that way most of the night, until we fall asleep sometime around two in the morning, tangled up together and exhausted in the best way possible.

I WAKE UP FEELING BETTER THAN I HAVE SINCE THE LAST time I spent the night with this woman.

Memories of how that morning played out, complete with the best morning sex of my life, makes me roll over, reaching for Sydney, but the sheets on the other side of the bed are cool.

I sit up, glancing around the large master bedroom, but there's no sign of her and the door to the master bath is open, so I can hear that she's not in there grabbing a shower.

Maybe she decided to go looking for food or coffee. Coffee, I have plenty of, but the food options are limited. But I can order us something delivered. There's a fabulous French place on Fifth Avenue that delivers brunch until two p.m.

That's one thing I'll never stop missing about the city, the food quality and selection are unparalleled. Burlington has a few nice places, but nothing like New York City.

I slide out of bed, pulling on linen pajama pants over my boxer briefs but deciding to skip the t-shirt. It's still warm for September and a part of me is hoping I'll be able to tempt Sydney back to bed before we eat.

Pushing aside the voice in my head trying to remind me that we said one *night* and it's already morning, I head into the kitchen to find Sydney sitting cross-legged on one of the stools at the island, the morning paper spread out on the counter in front of her. She's wearing my blue t-shirt and nothing else, exposing nearly every inch of her long, toned legs.

"You found the paper, I see." I cross to her, planning to skim my fingers up her thigh and discover if she decided panties were worth the trouble. But when she turns to me, her face is pale, and I freeze. "What is it? What's wrong?"

"Why do you have the paper delivered?" she asks, her voice strained. "No one gets the real paper anymore! We read it on our phones or in an app. And you don't even live here full time."

"I only get it on weekends when I'm in town. My assistant arranges it," I say, glancing down at the pages, but not seeing anything particularly terrifying in the headlines. But with the world these days, you never can tell. There's always something horrible unfolding in the news cycle. "Why? What's happened?"

She pulls in a shallow breath, shaking her head. "I'm an idiot, that's what happened. But in my defense, no one in the press seemed interested that I was back in the city." She drags a clawed hand through her wavy hair. "But that's probably because all I was doing was going to work and taking my work home with me and waking up in the middle of the night to work some more when the stress of not working got to be too much. I wasn't out on the town in a boob dress."

Still not understanding what she's upset about, but feeling compelled to defend her dress, I say, "It's not a boob dress. It's a leg dress. And you were beautiful in it."

"Thank you." She sighs. "But it's definitely a boob dress in pictures. If my father sees this, he's going to flip out. I'm supposed to be proving I'm mature enough to take over the company, not bouncing my bimbo boobs all over the city."

She pushes a picture-heavy section of the paper my way. The society section, I realize. Instantly, my gaze goes to the dazzling strawberry blonde in black with her hand propped on one hip. She's looking over her shoulder, laughing, while the man with his arm wrapped around her waist gazes at her profile adoringly. And yes, a good amount of her right breast is showing, but she looks classy and confident. There's nothing bimbo-ish about her.

It's a beautiful shot of Sydney...and my son.

His name is right there in black and white in the caption—Adrian Weathersfield (he uses my ex's last name) and Sydney Perry-Watson.

"Perry-Watson?" I blurt out, my gaze jerking up from the page. "You're a Perry-Watson?"

She blinks and a sheepish look creeps across her face. "Yes. I thought I told you."

"You said Watson, not Perry-Watson."

"Are you sure?" she squeaks in a way that makes me think the omission was deliberate.

"Positive. I would have remembered if there was a chance in hell that you were Silas Perry-Watson's daughter."

Her eyes widen. "You know my dad?"

"I used to work for your dad," I say, my stomach bottoming out as my mind races to connect the dots. I pace toward the cabinets and back again. "Right out of grad school. I interned at Watson Global for a few months before I was hired full time. I worked closely with your father for almost—" I freeze, my throat tightening as another memory leaps out at me, like a monster under the bed. "Almost two years. I was there when his wife and daughter stopped by on summer evenings to talk him into grabbing dinner instead of working late. I...I saw you. I think I might have even said hi. You were maybe eight? Nine?"

Her eyes are so wide now that she looks like one of those anime characters Adrian loved when he was a kid. "Oh my God, I remember you. You had a moustache!"

I wince. "I did. I'm so sorry. It was trendy at the time."

"No, I liked it," she murmurs. "I told my mom I liked it, and she said only the most handsome men can pull off a moustache without looking ridiculous. My mom met you and liked you... That's so nice." A soft smile curves her lips, but I'm too horrified to share her pleasure in that.

I lean against the island, my legs suddenly weak. "I was a grown man working my first job and you were a child."

"Well, I'm not a child anymore," she says, sitting up straighter. "So don't start freaking out about that again. We have bigger things to freak out about."

"Like?" I arch a brow. "You know any nine-year-olds? Do you like the idea of dating one of them in fifteen years?"

Her lips press together. "The only nine-year-old I know is my cousin Pearl, so no, I can't imagine dating her in fifteen years. But I'm sure she'll be a fabulous woman by then." She reaches over, pointing a finger at the picture of her and Adrian. "This, however, is not fabulous. Adrian doesn't know I'm a Perry-Watson. He doesn't know my father is ridiculously wealthy or that my grueling new job is setting me up to be a merciless titan of industry. He hates trust fund babies. He goes off about them all the time. He's going to think I'm an asshole and a liar."

I frown, trying to sort out why that troubles me.

Because she cares. She cares what Adrian thinks of her, my gut replies. Before I can decide whether or not I want to bring that to her attention, the front door slams open, and a voice booms, "What the fuck, bossman? I've been waiting downstairs for twenty minutes. I thought we were going for coffee in the park."

Sydney scrambles off her stool and starts toward the bedroom, but aborts the mission to hide behind a wing chair in the living room when Mitch emerges from the entryway. "I know you were out partying last night, but —" He cuts off abruptly as he spots Sydney, frozen like a deer in the headlights.

He takes a step back, jerks his gaze my way, then jerks it back toward Sydney before croaking, "Sydney?"

"Uncle Mitch," Sydney says, her voice breathy and pink creeping up her neck toward her cheeks. "Um, hi! How are you?"

eighteen

SYDNEY

I close my eyes for a beat, certain that when I open them, I'll be back in my apartment, and this will all have been a dream.

I didn't really spend the night with Adrian's dad, end up on the society page with half my breast out for show and tell with Adrian himself, or get caught wearing nothing but a t-shirt by a man I've known since I was practically a fetus.

Mitch McMillan isn't my *real* uncle, but he might as well be.

Mitch has been a member of my dad's cigar club for as long as I can remember. Most Sunday afternoons in the fall and winter, when society has abandoned their summer homes, Mitch is part of the circle of puffing professionals on our roof on the Upper East Side. Dad has the butler set up heaters like they have at outdoor restaurants when it's cool, and the cigar club sits under the pergola, contemplating how much better things were in "the good old days."

I never lingered up in the stinky smoke, not even when I was a kid and didn't realize the "good old days" they were talking about were the days when no one challenged their rich, white guy entitlement, but I know Mitch well. He's a gruff, but kind guy, who brought cookies or chocolates for Mom when he came by. After Mom's death, he brought stuffed animals for me and always made time to ask how I was doing before heading up to the roof. I was technically too old for stuffed animals, I guess, but I adored them.

By the time Dad finally told him to stop spoiling me, I had a menagerie of beautifully made toys that are still lined up on the bookshelves of my childhood room. Even as a teen, I liked to look at them. They reminded me that there are sweet people in the world who care about others and aren't afraid to show it.

But right now, Mitch doesn't look sweet.

He looks *pissed*.

"What the fuck, Gideon?" Mitch motions toward me, then flaps a hand at Gideon, before pressing a hand to his chest. "I think I'm having a heart attack."

"No, don't have a heart attack," I say, the words breaking through my frozen-in-fear response. "Sit down and take slow, deep breaths. Gideon, get him a glass of water. I'm going to put on pants. I'll be right back, and we'll talk this out calmly and rationally."

I dash into the bedroom, cursing myself when I arrive beside the rumpled bed, and remember all I have to wear is the boob dress. Deciding Gideon won't mind if I borrow something, I drag open drawers until I find a pair of khaki shorts. I pull them on, secure them with a belt from his closet, and pop into the bathroom to smooth my hands through my hair.

But there's nothing to be done with the wild curls floating around my shoulders, declaring to the entire world that I was fucked hard last night. I don't even have a hair tie in my purse. Clearly, I need to improve my "staying over at a man's house" preparations.

Only, I don't want to stay over at any other man's house and Gideon was already pushing me away, even before he realized that he used to work for my dad and is apparently good friends with Uncle Mitch.

"Fuck, fuck, fuck," I mutter, pacing back and forth in front of the mirror. I need advice, but it's way too early for Noelle to be awake after a party night, and no one else knows about Gideon.

Well, no one around here anyway…

Gambling that Elaina will be having a slow morning at the café, I grab my cell from the bedside table and call her, continuing to pace the soft carpet beside the bed as the phone rings, hoping Gideon and Mitch aren't coming to blows in the other room.

Everything sounds pretty quiet out there right now, but I know Mitch. He has a big temper, and I'm sure it'll make an appearance as soon as he's over the initial shock.

Thankfully, Elaina answers on the second ring with a cheery, "Sydney! What's up, woman? When are you coming in October? I want to plan a book club rager. I'm going to make a signature drink and make a spooky playlist and everything. I figure, if you can't beat the spooky weirdos, join 'em, right?"

"Listen, I can only talk for a second, but I'm in trouble," I whisper, quickly filling Elaina in on the situation, before hissing, "What do I do?"

"Shit," she whispers back. "I have no idea. I've never dated my uncle's best friend."

"He's not really my uncle," I remind her.

"Right, but that's not the point, is it?" She hums softly, her thinking hum.

I cross my fingers and pace faster, praying she'll come up with something. Because honestly, right now? I have nothing. Nothing but anxiety and the strong urge to climb out a window and flee down a fire escape.

"Okay, this is what you should do," she finally says, proceeding to outline a plan of action so outrageous, it just might work. "BDE? Got it?"

I exhale. "Um, yeah, but am I that girl? The girl with Big Dong Energy? I don't know if I am."

"You're the girl who went home with the one who got away last night, woman," she says. "Because he couldn't stay away from your sexy, boss bitch self. You are a powerhouse of sexy, a brilliant business mind, and your hair always smells amazing, even when you've been out in a bog counting butterflies all day."

"Thank you, my shampoo is really great," I say, my chest filling with warmth. "So are you. I love and miss you so much."

"Aw, I love and miss you, too," she says. "So do the girls. Sea Breeze isn't the same without our Syd. Good luck and call me as soon as you can to fill me in on what happens next. Oh, and don't forget to let me know about October. Any weekend is fine. We'll make it work. We know your schedule is a lot more hectic than ours."

My stomach tightens, but now isn't the time to tell her that I won't be able to make that October book club meeting.

I'll explain later, after I've put out my current, inter-personal fire and have hopefully made a plan to get up to Maine in November. Surely, the insanity at work will have slowed down a little by then.

I end the call, square my shoulders, and prepare to head back into the living room. At the last second, I slide into my borrowed stilettos and grab my purse and dress. I'm sure my borrowed t-shirt and khakis look ridiculous paired with high heels, but I feel at least ten times more powerful with shoes on.

Now, I can strut into the living room, and strutting is always better than tiptoeing into a confrontation on bare feet.

Or so I tell myself as I aim myself toward the door, doing my best to channel my inner badass.

nineteen

GIDEON

I fetch Mitch water, but when I set the glass in front of him on the coffee table, he only grunts and shakes his bowed head.

He doesn't even look at me.

"It isn't what you think," I say, though I'm actually not sure what Mitch is thinking.

If he's thinking that I'm taking advantage of a young woman, maybe he's right. I keep telling myself Sydney is wise beyond her years, but isn't that what every old creep tells himself as he chases a girl half his age?

And Mitch doesn't even know about Sydney's history with my son or my newly discovered history with her father. Though, he might remember that Silas and I have a connection...

Mitch and I didn't start working together until years after I left Watson Global, but we've discussed my time there. Silas is one of our many mutual connections. I worked for Silas, and Mitch, being nearly a decade older than myself, is one of his cigar club buddies.

I was actually invited to join the cigar club last year. They usually only allow men over forty, but Mitch said he could sneak me in a year or two early. I deferred, citing my deep loathing for the stomach-churning smell of cigar smoke. I held firm, even when he insisted the networking opportunities were worth a little nausea.

Now, I'm so glad I did. A closer connection than I already have to Silas would further doom my chances with Sydney.

What chances? She's probably on her way out the old servant's entrance right now, asshole.

The voice of panic is loud, but I know that's not Sydney's style. She's not the kind to run when things get hard. She'll face the problem, head-on, and probably tell me flat out that she can't see me again.

I have no idea what I'll do if that happens, but I already knew that our "one night" bargain wasn't going to hold. At least, not for me. Being with her feels too damned right.

I have a good life, great friends, and a job and hobbies I love. Until Sydney, I believed that was enough. I'd convinced myself that I wasn't lonely or longing for the kind of soul-deep connection I was certain had passed me by. But maybe it hasn't. Maybe all my previous attempts at happily-ever-after failed because the universe was waiting to bring me into the same orbit as this incredible woman.

The one strutting into my living room in shorts, a t-shirt, and three-inch heels…

"Okay, first things first, is Mitch actually having a

heart attack?" she asks, holding up her cell. "If so, I'm calling 911 and the rest of this can wait."

"No," Mitch grumbles, his elbows braced on his knees. "But it's still early days. Give me a few weeks of keeping a secret like this from your father, and I'm sure I'll be having chest pains on the regular."

Sydney comes to stand on the other side of the coffee table, her hands propped on her hips. "You aren't going to be keeping anything from my father. Because you never came up here this morning. You stayed downstairs and Gideon came down to meet you. You never saw me, I never saw you, and no one jumped to any wild conclusions."

Mitch looks up, arching a brow. "Wild conclusions? You're wearing his clothes, Syd. What other conclusion is there? And you can't Jedi mind trick me. I'm too old."

"You're not too old," she insists. "You're the perfect age to realize that discretion is the better part of valor, and that what my father doesn't know, can't needlessly upset him. Additionally, you're old enough to realize that I'm an adult and capable of making my own decisions without input from my father or anyone else."

"Your own mistakes, you mean?" Mitch nods toward me, but still doesn't shift his gaze my way. "He's old enough to be your father, kiddo. He has a son your age."

"I know," she says, without missing a beat. "Adrian and I went to school together. We're friends, actually. That's how Gideon and I ran into each other again last night. And yes, the age gap is an issue. It might even be a dealbreaker, but that's for us to decide. Until we make that call, I would appreciate you keeping this to yourself. Consider it a favor to an old friend." She paces past him toward the door before spinning back with a calm smile. "I do hope we can be friends, Mitch. I'll be head of Watson Global in a few years, and I know that business relationship has always meant a lot to you. Though I confess, I didn't realize you worked with Gideon until this morning. But now that I do, I'm even more excited to put future retrofitting projects in your company's care. Assuming, of course, that we're on the same page this morning."

Mitch's jaw drops, but there's new respect in his tone when he says, "Are you waving your business dick at me, Syd?"

She smiles, her eyes sparkling. "Maybe. A little dick-waving isn't out of order at times like these. A friend taught me that. And my father taught me to leave a negotiation while I still have the upper hand. I'll see you both later. Have a wonderful morning." She looks up, meeting my gaze, a softer note in her voice as she adds, "Call me? I'll leave my number at the desk downstairs."

"Absolutely," I promise.

Then, before I can offer to walk her to the door or tell her what a badass she is, she struts through the entryway and shuts the front door quietly behind her.

When she's gone, I turn back to Mitch.

He shakes his head. "You're crazy. You know that, right?"

My lips hook up. "You don't know the half of it." I nod toward the door, deciding the news that my son used to date Sydney can wait until we have coffee. And eggs. I'm suddenly starving. "Come on. I'll buy you breakfast and confess my sins. My treat."

"I don't know if I can handle more sin," he says, but he rises to his feet and smooths a hand over his impeccably gelled hair. "But I could eat. The diner on Eighteenth Street, though. None of that French shit."

"None of the French shit," I promise. I'd rather save that to share with Sydney anyway.

Sydney, who I will absolutely be calling. And likely, seeing again. I have zero self-control when it comes to this woman.

I suppose there's a chance that talking things through with an old friend will bring me to my senses, but I doubt it, not with her powerhouse of an exit still fresh in my mind.

I'm beginning to think that if anyone can make the transition from dating a son to dating his father without causing a scandal, it's Sydney.

twenty

SYDNEY

I decide to walk uptown, at least part of the way.

It's a gorgeous autumn morning, with the leaves just starting to change in the parks and a pleasant nip in the air. People are out walking dogs, taking their kids to playgrounds, or just wandering the streets with coffee in hand, soaking in the lazy weekend vibes.

It's my favorite kind of day in New York City, the kind I haven't had the chance to enjoy since returning home. I've been working straight through the weekends and the one Saturday I had "off" two weeks ago, my father roped me into an extended business brunch.

I love my dad, I really do, but he's bad for my digestion. By the time he gave me a fifteen-minute rundown on why our supply chain would need to be completely revamped in the next ten years, my stomach was in knots. I could barely eat two bites of my savory mushroom crepe, and I love a good mushroom crepe.

Though not as much as I loved those lemon souffle pancakes last night...

But I'm guessing any meal shared with Gideon would taste ten times more delicious. He's just fantastic. And he thinks *I'm* fantastic, too. He even approved of my handling of the Mitch situation. As I walked out, his eyes were shining with amusement and pride.

He was proud of me. And I liked it.

Maybe a little too much, which gets me to thinking...

I call Elaina again.

She picks up on the first ring with a breathless, "How did it go?"

"Amazing," I say, grinning as I drift into Bryant Park, admiring the sun on the white bark of the birch trees. "You were right. Big dong energy was the way to go."

"I knew it! I'm so smart," she crows, humble as ever. "BDE is always my go-to in a pinch. Works like a charm. Gertie says it doesn't, but that's because she doesn't understand the difference between confidence and conflict. Big dick energy isn't about starting a fight; it's about proving a fight isn't necessary because shit has already been handled by the Giant Schlong in Charge." She sighs. "I'm so proud of you."

"Weird you say that. That's sort of why I'm calling. I think Gideon was proud of me, too."

She emits a happy cooing sound. "See? He's a keeper. You have to keep dating and see where this goes, Syd! A man who appreciates big dick energy is a treasure. And not easy to find. Believe me, I've been looking. I thought Stettler might be down with my powerful side for a while, but once he found out how much the café makes a year, he dipped. Said he couldn't be with a woman who made more cash money than he did. That it made his dick shrivel up. Which would have been a deal-breaker for me, too, since it wasn't that big to start with." She makes a growling sound. "Ugh. Men are the worst. Except Gideon, of course. Does he have a twin?"

The question reminds me of one tiny detail I haven't shared yet. "Um, no, but he does have a son. A son I sort of maybe...*dated* for a little while last year?"

"What?" she squawks, loud enough to summon several outraged meowing sounds from the background. "And you left this out of the story because why? Don't you know by now that I live for drama like this, woman? You should have told us all at the lobster boil before you left. We could have watched Maya come unglued at the thought of all the conflict in your future. There is conflict, right? Or are they like...cool with sharing?"

"They're not *sharing*," I say, my nose wrinkling. "And I didn't tell you before because I didn't know until last night. Neither did Gideon. As soon as he realized Adrian and I used to be a thing, he wanted to call it off. But then we went for pancakes and one thing led to another and..."

"You ended up sleeping over at his place," she supplies. "Of course, you did. Pancakes are underrated as an aphrodisiac. Also salads. A fresh salad with a zesty dressing totally does it for me. I get frisky just walking through a farmer's market, buying ingredients. So, when are you going to see him again?"

I ease into an empty bench with a view of kids playing hopscotch on the pavement not far away. "I don't know. But he's going to call me. He said he would, and he's not the kind of guy to say something he doesn't mean."

She coos again. "I love him already. What about you? Are you still falling hard?"

"Yes," I whisper, even though there's no one close enough to hear. "But what if that's only because there's something wrong with me?"

She snorts. "What the hell are you talking about? There's nothing wrong with you. You're fabulous, not to mention one of my best friends. And I don't have lame best friends. I just don't. I'm too good at friendship."

I smile, but my stomach is tight as I say, "You are good at friendship. I'm good at friendship, too, but I'm not so great at dating. I managed to make it to twenty-four without getting laid, Elaina. And as soon as I started sleeping with someone, I developed a praise kink almost immediately."

"Woah," she says, letting out a long, slow breath. "That is so baller. You're my idol."

I laugh and roll my eyes. "Why? Because I'm a weirdo who likes to be told I'm a good girl while doing filthy things to an older man in bed? And who also really likes it when the man seems proud of me outside the bedroom? I'm no psychologist, obviously, but the daddy issues are practically slapping me in the face at this point."

"Do you think you have daddy issues?" she asks, not sounding as shocked as I thought she would.

She just sounds curious, which gives me the confidence to say, "I don't know. I didn't think so, but... maybe? I honestly can't remember my dad ever looking at me like that, Elaina. I mean, he's said he was proud of me before. Like when I graduated with honors, but I've never felt it. I've never looked into my dad's eyes and known that he thought I stuck the landing, you know?"

"Well, I don't want to overstep, but..."

"Go ahead," I urge after a moment. "We've been friends too long for you to hold back."

"Yes, we've been friends for a long time," she agrees. "But in all that time, you've maybe said...five sentences about your dad, Syd. I know more about your mom, and she's been gone since you were a kid. I have no idea what the story is with you and your father, but it might be worth a discussion with a professional."

I sigh. "That's what my last therapist said, but I thought I'd worked through all of that. I don't tie myself in knots to please him anymore."

"Says the woman who's working at her father's company because he told her that's what she would be doing after college, even though she wanted to look for a different job. Or stay on the bog with the butterflies..."

My stomach cramp intensifies. "Yes, but I'm not living with him. I said no to moving back home and to having lunch with him every day. And I wear pants to work on Fridays. Even though I know Dad wants women to 'look like women' in the office."

Eliana makes a gagging sound. "Oh my God. I think I want to punch your dad in the face. No offense. But wanting 'women to look like women?' What does that even mean? I'm a woman, no matter what I'm wearing. What century does he think he's living in?"

I shake my head, feeling more confused than before I placed this call. "He means well, and he's one of the most generous people I've ever met. He's just old-fashioned."

She grunts. Dubiously. "I think you should show him some of your Big Dick Energy. See how that shakes out."

I laugh. "Right."

"I'm serious."

My smile fades. "I should go. I have work to catch up on at home. Can't spend all day wandering the city, dissecting my likely doomed relationship and psychological shortcomings."

"Maybe you should," Elaina says. "Sometimes a person needs a day to just wander and think and live, you know? You're not mad at me, are you?"

"Not at all," I say, again deciding the news that I won't be able to make it up to Maine in October can wait. "I love and appreciate you."

"Love and appreciate you, too," she says. "And I will deeply appreciate more news on the Gideon front ASAP. I'm assuming I can share this gossip with Gertie and Maya?"

"Could I stop you?"

"Probably not," she says. "But if you asked me to, I would try. I really would."

"Don't worry about it," I assure her. "Tell the girls all, and I'll talk to you soon."

We end the call, but I don't get up right away. I sit on my bench, watching the people lounging around the park with nowhere to be with envy. Maybe Elaina's right. Maybe I do need a day to wander...

I'm on the verge of deciding that my work can wait until tonight, or even tomorrow morning if I'm feeling feisty, when a text pops through from the last person I'm expecting.

It's Adrian, and the text reads only—*We have to talk. Should I come up to your place or would you rather pop by mine?*

"Shit," I mutter, my pulse spiking.

I remind myself that there's no way he could know what I've been up to with his father—he was at the party when Gideon and I were at the diner, and we were inside the rest of the night—but my hands are still shaking as I text—*My place. Thirty minutes. Just need to grab a quick shower.*

Instead, I grab a taxi and fight the urge to pick apart my manicure in a fit of anxiety as the cab lurches north.

twenty-one

B ack at the apartment, Noelle is still asleep, as evidenced by the soft classical music drifting from her room.

Noelle always has music playing but there are different playlists for different activities. Lately, it's Florence and the Machine for designing, jazz for sewing, and murder podcasts for lying in bed, feeling angsty about whether or not she'll ever be able to make a living sewing for humans instead of hamsters.

She mixes things up occasionally, but classical is always sleepy time, so I tiptoe through the main living area and shut the door to my bedroom softly behind me.

Once I'm safely in my own space, I dash into the bathroom, whipping off my borrowed clothes and hanging Noelle's dress carefully on one of my empty towel hooks. Then I set the water on blast and jump into the shower while the water is still freezing cold.

I curse as the icy droplets hit my skin, but I don't

have the luxury of waiting the five minutes it takes for the hot water from our ancient system to reach the fifth floor. If Adrian's on time, I only have ten minutes to shower, get dressed, and get my game face on.

Hopefully, he won't ask me where I went last night after the party or anything else that might lead the conversation around to his father. I'm a terrible liar, even when I know the truth isn't the kindest choice.

Adrian doesn't need to know that I'm sleeping with his dad, at least not yet, not until Gideon and I decide our relationship is worth fighting for.

You're awfully confident this morning. You're skipping right over the "if" and going straight to "when."

The thought makes me hesitate a beat after shutting off the shower. I *am* confident. After last night, how could I not be? Every night with Gideon is better than the last. Being with him is so natural, so easy and wonderful and fun, and exactly what I've always wanted.

Surely, he has to feel it, too. Surely, he'll come around to seeing that what we could have together is worth an uncomfortable conversation and a blow to Adrian's ego.

An uncomfortable conversation? Remember who you're dealing with, girl. Adrian already has a Texas-sized chip on his shoulder when it comes to his dad. You think learning Gideon is sleeping with his ex-girlfriend is going to be something they sort out with a chat over coffee?

"That's not my problem," I mutter to my reflection as I sweep on a quick coat of mascara and some lip gloss. "Not today, anyway. Don't bite off more than you can chew. Just deal with Adrian as quickly and efficiently as possible, tell him you have to work, and then you can order coffee and a breakfast sandwich."

Buoyed by thoughts of my favorite goat cheese and avocado croissant from the deli on Madison Avenue, I whip my damp hair into a messy bun and breeze out into the living room. I have just enough time to grab a bottle of sparkling water from the fridge before there's a knock on the door.

Reminding myself again that there's no way Adrian could know that all my filthiest fantasies feature his father in a starring role, I slide the chain off the hook. By the time I unlock the deadbolt, Adrian is already turning the knob.

"Come in," I say dryly, arching a brow at him as he barges past.

But he doesn't notice. He's too busy barging.

I close the door behind me, preparing to defend myself against charges of being a dirty, lying trust fund kid, if that's what he's upset about.

But when Adrian spins to face me, he doesn't look angry.

He looks...scared.

My stomach drops, and I shift into crisis containment mode. "What's wrong? What happened?"

"It's bad, Syd," he mutters, dragging one hand down his pale face as he braces the other on the kitchen island. "It's so bad. I don't know what I'm going to do. I can't do this now. Maybe not ever, but especially not right now." He shakes his head numbly. "I just can't. I'm not ready."

"Not ready for what?" I ask, crossing to pull out one of the island chairs. "Sit down. Let me get you some tea."

"I don't want tea," he says, his voice strained. "I want to travel back in time and wear a condom every time. Every single time."

"Oh no," I murmur, sinking down into the chair myself as his meaning hits.

"Yeah." He croaks out a humorless laugh. "I should have known better than to trust that Gigi was remembering to take her pill every day. Gigi can't remember what day it is or how many drinks she's had or if she's supposed to be on set at three or five." He winces, his eyes squeezing shut. "I'm so stupid. So fucking stupid."

"You're not stupid."

He opens his eyes, shooting me a "play it straight with me" look.

"Okay," I amend with a sigh. "You're kind of stupid. But we're all stupid like that sometimes. In the heat of the moment, you're not always thinking about being safe and responsible. I get it."

His brow furrows. "You do?"

I nod, ignoring the guilty flutter behind my ribs. "Of course, I do."

"But you're *always* responsible."

"Not always. Sex is a powerful instinctive drive, Adrian. Our survival as a species depends on it. It's understandable that sometimes the urge to go at it without worrying about the consequences wins out."

He sighs as he sags onto the stool next to mine. "I still hate myself. I can't do this, Syd. I have no idea how to be a father. I'll screw this kid up even worse than my dad did with me. He'll probably become a serial killer or something."

Fuck. His father. He's mentioned his father.

And I know enough about Gideon to realize he'd love nothing more than to help his son learn how to be a dad. For the two of them to learn how to do that *together*.

But I can't say anything.

I'm not supposed to know his dad. There's no way I could.

At least, not until last night... But I can't lie to Adrian, not even to help him and Gideon repair their relationship. Can I?

"I know your dad wasn't always there for you as a kid," I say, my pulse racing as I ponder all the ways this could blow up in my face.

Adrian snorts as he studies his folded hands. "He was *never* there. He couldn't get rid of me fast enough. He sent me home early from almost every visit."

"Okay," I say, deciding the fact that his mother was manipulating things behind the scenes is something Gideon should explain to him. "But that was a long time ago. You're an adult now, and it seems like your dad really wants a relationship with you. I um, I talked to him a little last night. At the party."

Adrian's head snaps up. "You did? God, why? I knew I should have told him not to speak to anyone. He's always so damned extra."

I frown, fighting the urge to leap to Gideon's defense. If I'm going to win Adrian around to the idea of giving his father a chance, I have to tread lightly. If

Adrian doesn't think I'm on his side, he'll push me away. "I didn't find him extra. He was nice. And he seemed to really care about you."

"He doesn't even know me," Adrian mutters, his shoulders sagging.

"But he wants to," I say softly. "He flew in to support you and to help celebrate your success. He's ready to be there for you. All you have to do is…let him."

Adrian sighs, a pained sound that hurts my heart.

"Come on," I wheedle after a beat. "What do you have to lose? Maybe he'll have some good advice. At the very least, he can be a shoulder to lean on while you figure out a way forward with Gigi."

He swallows and the way his throat works reminds me of Gideon. He has his father's build and Gideon's wild, but perfect wavy hair. But it's his mother's dark eyes that lock on mine as he whispers, "But what if he still doesn't like me? What if he spends two days with me and bolts again? I couldn't handle it, Syd. Maybe I should be tough enough to let things like that roll off my back, but…I'm not."

"Oh, Adrian," I say, my chest aching as I wrap an arm around his shoulders. "That isn't going to happen. He loves you. So much. I could see it in his eyes. I know it's scary to put yourself out there, but if you reach out to your dad, he's not going to let you down. I promise."

He arches a brow. "Wow. He really got to you, didn't he?"

You have no idea, I think. Aloud, I say, "He made a good impression. Yes. But I think I'm a pretty good judge of character."

"Yeah, you are. That's why you broke up with me," he says, his lips twitching a little at the edges.

I smile. "We're obviously better as friends. But you trust me, right? That's why you came to me with this, instead of someone else?"

Sobering, he nods. "I do. Even though you lied your face off about being the richest girl in Nepo Babyville."

"You saw the society page." He nods, and I wrinkle my nose. "I'm not a nepo baby. You've seen how hard I work. My father pushes me harder than any of his other employees."

He grunts. "You still lied."

"I did, and I shouldn't have," I admit. "I just didn't want you to hate me for something I couldn't control."

"I could never hate you," he says with an affection that makes me feel warm and worried at the same time.

Surely, Adrian doesn't still have *those* kinds of feelings for me. He can't. If he does, the path forward just got even harder for Gideon and me.

"You're one of the good ones," he continues in that same soft voice, making my empty stomach start to burn. "I wish I'd had my shit together when we dated."

"It's better this way," I say. "Friendships don't have expiration dates. Most college relationships do."

He laughs, easing my fears. "No doubt. And you being perfect all the time would have driven me crazy, eventually. No offense, but no one should be this perfect, Syd. It's annoying."

I arch a wry brow. "Thanks."

He laughs again. "You're welcome. And...you're probably right. Again. I should at least try reaching out to Gideon. He's in town for a few more days and wanted to talk anyway, so…"

I nod, excited and nervous at the same time. "I think that sounds smart. I'm sure he'll have better advice for you than I will. I have no idea how I'd handle being a mom right now. Becoming a parent is a huge deal."

His expression sobers. "Fuck, I know. I've been reeling since Gigi texted last night. It just gets scarier and scarier."

"She *texted* the news that you two were having a baby?" I ask incredulously. "She didn't tell you in person? Or at least call?"

He shoots me a sideways glance. "No one calls anyone anymore, woman."

"*I* call people," I say, thinking how much I wish I had Gideon's number, so I could call him as soon as Adrian leaves and give him a heads-up about what's going on with his son. "I call people all the time."

He pats my arm with exaggerated care. "Yes, you do. And it's a testimony to how sweet you are that we haven't all ghosted you for it. See, you do have flaws. No one's perfect, after all. Thanks for the reminder." He rises from the stool, rolling his shoulders back.

"You're welcome," I say dryly. "But you should call your dad. Or better yet, meet up. This isn't a texting matter."

"Yes, Mom, I know," he says, the words like cold water tossed in my face.

If Gideon and I end up living happily ever after, I could be Adrian's *stepmother* someday. It's not something I've thought about until this exact moment.

This sobering, chilling, borderline horrific moment...

I'm still reeling when Adrian pulls me in for a friendly hug. "I'll hit you up later. Tell Ben the cleaner is coming this afternoon instead of tomorrow for me, will you? He's in there with Noelle, but they'll probably be asleep for a while. They got hopped up on chocolate-covered espresso beans and shut down the dance floor at three a.m."

I smile as he pulls back. "Will do."

When he's gone, I dash into my room and flip open my computer. A little googling reveals numbers for Gideon's offices in New York and Burlington, but no home phone or cell phone or anything that looks like a personal email. But I know where he lives, and the doorman was really nice this morning when I left my number.

Crossing my fingers that the same man is still on duty, I track down the number and place my call, hoping I can give a heads-up to Gideon before it's too late.

twenty-two

GIDEON

Mitch and I cross Union Square Park, get seated at the diner, and inhale our food in near silence. It isn't until we're nursing our third cup of coffee after the food has been cleared that he finally speaks his mind.

But that's Mitch. He's a hothead in many ways, but when it comes to his friends, he always chooses his words carefully.

"This could ruin the Bronx deal with Watson Global," he says, lifting a hand to stop me before I can respond. "Which is fine. I'm okay with losing the contract, I really am. I don't think Silas is as on board with sustainable retrofitting as he pretends to be. He's a great guy and I love him, don't get me wrong, but he's old-school and profit is still his number one concern. And we've never done a shelter before. It was going to be a bear of a project, anyway, and a permitting nightmare, I'm sure." He threads his fingers together into a single, massive fist beside his coffee mug. "But what if one deal becomes two deals, three deals, four? We do a lot of work for them, Gideon. It's a significant chunk of our bottom line."

"I know," I say, wishing I'd had time to discuss this with Sydney.

But I can't deny that I'm glad I didn't realize who she was when we met. If I'd known, I might have succeeded at holding her at a distance, and I don't want to imagine a world where I don't know how she feels wrapped around me or the sounds she makes when she's about to come on my cock.

Pushing memories of last night aside, I add, "But Silas is grooming Sydney to take over the company. If he trusts her business sense enough to turn over his life's work to her in a year or two, surely, he can be convinced to trust her judgment when it comes to her personal life, as well."

Mitch studies me for a beat, his dark eyes worried, before he asks, "So this is more than fucking?"

My brows lift at the blunt words, but I nod. "Yeah. I can't stop thinking about her, no matter how hard I've tried." I briefly explain how Sydney and I met, how we tried to put a stop to things after that one night in Maine, and how we reconnected at Adrian's party last night. "That's when we discovered our first...awkward connection. She and Adrian dated last year when they were both at BU."

Mitch curses and rolls his eyes, muttering beneath his breath.

"I know," I say. "It's not great."

"It's a mess," Mitch says. "A hot fucking mess. I'll be

honest, man, I don't see a world where this *doesn't* blow up in your face. I know you're the smooth talker around here, but no one is this smooth. Not even you." He pushes his mug toward the table's edge as our waitress walks by with the coffeepot. As she tops him off, he adds, "Betsy told me about your Coney Island visit, by the way. She thinks I should let you handle the Wednesday meeting on your own."

I wave our server's offer of more coffee away, waiting until she leaves before asking, "Are you okay with that? You still trust me?"

At the end of the day, I'm the owner of G.P.G. Green and technically Mitch's boss, but we've worked together for over a decade. I couldn't run the New York office without him, and I'm not about to pull rank. If he wants in on the meeting, he'll be included. End of story.

"Of course, I trust you, asshole." He dumps creamer into his cup with a sigh. "And I understand falling for the wrong girl, but...fuck, she's young. And such a good kid. I've known her since she was this big." He holds out a hand, just a few inches taller than the top of our booth. "She had to grow up so fast after her mom died. Silas tried, but feelings aren't his thing. He hired people to handle that part of parenting, but what Sydney needed was love. A father's love. And she didn't get it. It made me sad for her."

"And protective," I add. "I get it. I know she's young, but...I haven't felt this way in so long, Mitch. I don't know if I ever have, honestly. She's special."

"The heart wants what it wants," he murmurs. "I get it."

It's a strangely romantic thing to hear from my curmudgeonly friend and colleague. But Mitch and Amy, his wife, have been together for nearly twenty years, and she's still the only one who can make his eyes light up when he smiles.

"Well, let me know how it goes with the Coney Island dick," Mitch adds as he scoots out of the booth. "And with all the rest of it." He stands, motioning toward the table with a crooked grin. "You're buying, by the way. We'll consider it your apology for nearly giving me a heart attack in your apartment."

"Absolutely. Thanks for your trust. I'll figure this out, Mitch. I promise."

He sighs, clearly still dubious, but more relaxed than when we first sat down. "I'll have Amy light a candle for you at church tomorrow. You're going to need it."

He leaves and I pull out my wallet. Before I can set down my credit card, however, my cell dings. I glance down to see a message from Derrick, my doorman. He has my number in case of emergencies, but he's never used it.

Not until today.

I read the text—*Your guest from last night called with a message, sir. She said your son is in crisis and is going to be reaching out to you soon. She also said she has more information if you wanted to call her at the number she left at the desk. I wouldn't usually reach out like this, but she sounded worried, and she seemed like a nice lady.*

Cursing myself for forgetting to get Sydney's number on my way out with Mitch, I shoot back—*Of course, please forward the number, Derrick. Sydney's abso-*

lutely someone I trust. Thank you so much. I appreciate your time.

I'm still waiting for a reply when another text pops through. This one is from Adrian and reads only—*Talk? About family stuff?*

It's not much, but it's the first time Adrian's reached out to ask me for something other than money or a hookup with one of my connections in a long time. I don't know what this "crisis" is, but I know I want to be there for him. And that I don't want to drop the ball on a chance to show him that I'm someone he can count on.

Thankfully, Derrick comes through with Sydney's number a moment later.

I drop a hundred-dollar bill on the table and leave the diner. As soon as I'm out on the sidewalk, I text Adrian—*Absolutely. Noon? By the obelisk in Central Park?*

While I'm waiting for him to reply, I text Sydney—*Can you talk? I just heard from Adrian. He didn't say what's going on, but it seems serious, and I'd really love to get this right.*

She replies quickly. *Yes, give me a second. My roommate and her boyfriend just woke up, and I don't want them to overhear. I'll go up to the roof and call you in a few?*

Some of the tension easing from my shoulders, I reply, *Perfect. Thank you. You were amazing this morning, by the way. As I thought, one hell of a businesswoman.*

She sends over a blushing smiling face. *Thanks. It felt good. Call you when I'm alone.*

Smiling, I reply—*Yes, please. Looking forward to it.*

I'm still smiling when Adrian texts a second later,

confirming our meeting time, which gives me approximately two hours to talk to Sydney, formulate a plan, and get uptown.

But that's doable.

Everything feels a little more doable this morning, even staying in New York on more of a full-time basis. As long as Sydney's in the picture, many previously unthinkable things suddenly seem possible.

twenty-three

U
p on the roof, I cross to the southwest edge of the building, gazing across Manhattan toward Chelsea and Gideon.

The city feels different with him in it.

I feel different.

This morning, my workaholic new life seems silly, the actions of a scared kid, not a competent business-woman. Part of being a grown-up is drawing bound-aries and letting the people around you know what you will (or won't) tolerate moving forward. No one else at Watson Global is working this hard, not even the most ambitious junior exec, determined to be promoted to management before he turns twenty-eight.

I've been killing myself to prove myself to my father, but...there's nothing to prove. I graduated top of my class and I've been rising to every challenge presented to me at Watson Global. I've got this. The only problem is time. I need more of it, and I intend to make that clear to my father on Monday.

No more staying at the office until seven or eight at night or working through the weekends. And if that means it takes longer for me to transition into a leadership role in the company...that's okay. My father is getting older, but he's still in great health. There's no need to rush this at the expense of my well-being or sanity. I should have time to hit the gym three times a week, take a walk in Central Park after work every once and a while, and spend time with the people who matter to me, like my friends and...

"Hey," I say when Gideon answers on the first ring, the sound of his voice enough to make my chest fill with fizzing bubbles. "How did things go with Mitch?"

"Good. Better than expected, actually. I think he understands this isn't what he thought it was. That it's... more serious. At least for me."

My fizzy bubbles transform into giant helium balloons capable of ferrying me across the rooftops to Gideon's door. "Me, too. So, we're done pretending this is a one- or two-night thing?"

There's a smile in his voice as he says, "Yeah. That sounds good. I can't wait to see you again."

"Same," I say, lifting my face to the warm autumn sun. "Maybe we could get dinner tonight? If you're free?"

"I'm free. Assuming Adrian doesn't need me. Thanks for the heads-up, by the way. If he's finally turning to me for something other than financial support, I want to prove I'm up to the task."

I sigh, my happy glow fading as I remember why we're on this call. "You're welcome. I don't feel comfortable sharing exactly what's going on—that feels like Adrian's story to tell—but I wanted you to know that he's scared, Gideon. He may play it tough around you, but you should have seen his face this morning. He was like a little kid. I think the stuff in the past, when his mom cut the visitations short when he was younger and the things she said to him about you, really messed him up. He seems to think you don't like him. And that you *really* won't like him if he gives you the chance to get to know him. Rejection seems to loom pretty large for him."

"I would never reject him," Gideon says, the hurt in his voice making my throat tight. "He's my son. I love him. He drives me crazy sometimes, and I wish I could rewrite so many things about our past, but...he's my baby."

Unexpected tears sting at the backs of my eyes.

Damn, this man...

He's such a good one, the perfect mixture of strong and tender, with such a beautiful heart. I don't know what Adrian's mother was smoking. If Gideon was the father of my child, I'd feel like the luckiest woman in the world.

The thought sends a pang through my stomach I don't fully understand until several minutes later, after Gideon and I have said our goodbyes and he's promised to touch base about dinner later. It's only as I'm stretching out on a cushioned lounge chair to stare at the robin's egg blue sky that I realize the pang is about children.

I want them, someday. I always have, ever since I

was a little girl and wasted years fruitlessly begging my mother for a baby sister. When it became clear a sibling wasn't coming, I shifted my focus to planning my own family. When I grew up, I would have at least two kids, but hopefully three or four, so they'd never be lonely or without someone to play with.

And they wouldn't have to hold the hopes of the entire family alone on their shoulders...

But Gideon already did the whole "dad" thing and has a grown son. Chances are, he considers kids a part of his past, not his future. It's something we'd have to discuss if things got serious between us, but even the chance that he wouldn't be interested in starting another family isn't enough to scare me away. Gideon's too special for that. So is the way I feel when I'm with him, like the bravest, best version of myself.

On impulse, I text my dad, suddenly not wanting to leave this conversation until Monday at the office—*Hi, Dad, I hope you're having a great weekend. I just wanted to let you know that my audit of the company structure is taking longer than expected. Now that I'm in the weeds, it's clear things are more complicated than I anticipated, and I don't want to miss anything. But I feel confident I'll have this tied up and my suggestions for reorganization to you by mid-October.*

My thumb hovers over the screen, my pulse picking up as I imagine my father's reaction, but I push the anxiety aside and hit send. Then, just to prove to myself that I'm serious about my new, boundary-friendly lifestyle, I add—*And I'd love to be more involved in the retrofitting project for the shelter in the Bronx. I think it would be a great way to learn more about the charitable wing of the organization and put my area of expertise to use.*

It's true—reimagining spaces to make them more energy efficient and sustainable in a warming world, *is* my area of expertise. But a quick search of the company database after Adrian left also confirmed my suspicion that G.P.G. Green is our contractor on that project. Taking a more active role in the reimagining of the space will give me the chance to prove to Mitch that I'm a worthy new ally and maybe...if Gideon ends up staying in town...

The thought of working with him is exciting.

Nearly as exciting as the thought of seeing him again tonight.

Crossing my fingers that Gideon's talk with Adrian goes well—and that my dad decides to return my texts in a speedier fashion than his usual five to six hours—I stretch out on the lounge chair and pull up the October book club pick in audio.

I'm still listening an hour later when my phone dings with a new message.

I lift my cell to see a text from my dad saying—*That sounds wise. Better to be measured and thorough with something like this. Let's circle up about the Bronx project on Monday. Enjoy your weekend. And think about coming to the beach house with me next weekend if the weather's still good. We haven't been out on the water in ages and the fishing is incredible this year.*

Smiling at my father's uncrushable belief that I'm eventually going to learn to love fishing as much as he does, I reply—*Thanks, Dad. I'll think about it. And thanks for your support. Have a great rest of your weekend. Hope you catch a big one.*

I rise from the lounger, heading back downstairs, marveling at how much easier that was than I was expecting. Hopefully, Gideon's talk with Adrian is going even half as well.

I keep hoping that right up until the moment Adrian slams into my apartment a little after one p.m., shouting for Ben to "Get dressed, Benjamin. We're going day drinking. I need approximately ten shots of whiskey to erase this shitty day from my head."

Before I can ask him what happened with Gideon, he turns to me and says, "You're a great person, Syd, and I know you give solid advice about most things, but don't ever suggest I talk to my dad again. He doesn't get me, and he never will. Some people don't deserve second chances." He spins, motioning for Ben, who's still reeling from being startled out of a nap on the couch with Noelle, to follow him. "Now, Ben. Best friend emergency, bro. Your lady will still be here in a few hours when we're wasted and feeling no pain."

Speaking of pain…

I text Gideon, asking—*Where are you? I can be there as fast as the subway allows.*

Seconds later, he answers. *I'm not far, actually. By the obelisk in Central Park. Saddest bench on the path. You can't miss me.*

Chest aching for him, I promise—*Be there in ten minutes. I'll jog.*

And jog, I do.

T it's been a long time since I had someone care enough to drop everything and come running for me.

Literally, running.

Sydney jogs into sight just a few minutes after her text, looking stunning in black leggings and a burnt orange tank top that brings out the strawberry notes in her hair. Heads turn as she cuts across the grass to join me on my bench, but she doesn't notice.

Her focus is all for me. Despite the shitty way things ended with Adrian, I can't help feeling lucky. And so damned grateful to have someone to talk to.

"Hey," she says, voice breathy from her run as she slides onto the bench beside me.

"How did you know?"

"Adrian stopped by my place to get Ben and he was…clearly not happy," she says diplomatically. "What happened? He seemed open to connecting when I spoke to him this morning. I thought this was going to be a good thing for you two. I mean, as good as things could be considering the situation."

"Considering my son is making the same mistake I did?" I ask with a sigh. "Yeah, I guess I should have known what to say, seeing as I went through the same thing, but I didn't. Or I did, I guess, but my advice wasn't what Adrian wanted to hear."

Her features tighten sympathetically. "What did you say?"

"I told him not to propose to Gigi."

Her brows shoot up. "What? I didn't realize that was even on the table. He didn't mention about proposing this morning."

"Yeah, well, apparently, he and Gigi talked again before we met up. She hinted they should take the baby as 'a sign' and think about making the relationship official. He was already looking at rings."

"What? Is he insane?" Sydney squeaks, the fact that she's as shocked by this as I was making me feel better about my less-than-supportive reaction. "He and Gigi have only been dating for a few months, and she's cheated on him at least twice. That we know of! The baby might not even be his. I didn't want to bring that up when we spoke because I knew it would put him on the defensive, but someone needs to say something before he marries a woman he barely knows and absolutely can't trust."

"Agreed, but I doubt that conversation will go well." I drag a hand through my hair. "My suggestion that he wait for the results of a paternity test before making any big decisions was the beginning of the end. He stopped listening to anything I had to say after that. He accused me of projecting my issues with his mother onto other people's relationships and dragging everyone down with my negative vibes."

Sydney rolls her eyes. "Ugh, the toxic positivity in his new friend group drives me crazy. Sometimes the vibes are bad. That's just reality. Bad vibes are part of life! And that's okay. Negative experiences help us grow and appreciate good things more than we did before."

My lips curve. "Well, at least *we're* on the same page."

Her shoulders slump. "I'm sorry. I was hoping this would be a fresh start for you two. But I probably should have known better. I think Adrian needs more help than even the most supportive father could provide."

"I've offered to pay for therapy at least a dozen times. I even offered to go with him if he thought that would be helpful, but he wasn't interested. His mom thinks therapy is a waste of time and 'destructive to the artistic soul,' so…"

Sydney hums judgmentally beneath her breath.

"Agreed." I lean back on the bench, until my shoulder brushes hers. "But I tried, that's all I can do. At least I managed to convince him to put off proposing until he has proof the baby is his."

"Really?" Her eyes widen. "How did you do that? I thought you said he stopped listening after the paternity test suggestion?"

"He did. But he listened long enough to hear that my continued financial assistance is dependent upon him remaining single until he and Gigi get the results of a DNA test."

Sydney exhales a breathy laugh. "Wow. No wonder he's pissed."

"You think I went too hard on him?"

She shakes her head. "No, but...I know Adrian. He likes to be in control. Nothing makes him angrier than feeling like someone else is calling the shots for him."

I grunt. "Yeah, I can see that."

She rests a gentle hand on my knee. "But he's not a kid anymore. You aren't obligated to help him financially. If he wants control that much, he should be paying his own bills." She wrinkles her nose before adding, "But maybe that's entitled of me to say. I've never had to worry about finances. Even if my father cut me off, I have a trust fund from my mother and another from my maternal grandmother that I'll have access to when I'm twenty-five. I'll never have to worry about money so...I should probably keep my opinions about things like that to myself."

I shift on the bench, studying her face for a beat. "You're an extraordinary person, Sydney Perry-Watson."

She blushes. "I don't know about that, but I did just tell my father that my audit of the company structure was going to take longer than expected. I clawed myself out of the workaholic hole. From now on, I won't be working straight through the weekend anymore."

I arch a brow. "So, if a guy relocated to the city for a while, he'd get to see you at least once a week?"

She beams, sending another rush of warmth through my chest. "At least. Probably more than once. I'm determined to leave the office by six-thirty at the latest. I'm going to try some of that work-life balance people talk about."

"You continue to be wise beyond your years."

"And you continue to be really sexy," she says, making me laugh. "No, seriously. I can't stop thinking about being naked with you, even when we're having serious discussions. Is that normal?"

I lean in until my lips are inches from hers. "Who cares about normal?"

"You're really going to move here for a while?" she whispers. "For me?"

"Well, my son lives here now, too. And maybe, someday soon, my grandchild, but…"

She pulls back. "Ugh."

I arch a brow. "Grampa talk kill the mood?"

"A little, but it's for the best." She glances around the park, her gaze skimming over the various singletons and couples roaming past. "We shouldn't be making out in public. At least not in Central Park. I grew up not too far from here. Half the old ladies walking their dogs know my dad and all of them like to gossip. If we want to control the message, we should be careful."

I shift a few inches away from her on the bench. "You're right. And we shouldn't come out to Adrian until he has some clarity on his current situation. Call me crazy, but I don't think he'd be open-minded about his ex dating his father right now."

Sydney winces. "You're not crazy. Not at all. I'd prefer to put off that conversation with my dad, too."

"Until we see if this is worth a big family blow up?"

"There won't be a blow up," she says with more confidence than I'm expecting. But maybe Silas has changed since I knew him, softened, become less overbearing with age. "But Dad and I are still finding our footing in our working relationship. I think it's best if we give that time to settle before I introduce another big change."

I exhale. "I'd certainly be a big change."

She nudges my foot with hers. "You would be, but not because my dad knows you. Or not *just* because of that. I've never had a serious adult boyfriend in New York before; let alone a man I can't get enough of." A hint of uncertainty flashes in her gaze. "Should I have kept that last part to myself? Played it cool?"

"Never," I assure her, threading my fingers discreetly through hers. "I love knowing you want me even half as much as I want you."

She bites her lip and suddenly the day isn't a complete disaster. I failed with Adrian, but what else is new? I can always try again. Hopefully, my son heard how much I love him and want to support him, as well as my words of caution, and he'll remember them when the time is right.

But in the meantime, I get to spend more time with this amazing woman. "Come home with me?" I ask. "Let me feed you something fantastic for lunch and tie you to my headboard?"

She smiles and her voice is pure auditory foreplay as she whispers, "Tie me up first and feed me after, and you've got a deal. I don't want to wait for the fun part."

"Yes ma'am," I murmur. "I promise, I'll never make you wait."

She gives my hand a squeeze before rising to her feet. "I'll grab a cab and meet you there in fifteen or twenty?"

"I'll take the subway and see you there," I say, my gaze raking up and down her frame as she backs away, devouring every inch of her with my eyes.

Soon, I'll have my hands on her, my mouth...

Despite my worry for Adrian, I can't help feeling like the luckiest man in New York. The feeling lasts until I reach my apartment building twenty minutes later to find a woman in a dramatic palm-print dress and a giant straw hat pacing in front of the door.

It's Angela, my ex, and she's clearly heard the news.

There's an open manhole on Fifth Avenue and a street festival blocking the alternate route my driver tries on the way to Gideon's place. It takes nearly twenty minutes to get to Twenty-First Street, where I finally decide to get out and walk.

I expect Gideon will already be upstairs when I arrive, but...he's not.

He's standing under the restaurant awning next to his building's entrance, in a heated conversation with the most beautiful woman I've ever seen.

She's nearly as tall as Gideon and slim, but with the tanned, toned arms of an athlete. Her dress and hat are clearly designer originals as is her chunky jewelry. The bracelet and large necklace bring out the silver streaks in her long brown hair, but the gray doesn't age her. It adds to her exotic, artsy vibe.

I'm instantly intimidated.

If this is the kind of woman Gideon usually dates, what the hell is he doing with me?

Yes, I have the money to buy expensive clothes—I have several suits in my closet that, even on the resale market, could pay my rent for a month—but I'm one of the least fashionable people I know. Sure, I enjoy dressing up now and then, but I'm happiest in athletic wear and whatever gear I need to stay warm and dry out in the wild. I'm a person who enjoys looking out at the world more than gazing at my own reflection.

But this woman clearly puts in the time in front of her mirror. Her makeup is subtle but perfect, from her dewy complexion to her contoured cheekbones and full, berry-stained lips.

I shift into the shelter of the awning of a nearby makeup store, wondering if I should duck inside. I'm wearing mascara, as usual, since my blond eyelashes are invisible without it, but I was in such a rush to get to Gideon, I didn't bother with anything else.

Besides, he's seen me without makeup and didn't seem to care, one way or the other. I figured he was an outdoorsy guy who wasn't into fashionista women.

But maybe I was wrong...

He and this glamorous human have history, it's there in every tense line of their bodies and the ease with which they shoot verbal darts back and forth. They clearly aren't friends anymore, but they're...familiar.

And this woman is familiar to me, too, I realize as she turns with a dramatic flail of her arms, sending her skirt swirling around her legs. The pose is just like a picture Adrian had on his bookcase back in college. It was a black-and-white photo of a gorgeous woman with long brown hair, swirling in a black dance dress while a naked toddler—Adrian—ran in a giggling blur through the front of the shot.

This must be Angela, his mother.

My hunch is confirmed a moment later, when Gideon brings his phone to his ear and my cell starts to ring.

"Hey," I say. "What's up?"

"My ex was waiting for me when I got home," he says, a tension in his voice I've never heard before. "She flew in from Florida this morning, as soon as Adrian texted her about the baby. She thinks we should be supporting him by giving him my apartment, so he and Gigi can raise the baby in a safer part of town."

My brows lift. "Wow, that's...quick. She doesn't want to make sure the baby's his first? And she does know he currently lives in one of the safest buildings in the sleepiest part of the Upper East Side, right? We have a doorman, too."

"She knows," he says with a sigh. "This is just an excuse to try to force me to sign the apartment over to Adrian and, by extension, to her. She's been angry about it for close to a decade. My business didn't take off until a few years after our divorce was final. She didn't get as much from me in the settlement as she felt she deserved."

I make a sound I've never heard before, somewhere between a grunt and a squawk of outrage.

Across the street, Gideon laughs.

"Couldn't agree more," he says, the affection in his voice mirrored on his face. "Where are you?"

I feel a little guilty for spying on him, but this stolen

moment is worth it. That's not the face of a man who wishes I were more glamorous or spent more time on my makeup. That's the face of a man who likes me just the way I am, weird noises and all.

"I'm almost there," I say, launching into motion. I lift my hand as I stride toward the crosswalk. "Traffic was so bad, I had to get out and walk."

His gaze finds mine and his smile widens. "There you are. Meet me upstairs? I'll tell Derrick to put your name on my approved visitor list until I can get you a key."

"Sounds good. See you in a few," I say before ending the call.

I fight to keep my composure until Gideon disappears inside his building. Only then do I do a giddy happy dance on the corner, my smile spreading so wide it hurts my jaw.

He wants to give me a key to his place! Already!

If that's not a sign he's feeling the same "this could be something special" vibes I'm feeling, I don't know what is.

When the crosswalk light changes, I practically dance across the street, happier than I've been since I left Maine at the end of the summer.

The next morning, as Gideon and I are feasting on pastries from the best French bakery in town, the doorbell rings.

"Just a second," he says, an eager light in his eyes. "I'm expecting a special delivery." Moments later he returns to the balcony, placing a gorgeous, old-fashioned-looking key beside my now-empty plate.

My brows shoot up. "You found a hardware store that delivers on a Sunday?"

"I did. One of the best things about New York City—it never sleeps. And even when it does, a bribe can usually wake it up again."

I fight a smile. "You bribed a hardware store for me?"

"Too much?"

I shake my head, shifting off my seat and into his lap, wrapping my arms around his neck. "No. It's very sweet. Very comforting."

"Comforting?" he asks, his big hand molding to the curve of my hip in a way that makes me ache for him again, even though we christened his shower less than an hour ago.

I nod and brush his hair from his forehead. "Knowing you want to eliminate barriers between us." I bite my lip, my nipples tightening as his hand drifts lower. "Speaking of barriers, I was thinking about seeing my doctor this week, about an IUD. Then we wouldn't have to worry about condoms."

"That sounds amazing." He reaches up, loosening the top of my robe until the V shows my cleavage. "As long as your doctor thinks it's safe."

"They're completely safe, most of my friends have them," I assure him, my breath catching as he slips a hand into my robe, rolling my nipple between his fingers. "We're outside. Someone could see."

"They could," he agrees, continuing to touch me in ways that make my well-used body ache. "We could go inside. Or..."

"Or what?" I ask, my voice breathy.

"Or you could sit on the edge of your chair like a good girl while I duck under the tablecloth," he murmurs. "Do you think you could do that? Keep your composure while I devour your pussy out here in the morning sun, butterfly?"

I should say no, or at the very least hesitate a beat or two—there are at least three nearby balconies with views of Gideon's and God only knows how many other apartments—but I want him too much. I want to please him, and he knows it. That's why he made his wicked offer the way he did.

"I don't know," I murmur, my thighs already slick with wanting him, "but I would certainly try my very best, Mr. Gabaldon."

"That, Miss Perry-Watson is all anyone could ask." He squeezes my thigh before shifting me back onto my chair and coming to his knees. "Lift up your robe and spread your legs under the tablecloth, baby."

Blood rushes to my head as he disappears under the table, making me glad I'm seated. I spread my robe open wide, breath hitching as Gideon grips my ass in both hands, dragging me closer to the edge of my seat.

"No panties," he murmurs. "That's my good girl."

I bite my lip and mutter, "Don't start with that. Not yet."

He chuckles, a low rumble that has me gripping the table for support as it vibrates against my thigh. He kisses me there, just inches from where I'm soaked for him before whispering, "All right. No more good girl until you've come for me without putting on a show.

Fuck, I love the way you smell when you're salty and hot for me, Sydney. Your pussy's so damned beautiful."

Pulling in a bracing breath, I grip the table even harder as his tongue slides up the seam of my sex. I tuck my chin to my chest, fighting to look respectable from the chest up as Gideon ravages me from the waist down.

He licks and sucks, swirls and teases, stoking the fire building between my hips before penetrating me with two fingers, delivering the perfect pressure inside my molten core. I tremble and press my lips together, swallowing my coming sounds as I spiral out on Gideon's talented mouth. He licks up every bit of my slick heat, murmuring encouragement between each swipe of his tongue.

He tells me how delicious I taste.

How much he loves fucking me.

And, of course, what a good girl I am.

By the time he emerges from beneath the table, looking very pleased with himself, I'm already dying for more of him. *All* of him. "Bedroom," I whisper. "I need your cock, Mr. Gabaldon."

"I believe that can be arranged, Miss Perry-Watson," he murmurs. "I'm enjoying our formality this morning. Perhaps you could call me Mr. Gabaldon while you're telling me how you'd liked to be fucked next?"

Before I can reply, Gideon's cell vibrates on the table.

I look over, horror banishing my lust as I read the message.

The text is from Adrian.

And he's on his way up.

twenty-six

I can count the times Adrian has stopped at my place unannounced on one hand. One finger, in fact, and that was only because a pigeon pooped on his head on his way out of the Union Square subway station and he didn't have time to get back uptown to his hotel before he was due at a DJ gig.

I assumed Sydney and I would be safe from discovery here.

Instead, she's hiding under the tablecloth on the patio, the same tablecloth I was under a few moments ago while I was devouring her pussy, and my son is going to be letting himself in any moment.

In the kitchen, I wash my hands and splash water on my face. Then, I pour myself another cup of coffee and do my best to play it cool. I nearly have myself talked down from the edge when I glance out toward the table to see Sydney's arm emerging from under the table-cloth. She grabs her plate, drawing it under the table with her, before reaching for her water glass.

Smart. If Adrian notices I was having breakfast outside and sees two sets of plates, he'll wonder what's up. But I'm not sure she has time to get rid of all the evidence before he reaches the top floor.

I start outside to help her, but the sound of the key turning in the lock stops me in my tracks. I spin, clutching my coffee mug like a lifeline, and pray I'm blocking Adrian's view of the patio with my body as he slams inside.

"Ouch, shit," he curses, wincing as he brings a hand to his head. "Drank too much yesterday."

"Can I get you an ibuprofen?" I ask, sounding remarkably calm considering the state of my blood pressure. "Or some Pedialyte? I think I still have some in the fridge from last New Year's Eve."

"No, thanks, I'll be fine." He drags a hand down his face as he shuffles in. "Just water would be great. Or one of those orange sodas, if you have them."

"I do," I say, relief rushing through my chest as he sags into one of the stools at the island with his back to the windows. A quick glance outside reveals Sydney's finished clearing her plates, as well. I grab a soda from the fridge and crack the top before setting it in front of my son. "To what do I owe this surprise visit? Not that I'm not happy to see you, but after the way our discussion ended yesterday, I didn't expect to hear from you for a while."

"Mom flew in and met us at the bar," he says, pausing to take a sip of his drink. His eyes slide closed as he sighs. "Fuck, that's good. I haven't had an orange soda in forever. Not since that last weekend with you in Burlington."

His words make my throat tight. I remember that visit. He was fourteen and so angry all the time. The only thing he seemed to enjoy was hitting the rock-climbing wall at my gym with me and orange sodas on the porch after. But even those memories are marred by tension and stress. Every conversation was strained, every smile hard won. He worked so hard not to let me in.

His eyes open, the dark circles beneath them making him look even more like his mother. Angela's a beautiful woman, but she's always had dark circles under her eyes, even when she was pregnant with Adrian, and stopped staying up late and surviving on lemon water and diet yogurt to maintain her dancer's figure.

"Mom mentioned you were thinking about giving Gigi and me the apartment, so we could have a safe place to raise the baby," he says, sending a rush of heat up my neck.

My fucking ex. She never stops. This is part of the reason I moved to Vermont; a state Angela has no interest in visiting. Even nearly twenty years after the end of our marriage, she seems determined to stick her nose into areas of my life where it absolutely doesn't belong.

Before I can tell Adrian that there's been a misunderstanding, he adds, "But she was lying, wasn't she?"

My brows lift. "Well…yes. She asked me about the apartment yesterday, but I said no. This is my home when I'm in the city, and I'm going to need to be in New

York more for work this year. But if you need a place to stay, you're welcome to the guest room."

That would make being with Sydney awkward to say the least, but I already know Adrian has no interest in being roommates, a fact he proves by emitting a sharp burst of laughter.

"Ow," he says, wincing again. "Sorry. Didn't mean to be a dick, but we'd be terrible roommates. You have OCD and I'm a slob. A hot, talented slob, but…"

I smile. "We're all a little messier in our twenties. I certainly was. You should have seen our apartment when you were a kid. It looked like a bomb exploded most days."

"Yeah, I've seen pictures. Mom has some in my baby book." He sighs. "There aren't any pictures of you in it, though. Not a single one, but I remember you being around. I remember going to the park and museums and stuff with you. And dinners with grandma and grandpa when Mom was at dance practice or whatever."

I nod, but don't speak. I'm not sure where he's going with this, but I don't want to say anything to interrupt his flow. The sense that something happened with him yesterday, something big, continues to grow as he takes another drink of his soda and shakes his head with a tight laugh.

"She always did that," he says. "Just…rewrote history. But so did her dancer friends and the losers she dated. For a long time, I thought it was something everyone did. Hell, I did it, too, until enough friends called me on it that I figured out creatively editing your past whenever you felt like it wasn't kosher. Still, with Mom, I just…" He shrugs. "It was a part of her. I was so used to it, I didn't think about it much. Didn't even notice it, really. But yesterday, watching her sip absinthe with my friends and make touring around the country when I was a kid sound so glamorous, it just…hit me. It *wasn't* glamorous. It sucked. I didn't have any kids my age to play with, I missed my home and my daycare and Central Park and my grandparents. And I really, *really* missed my dad." His tired eyes meet mine and the lump growing in my throat swells larger. "I knew you missed me, too. Even though Mom said you were too busy with law school to care."

"I did," I say, my voice thick with emotion. "I missed you every day. I still do."

His eyes begin to shine. "Gigi's a lot like Mom. In the good ways, but…also the bad. What if the same thing happens with us? What if we have the baby and it doesn't work out and she just…takes my kid away. What if my son or daughter learns to hate me for no reason?"

I move around the island, wanting to pull him in for a hug so badly, but I'm not sure we're there yet. I pause just a few inches away and promise him, "That's not going to happen. We won't let it. If the baby's yours, we'll lawyer up immediately and make sure you always have access to your child. I messed up with your mom. I didn't see what was coming until it was too late. We won't let that happen to you. I won't and your mom won't. As flawed as she is, she loves you more than anything in the world. She'll tear the stars out of the sky before she lets you suffer that kind of pain."

He swipes at his face, smearing the tears slipping quietly down his cheeks. "How can you do that?"

"Do what?"

"Say nice things about her? She never says anything nice about you. You're always the villain or the fool. She made your kid think you were pathetic and embarrassing." He hitches in a breath. "And yeah, that orange shirt you were wearing at my party was awful, but you're not pathetic. And you're not a bad guy, not even close. I'm sorry, Dad. I'm just so fucking sorry."

I'm not sure who moves first, him or me, but we meet in the middle, standing beside the island, hugging each other tight. He's still a couple inches shorter than I am, but so much broader than the last time I held him. He's really a man now, a fact he's proven this morning.

"It's okay, son," I say to the top of his head, the one I used to love kissing when he napped on my chest as a baby. "I love you, Adrian. I always have and I always will. It's not too late. We can make things right. No doubt in my mind."

"I want that," he says, sniffing. "But fuck, Dad. I have no idea how to be a good son, let alone a good father. And Gigi didn't answer my texts this morning about the paternity test. I'm afraid she's going to push me out of her life entirely, and I'll never know if the baby is mine."

I pull back, giving his shoulders a gentle squeeze. "Give her time. Maybe she's just scared and overwhelmed." I pause, choosing my words carefully before I add, "And if she refuses to take the test, that's a pretty strong sign that she doesn't think the results will be what you want them to be."

He swipes at his face again with a grunt. "Yeah. You're probably right, but still...I want to know. I wasn't sure I even wanted to be a dad before this, but if that's my kid, I don't want to let them down."

"Then you won't," I say, prouder of him than I've been in a long time. "You've shown you can accomplish anything you set your mind to, Adrian. This won't be any different, and I'll be here to support you every step of the way."

His lips twitch at the edges. "Thanks. I'm glad you're going to be in the city more. Maybe we could hang out sometimes. Do lame father-son shit."

"You mean kick-ass father-son shit," I say, giving his shoulder a playful nudge as I release him. "I could give you cleaning tips and you can help me avoid embarrassing party outfits."

He rolls his eyes. "You weren't really embarrassing. My friend, Summer, actually thought you were hot. It was gross."

I pull in a breath to agree with him but stop myself. Adrian's here being honest with me. Don't I owe him the same? I'm not about to out Sydney right now, but when we're ready to come forward, I don't want Adrian to have any contradictory information out of my own mouth to use against me.

"Well, maybe not so gross," I say gently. "I did become a father when I was very young."

Adrian snorts. "Not *that* young. Summer's a freshman at NYU. She's one of the kids I'm mentoring for the DJ stuff."

Pride swelling in my chest again, I agree, "Yeah,

that's way too young. But I'm proud of you. It's great to hear that you're giving back."

"I'm not always a spoiled brat," he says with a self-deprecating grin. "Just with you, Pops and...I'm going to do better with that. I don't know why it took my girl-friend getting pregnant to make me put myself in your shoes, but it did. I guess it's like my friend Sydney says, I need to practice using my empathy muscle more often." Before I can recover from the shock of hearing Sydney's name on his lips, he adds with a sigh, "Which reminds me, I owe her an apology. She was the one who told me I should talk to you yesterday. When it didn't go well, I...kind of gave her shit about it. Shit she absolutely didn't deserve. She's one of the best people I know. Always ready to drop everything for a friend." He pauses, considering me out of the corners of his eyes, making my anxiety spike higher. "You'd probably like her. She's more of a grown-up than the rest of us hooli-gans. Probably because her mom died when she was young, and she practically had to raise herself. Her dad sounds like a huge dick."

"Parental relationships can be hard," I say, torn between the voice in my head screaming that I have to come clean—he mentioned Sydney *by name* and she's literally hiding under my table right now—and the certainty that this isn't the time. "I still don't talk to your grandma more than once or twice a year. She never forgave me for losing physical custody of her only grandson. She warned me not to let your mom leave the city with you, but I was young and naïve and thought I knew Angela better than she did."

Adrian's nose wrinkles. "No one knows Mom. Except me, and after yesterday..." He sighs. "I don't know. I love Mom. I'll always love her. She's my best friend. But she's always hustling, trying to rearrange the world to her liking, and she doesn't care who she has to steamroll to get what she wants." His lips curve in a wry smile. "But I'm the same way a lot of the time, so..."

"You don't have to be," I say. "You're still young. Nothing about you is set in stone. You can choose to be whoever you want to be."

He pulls in a breath, but before he can respond, his cell dings. He pulls it out of his jeans pocket, his shoulders inching closer to his ears as he reads. "It's Gigi. She wants to talk. At her place in the Village."

I rest a hand on his shoulder, giving the tight muscles a gentle squeeze. "Good. You've got this. And if you want to talk after, we could grab an early dinner later. Maybe sushi at that place you liked when you were in junior high, the one that sends the rolls by on the toy train?"

Adrian laughs and rolls his eyes. "I think we're both too old for that one now, but there's a kick-ass Thai place not far from here. Maybe Thai later? If I'm not crying in my beer somewhere because Gigi told me she lied about me being her baby daddy?"

I tip my head down until my gaze is level with his. "You already have a hangover. I would suggest a moratorium on beer for the rest of the weekend. And Thai food is a great choice on a hard day. If you start crying, you can always blame the spicy curry. Or you could come here, and we could order takeout."

"Yeah, takeout sounds good," he says. "I'll text you if I can make it. And thanks. For the talk. It was good."

"It was great," I say, meaning it with everything in me. "I love you. And you've got this. I believe in you."

He leans in and we hug again—two hugs in less than thirty minutes after years of being held at a distance in every way possible. It's almost more than I can handle, a fact proven when I stand staring at the door for several seconds after Adrian leaves before I remember—"Sydney. Fuck."

I hurry out onto the balcony. "Hey, I'm sorry. Are you okay? He just left."

"I'm fine," she says, crawling out from under the tablecloth. I reach to help her up, but she's already on her feet. "So, what's up? Is he okay?" she asks, running both hands quickly through her hair. "Sorry. There was a spider under there. I'm pretty sure it was in my hair at some point."

"I'm sorry. Here, turn around, let me check for you."

She smiles as she tosses her hair over her shoulder and turns. "Checking your lady friend for spiders. Is that one of the many services you provide?"

"For you, yes," I say, running my hands over her soft curls. "Any other woman, I'd toss her an electric razor and encourage a buzz cut."

She laughs. "Really? You're scared of spiders?"

"No, I was kidding. I'm good with bugs and rodents. Snakes aren't my favorite, but as long as they're not crawling into my bed, I figure live and let live." I lift her hair, checking under the collar of her robe. "You're safe,

I think. But I'd need you naked in my bed coming on my cock to be completely sure."

She giggles as she spins back to face me. "Tempting, but I should get home. I have laundry to do and finding a free machine in our building on a Sunday is always an adventure."

"Bring your laundry here next weekend," I say. "I have a washer and dryer in the guest bathroom."

Her eyes widen. "Wow. Aren't you fancy? My dad doesn't even have a washer and dryer at his place. He used to have one, but when it broke, he never replaced it. He likes sending his laundry out. Our maid could never make it smell as good as the place on Eighty-First Street." She crosses her arms. "So, are we going to keep making small talk about spiders and laundry or are you going to tell me why you look so happy?"

I smile. "I *am* happy. Adrian and I had a really good talk. Best one we've had since before he was in middle school, actually. I think we might have finally turned a corner. He's going to call later, and we might do Thai takeout tonight for dinner."

"Oh, Gideon, that's so great," she says, her eyes shining with relief. "What amazing news. I'll keep my fingers crossed for you."

"Thanks," I say. "He actually mentioned you while we were talking. Said he owed you an apology and that…he thinks I would really like you."

She winces and bares her teeth in something too pained to be a smile. "Wow. And you didn't break from the guilt and tell him I was under the table?"

"No, but I was close," I confess. "Would you have killed me?"

"No, but I'm glad you waited. He has enough going on right now. I think we should wait until after things settle with Gigi, at least a little." She presses her lips together for a beat before she adds, "And I think I should be the one to tell him. I think it will be easier to digest coming from me. I can even make it clear that *I* seduced *you*."

I arch a brow as I draw her closer. "Oh yeah?"

"Yeah. I'll tell him that you tried to resist, but I was a virgin on a mission and practically leapt on you like a starving animal."

I snort. "Yeah, that'll go over well. I think the less said about virginity or anything else remotely sexual, the better."

"I know." She loops her arms around my neck. "I was kidding. Mostly. I do think I should be the one to break the news that we're dating, but we can discuss that further at a later date." Her lips turn down. "I'm going to miss you. When do I get to see you again?"

"Tonight?" I ask, my hands drifting down to squeeze her ass through her robe. "As soon as Adrian leaves, I'll text you with the all clear?"

Sydney grins. "I think I need to sleep in my own bed tonight, but I love the enthusiasm."

"Do you?" I ask in a softer voice. "I'm not coming on too strong?"

She shakes her head. "No. Am I?"

"Not a chance. I want as much of you as I can get while I'm in the city. I'm extending my trip indefinitely.

Any night you want to get together this week, let me know. I have an early meeting in Brooklyn on Wednesday, so I'll have to leave the apartment by six or so, but you have a key now. You can stay as late as you want and lock up on your way to the office."

"I have a key to your place," she says, sounding as delighted by that news as I feel. She sighs. "Life surprises you in good ways sometimes."

"Which is good. Helps make up for the bad surprises."

I kiss her and we sway inside, bound for the bedroom despite her insistence that she needs to go, and I forget all about "bad surprises" for a while.

But I really shouldn't have.

Whenever my ex is within a two-hundred-mile radius, bad surprises are always right around the corner.

twenty-seven

I don't think I've ever been so sad to see a weekend end.

Not even back in Maine, when the girls and I spent an amazing weekend kayaking, having bonfires on the beach, and sleeping over in the lighthouse's lamp room.

But not even the ultimate girls' weekend can compare to Gideon.

Elaina would chock that up to the power of new peen and assure me the infatuation will fade in a month or two. But when I told Noelle how much I'm dreading being apart from Gideon, she just hugged me tight, whispering, "Isn't love amazing?"

Love…

I don't know if it's love yet. Surely, love takes longer to develop than a few days. But who knows? I've never been in love before.

Maybe when you know, you just…know.

All I know for sure is that I'm daydreaming about

Gideon's touch, his kiss, the soft rumble of his voice in my ear as he tells me I'm his "good girl" all the way to work. I arrive in an agitated state that isn't kosher for Monday morning at the office and grab an iced coffee from the coffee bar downstairs instead of my usual hot Americano.

Clearly, my inner sex fiend needs something to cool her off before I head into Dad's office for our weekly, Monday morning battle strategy meeting.

On the way up to the forty-fifth floor, I make a mental list of all the things I'll need to delegate if I'm going to take more of a role in the Bronx shelter project. Though that could be putting the cart before the horse. Dad hasn't given me the green light to get more involved yet. He might decide my time is better spent going full bore on my corporate structure investigation.

But in any event, the mental list has the desired effect—it gets my mind off Gideon under the tablecloth and back on business, where it belongs.

For now, at least. Barring a work emergency, I'll be up close and personal with Gideon's fabulous hands and lips and brain and all his other parts later tonight. He texted me first thing, asking if I'd be able to meet him for dinner at six-thirty at his favorite steakhouse in the Village. I, of course, said yes.

No more staying late at the office for this girl.

Not when my man is in town...

Silently thrilling to the idea of Gideon as "mine," I breeze through reception, wiggling fingers at Therese, goddess of the Watson Global phones, and head toward my father's corner office. The rest of the executive floor was remodeled ten years ago, opened up and filled with glass walls to make the most of the incredible views. Now, as I walk past the various VP offices, I can see my father's (almost entirely male) employees hard at work in their posh spaces, like well-dressed goldfish in a bowl.

Only my father's office remains encased in pale, polished wood, guarded by an ornately carved door with "Perry-Watson" etched in the center. Dad retains his privacy, while having a clear view of his kingdom every time he sticks his head out of his inner sanctum.

It's very Silas Perry-Watson. As is the beautiful, young secretary positioned at a tiny desk outside his door, guarding his office. In many ways, my father never left the 1950s, despite being born in the late 60s.

"Good morning, Elle," I say, smiling at the bleached blonde only a year or two younger than I am. "How was your weekend?"

"So good!" she enthuses with a bubbly giggle. "I went to the beach and the water was still so warm! I love fall, but I'm not going to complain about summer holding on for a little bit longer."

"Me, either," I say, already looking forward to a walk around the Village with Gideon after dinner in the warm, late-summer night.

"Mr. Perry-Watson is ready for you," Elle says, motioning over her shoulder. "I just brought him his second coffee ten minutes ago. He should be caffeinated and ready to conquer the world with his favorite girl."

I force a smile, thank her, and move past her desk.

Elle has a habit of saying things like that, things that make it clear she assumes my father dotes on me like the proud papa from a Disney cartoon. That's nowhere close to reality, but I'm not sure how one pushes back on those sorts of assumptions. I can't very well tell her, "My father and I actually have more of a businesslike vibe, Elle, with all doting and other emotional burdens outsourced to third parties, like my childhood nanny or my therapist."

So, I keep my peace and let her maintain her illusions. But in reality, I'm already reigning in the full force of my personality, narrowing my emotional range to those considered acceptable by my father.

"Good morning, Dad," I say with a warm, but not too warm, smile. "What a beautiful day."

He looks up from his desk, shooting me a quick smile before glancing toward the window, as if he's just noticed the glorious sunny day and clear blue sky. "Yes, it is. Maybe I'll ask Petrie to serve dinner on the terrace tonight. I'm having a few old friends over for tapas. You're invited, of course. If you don't have other plans."

"I'm actually meeting a friend for dinner, too," I say. "So, I'll be leaving by six, at the latest."

He grunts, a bit disapprovingly—Dad never leaves until six-thirty—but doesn't comment on my departure time. He launches straight into a list of the objectives he'd like to see me conquer this week, on top of my continuing research into the corporate structure. It's a lot, but I don't let that stop me from asking for more when he's done.

"That sounds doable, especially if I stay late one

night," I say, deciding one late night is acceptable in my new, better-balanced life. "Have you thought more about adding me to the shelter renovation team in some capacity? I'd really love to be a part of that. I think it would give me a chance to put my area of academic expertise to the test in a real-world setting."

"I have." Dad sits back in his chair, crossing his arms over his broad chest.

In his late fifties, Dad is now almost completely gray, but he's still as strong as I remember from when I was a kid and always tanned a golden brown. He puts the gym in my childhood home to use every other day and spends as much of his weekend out on the water as nature allows. He might not be in the prime of his life, but he's pretty close, bolstering my confidence that a slower transition of power will be just fine, if it comes to that.

Dad is clearly still a capable man and the master of all he surveys, a fact he proves by adding, "And I think it's worth a try, provided you can manage the rest of your workload, as well."

"I'm sure I can," I assure him, determined to prove it.

He grunts, more approvingly this time. "Dave's heading up the project. I put in a call to his office this morning and he's happy to loop you in. Touch base with him at your leisure to schedule a jobsite visit and discuss the next steps."

I smile, but not too widely. As far as my father is concerned, even joy is something best expressed with restraint. "Wonderful. Thanks for that. I'll follow up with him later today. Any other business before I get to work?"

His brow furrows as he leans forward. "Yes, actually. I know this isn't technically work related, but..." He shifts his keyboard to one side, pulling a familiar newspaper clipping from underneath, making my mouth go dry. "Is this who you're dating these days? This...DJ?"

I shake my head. "No, Adrian is just a friend," I say, deciding to keep the fact that Adrian and I were romantically connected in the past to myself. Coming out to Dad about Gideon is going to be tricky enough without adding further complications. "He needed a plus-one for his fundraising party and asked me to join him."

Dad's forehead smooths as he sits back. "Good. We do business with his father's company, G.P.G. Green, the one Uncle Mitch works for. They're actually the contractor on the shelter project, and I'd prefer you didn't mix business with pleasure. Not with the Gabaldons."

"Really?" I ask, surprised. "Why's that?"

"G.P.G. Green started as a retrofitting organization, but in the past ten years, they've moved more heavily into acquisitions and development. They opened an office in Vermont and rumor has it a third location in southeast Asia is in the works. They're still a valuable partner, but a partner with...ambition." He arches an ominous brow. "Ambition that might need to be tamped down in the future, should it continue to interfere with our own goals."

I nod, my stomach tightening. "I see."

I do see, but I don't like what I'm seeing, not one little bit.

"Good," Dad says. "I wouldn't want you to end up in the middle of something uncomfortable." His lips curve. "But do keep your ear to the ground with your friend. He's not involved with his father's business, but you never know when useful information might slip out in a casual conversation. That's one of the reasons I've remained close with your uncle Mitch. He's a friend, yes, but he's a friend who gets chatty about his business victories when he's had a few tumblers of scotch. That's been useful over the years."

Useful. People who aren't "useful" in some way don't last long in my father's social circle, but still…it hurts to hear him talk that way about a man who has gone out of his way to show me kindness. Mitch is a good man and Gideon's friend, which makes me feel even more caught in the middle than I normally would.

But I can't flat out tell my father that I don't "use" my friends. That would only lead to a fight and wouldn't change anything in the long run. My father is who he is, and he doesn't see anything wrong with exploiting the loose lips of friends and co-workers alike. In his mind, if you don't want your words used against you, you should keep your mouth shut.

So, I keep my mouth shut, simply nodding and saying, "I'll keep that in mind, but Adrian and I really aren't that close. I wouldn't spend much time with him at all if my roommate weren't dating his best friend."

"How is Noelle?" Dad asks. "I saw her father on the

links on Saturday. He was caddying again and seemed in good spirits. I assume the cancer is in remission?"

"Yeah, it is," I say, comforted by the glimpse of my father's softer side. "He's still in remission and training to run the marathon this year. Noelle and her mom are so proud of him."

Dad nods, his lips curving. "Wonderful. I wanted to make sure he was in good health before asking him to join the board for the charity fundraiser event this year. Peter doesn't have much to give personally, but he brings in donors from the cancer charities we can't reach without a connection to that community."

So much for his softer side. But that's Dad for you. I really should know better than to expect anything but friendship-for-profit from him by now.

"I'm sure he'd be happy to join the board. Noelle's family has always been supportive of charities that help women and children in need," I say, rising from my chair. "Thanks for the meeting. I'll touch base with you end of day Thursday to give you an update on where I am with this week's objectives."

"Excellent," he says. "And let me know if you're interested in joining me in The Hamptons this weekend by Wednesday. If not, I may invite a friend to join me. Can't let what could be the last good fishing weekend of the summer go to waste."

I smile. "Will do. I'll see if I can make it work."

I already know I won't be joining him, but I don't want to hurt his feelings. I'll come up with a good excuse by Wednesday and ask him if he wants to meet up this coming Sunday evening for dinner. That should strike a nice balance between time for my personal life and time with my father. And honestly, we both enjoy each other's company in smaller doses. Every time I've joined him at the beach house, we run out of things to talk about by Saturday afternoon, and he ends up inviting our neighbors over for dinner anyway.

I leave Dad's office and head over to my smaller, fishbowl office on the opposite side of the open seating area in the middle of the floor. The overstuffed couches, armchairs, and glass tables for holding coffee and snacks were meant to create a gathering space for the executives to network during the day. In reality, they mostly sit empty, while my father's VPs remain glued to their computers and cell phones in their offices, none of them wanting to risk a rival overhearing the details of their latest deal.

I wouldn't say the environment at Watson Global is toxic, but it's absolutely competitive, and anyone who's made it to the forty-fifth floor knows to watch their back.

I should watch mine. If anyone from the company sees me with Gideon, I'm sure my father will know all about it by the time I make it home on the subway. And then I would be scrambling to explain myself instead of controlling the conversation.

I need to hit the timing on this just right...

If Gideon and I are still going strong in a few weeks, I'll have to find a way to break the news to my father before anyone else does. After this morning's revelations, the thought is enough to put a knot in my stomach, but not enough to consider calling this off.

Gideon is already too important to me to even *think* about that.

We'll just have to be careful for a little while. And that's not such a big deal. I'd rather be alone with him than out at a fancy restaurant anyway.

I text him, asking if he'd be okay with getting takeout and eating at his place tonight. He texts back in a few seconds, saying—*Absolutely. I'll take as much alone time with you as I can get. I just didn't want you to think I wasn't interested in courting you properly.*

I grin, charmed by the idea of being "courted," and text back—*We can save the courting for after we aren't on the down-low. As big as this city is, it's also remarkably small. And apparently, we run in the same circles.*

Agreed, he says. *And things are going so well with Adrian, I don't want to flub the ball on this. We had a nice talk again last night.*

That's great! I shoot back, happy for him and Adrian.

It is, he replies. *I see a path forward to a real relationship with my son for the first time in a long time. I want to break the news that we're dating with thoughtfulness and finesse, when the time is right. And that isn't right now. Gigi finally agreed to the paternity test. Adrian's going with her to the doctor's office on Thursday.*

There's a knock on my glass door and I look up to see Dave, the project manager for the shelter. I lift a hand and motion toward my cell, indicating I'll be with him in just a second.

Good news! I type quickly. *I'll keep my fingers crossed and see you tonight at your place at six-thirty. Have a great day.*

Turning my phone on silent, I leave it face down on my desk as I move to let Dave in. I've named Gideon "Puppy Pilot" in my phone, but I don't want Dave to see a personal notification popping through during work hours. Dave is in his mid-thirties, but he's as old-school as my father. Personal calls and texts are for *personal* time, outside the office. I'm sure he's instructed his wife not to contact him during working hours unless it's a life-or-death emergency.

When I'm at the helm, that's something I want to change. People's lives are too complicated to have such a harsh divide between personal and professional time. I'd also like to see parental leave extended by two weeks and offered to both mothers *and* fathers.

That's actually at the top of my list of changes to discuss with Dad once I've found my footing with the company and proven I'm an asset to Watson Global.

Changes to Watson Global are still top of mind on Wednesday when I go straight from my cozy bed to a high stress jobsite in the north Bronx.

It takes approximately ten seconds in my hard hat to realize Dave's presence isn't appreciated—or necessary. Mitch, the foreman, and the rest of the construction team have things well in hand. Dave's attempts at "oversight" are only slowing things down and impeding innovation.

After hearing him shut down Mitch's proposal to add a dog grooming and kennel area near the back entrance, to help families needing to flee domestic violence with their animals in tow, I can't help stepping in.

I draw Dave aside, sharing the research on how many abused partners put off leaving dangerous situations because most shelters don't accept animals. "I only know that because I did a project on creating community refuge spaces in grad school," I say, hoping to soften the blow of knowing more about the needs of domestic violence victims than the man leading this project. "But I think we could really help fill a void here, Dave. Make this project stand out. Could be great for the company's charity and you as the leader of the project."

He seems to consider that for a beat, before adding, "But we're already over budget for plumbing. This would take us another ten-thousand into the red."

"What if I can find a workaround?" I ask. "Would you consider it then?"

Dave expresses he's agreeable to that and I huddle up with Mitch to find a solution, deciding to go with a slightly cheaper vinyl flooring in the dorms to stretch the budget.

When we're done, Mitch beams at me. "Thanks for advocating for the change, Syd. I think it'll be great for the shelter. Help give people comfort in a hard time. I know I wouldn't even think about leaving home without Wendy. That dog is like my third daughter."

"My pleasure," I say with a smile. "That's what we're here for, right? To think outside the box and try to make this the best place possible for the people who need it."

"That's what *we're* here for, anyway," he says, casting a pointed look at Dave, who is currently interfering with the HVAC installer for some unknown reason. He shifts his focus back to me, smiling as he adds, "Glad to see you living the dream, though. Your dad has been looking forward to this for years. He couldn't wait to have you home and working for the family business."

"Happy to be here," I say. And…I am. Mostly.

But as I catch a cab back to the office with Dave an hour later, Mitch's words continue to haunt me. I'm "living the dream," all right.

But is it my dream? Or my father's?

Suddenly, that distinction feels very important.

I suspect it has something to do with the man waiting for me at the speakeasy on Tenth Avenue after work on Wednesday, the one who makes it clear every time he touches me that what I want matters to him.

That *I* matter…

On impulse, I hurry across the bar, into the shadows in the back of the dimly lit space, and right into Gideon's arms.

twenty-eight
GIDEON

Her lips press against mine and the stress of the day vanishes in a rush of gratitude.

I've never felt this lucky, not in my entire life.

I'm a billionaire with a thriving business, in excellent health, and even on my darkest days, I've been able to count on a natural emotional and mental resilience I know isn't the norm for a lot of people. I have a gorgeous home in Vermont, a stunning apartment in the city, and the option of retiring by forty if I want to.

But it's this woman who makes me feel like I won the life lottery.

I can't believe I almost let her slip away.

The thought makes my arms tighten around her, holding her close as the kiss ends. "I guess you missed me, too?"

She nods. "So much. Tuesday night was lame without you."

"So lame," I agree, wishing it wasn't too soon to ask

her to move in with me. But it is. But in a month or two, things will be different. In a month or two, it won't be untoward to suggest cohabitation or to ask her if she might consider Christmas in Vermont...or to tell her that I'm in love with her. Because I am, and I don't give a shit if that seems crazy to anyone else. I've been looking for a love like this long enough to know when I've found it. "You should definitely sleep over tonight."

Her lips turn down. "Sadly, I can't. Noelle needs help boxing hamster fashion. She had a ton of orders come in last week and is so busy sewing she hasn't had time to get things ready to ship. I told her I'd come home early tonight and help her knock it all out before the panic attacks get any worse."

"You're a good friend," I say, squashing the disappointment rising in my chest. At least I get to see her and touch her, even if it's just for a little while. I nod toward the bar. "Should we go somewhere else, then? Will an old-fashioned interfere with your ability to ship hamster fashion?"

"Hell, no," she scoffs. "I need that old-fashioned. I spent the afternoon playing 'Please Stop Being a Jerk and Let me Make This Project Awesome' with Dave again. I thought Mitch was going to have a heart attack at one point, when Dave suggested the homeless children didn't need a playground in the courtyard."

I scowl, shaking my head as we make our way to the front. "What's wrong with that man? The project is coming in right on budget."

"He wants it under budget, I guess," she says, leaning against the gleaming mahogany bar beside me. "He thinks that's what wins brownie points with my father. And I guess it is. I mean, Dave's been with the company for seven years. Dad clearly knows how he operates and still selected him to take the lead on this project, so..."

"Two old-fashioned please," I tell the bartender before turning back to Sydney. "You're disappointed in your dad?"

"A little, yeah. I don't know... The longer I'm at the office, the more it feels like I don't fit in there. I knew that my father was old-school, but I didn't realize how...transactional everything was. I'm not sure he even has friends outside of work who can't boost business for him in some way."

I consider that as I pay for our drinks and Sydney leads the way back to the corner booth. Once we're seated, I say, "But that's something you could change, eventually. Your dad wants you to take over the company, right? And once you're in charge, you can build a new company culture."

She sighs, swirling her tiny black straw around in her drink. "Yeah, I could, I guess. But you know what they say in business school: Culture eats strategy for breakfast and culture is the hardest thing to change."

"True," I agree.

"And what if..."

"What if?" I prompt after a moment.

She looks up, her gaze troubled. "What if I don't want to fight to change the culture at my father's company? What if nothing about working there feels right? This summer, I thought I could push aside my reservations and be what my family needs me to be, but now...I'm not sure. That voice inside, telling me this isn't where I belong or what I want to do with my one precious life, just keeps getting louder and louder." She narrows her eyes on mine, "And it's at least partly your fault."

My brows lift. "My fault?"

"Yes," she says, scooting closer, until her thigh presses against mine beneath the table. "This feels so right. It makes wrong things feel even more wrong."

I put my arm around her shoulders, nestling her more firmly against my side. "Agreed. Not to change the subject, but I don't think I can keep this from Adrian much longer. That also feels wrong. I was thinking of telling him this weekend. I initially wanted to wait until he knew the results of the DNA test, but that's going to take at least two weeks, and I don't think I can wait that long."

Sydney pulls in a breath, letting it out in a rush. "Okay."

"If you want to wait, we can wait."

"No, I'm just dreading it. But you're right. The longer we put it off, the weirder it's going to feel. And at least it will be one uncomfortable thing off my plate. Then I'll just have to figure out how to tell my father that not only am I dating one of his business partners, but I'm also seriously considering running away to live in the marsh with the swamp birds and butterflies."

"Can I run with you?" I ask, loving the way she smiles at the thought.

"Yes, please."

"Or you could find a company that aligns more with

your values. Not to overstep, but I pride myself on putting the well-being of the people who will eventually be living in my buildings above the bottom line. Way above it. And I regularly give project managers time off to pursue other goals. Nigel went to Tibet for two months last year and Sierra took a sabbatical to build a yurt out of old soda bottles. I could absolutely find a way to give a valuable employee time off in the summers to roam the bog like the butterfly goddess she is."

Her gaze softens. "I appreciate the offer, but I'm not sure working for you would be a good idea, Gideon. I'd have to think about it, but I think I'd rather come home to you."

"Yeah, I'd like that, too," I say, my throat tight with emotion.

I'm about to say it, to tell her that I'm falling in love with her, when my cell dings. "Sorry," I apologize, "but that might be Mitch, checking in on the Coney Island project. I promised him I'd be available to chat tonight in case he couldn't wait until tomorrow morning at the office. If it is, I'll tell him I'll call him later, after you head home. I just need to touch base really quick."

But when I check my phone, it isn't Mitch.

It's Derrick the doorman with some unexpected news.

I grunt, perplexed.

"What is it?" Sydney asks.

"Apparently, my ex was just at my building and left a floral arrangement at the front desk. Derrick wants to know if I'd like him to take it up to the apartment for me."

She hums beneath her breath. "I take it she doesn't usually send flowers when she's in town?"

"Never," I say. "One time she threw a vase at me when we were married, but it was empty at the time."

Sydney's eyes widen. "Wow. Were you a completely different person back then? Because, honestly, I can't imagine you doing anything that would make me mad enough to throw something at you. Especially something capable of doing real damage."

I laugh. "Thanks. Looking back, I probably could have empathized more with how hard it was for Angela to be at home alone with the baby on nights when I had class until nine or ten, but no, I didn't do anything worth having glass thrown at my head. We were just... volatile together. If Adrian hadn't come along, I doubt our relationship would have lasted through our senior year of high school." I frown at my phone. "I wonder what she's up to."

"Hopefully there's a note with the flowers that will give you a clue," Sydney says. "Either way, I say you should keep them. Flowers are always nice. I prefer them in a heath at the edge of the ocean, but a vase is nice, too."

"You're missing Maine," I say as I text Derrick to go ahead and take the flowers up to my place.

Sydney sighs. "I am. Life is just so much simpler there."

"I get it," I say. "That's how I feel about Vermont. And in Maine, you're so close to the ocean. If I lived there, I might truly never come back to New York again. Except to see a certain woman."

Her lips curve. "A certain woman who is me?"

"Who else?" I ask, blood pumping faster as she leans in, brushing a kiss on my cheek. It pumps even faster when she whispers in my ear, "Is it bad that I'd rather be alone at your place right now than out on the town?"

"Is it wrong that I want to take you home and make you come on my cock?" I ask, the organ in question already thickening behind my fly. "And hire someone else to help your friend pack up her hamster clothes?"

Sydney pulls back, her eyes glittering. "We could do that, couldn't we? I don't think Noelle would mind. She already warned me that she wouldn't be able to talk while we work anyway. She's going to be sewing all night and she can't talk over the sound of the machine."

"I have the Task it Out app on my phone. I can have someone over there in thirty minutes."

She grins. "Me, too. Let me text her and make sure it's okay. Then, I can hire someone while you get us a car back to your place?"

"Let's do it," I say, picking my drink up and draining the last of the brown liquid.

Smith is already off duty for the day, so I pull up a ride-share app and order a car.

Ten minutes later a Task It Out worker with a hundred five-star reviews is on her way to help Noelle, and Sydney and I are kissing in the car back to my place. We stop making out long enough to breeze through the entryway, thanking Derrick for taking care of the flowers on our way past, and then we're all over each other in the elevator.

I know I'm acting like a kid with his first crush, but I can't help it. I can't keep my hands off Sydney. I crave her body like a drug. When we're finally alone behind closed doors, it's all I can do not to fuck her against the wall in the foyer.

The need to be close to her is that intense.

"I missed you," she murmurs against my lips as I half carry her through the entryway, my hands everywhere they've been dying to be.

I squeeze her ass, loving the way she wiggles her hips closer to where I'm hard for her. "Missed you, too. I don't like spending the night away from you."

"Me, either," she says, moaning as I cup her breast through her sheath dress. "I wake up wet and dying to feel you inside me."

I curse as we bump into the couch. I'm so desperate to have her naked and under me, I've lost all sense of spatial awareness. I pull back, guiding her thin green sweater off her shoulders and ripping it down her arms. She reaches for the buttons on my shirt, but I'm already jerking the stretchy material of her black dress down her arms, revealing a delicate lace bra that sends another jolt of need straight to my dick.

"Zipper," she murmurs, her arms now trapped by her sides. "In the back."

"Turn," I say, spinning her around. I drag my teeth over her bare shoulder as I find the zipper and pull it down. "How do you smell so good after a day running around the city?"

"I don't think it's me," she says, her voice breathy. "I think it's the flowers. Look at them. They're enormous."

I glance up, grunting at the obscene display of fall blooms on the kitchen island, everything from pansies and asters to violets and pale pink roses, topped off by giant fake butterflies made of tissue paper and clay. It's beautiful, unique, and expensive—all the things Angela values most—and appears to be a genuine effort at making amends.

The jaded voice In my head Instantly wonders what she's up to, what kind of angle she's working, but the rest of me is too eager to be with Sydney to worry about it now. Whatever Angela's up to, figuring it out can wait until I've made love to the gorgeous woman turning in my arms.

I kiss my way down her throat, kneading her breasts in my hands as I go.

"Don't you want to read the card?" she asks, her nails digging into the back of my neck as I suck her nipple into my mouth through her lace bra.

"No," I say. "I have other priorities at the moment." I drag my teeth over her sensitive skin, making her gasp.

"God, Gideon. How do you do that?"

"Do what, baby?" I ask.

"Make my head feel like it's literally spinning?"

"I haven't even gotten started yet." I pull her dress down around her hips and push it the rest of the way to the floor. I kneel in front of her, leaning in to press my face against the front of her matching lace panties, inhaling the salty tang of her arousal. "Fuck, I missed the smell of you. Spread your legs, butterfly, let me show you how much."

"No," she says, surprising me. When I look up, she adds in a whisper, "It's my turn. I want to put my mouth on you. I want to make you as crazy as you make me."

"You do," I promise. "And you don't have to return any favors if you don't want to. I love fucking you with my mouth, I promise. It's not something I do because I'm expecting payback."

She shakes her head, a bemused smile on her face. "I think you're the only man in the world who would try to talk a woman out of giving him a blow job."

"I just don't want you to feel pressured. If you don't enjoy blow jobs."

"I don't know if I enjoy them," she says. "Why don't we find out?" She reaches down, tugging at my arms until I'm on my feet before she guides me to lean against the couch.

"You've never?" I ask, my pulse racing faster as she reaches for the close of my pants, guiding the button through the hole.

She shakes her head. "No, but I understand how they work. I've just never been...inspired to try it myself before." She hooks her thumbs around my boxer briefs and the back of my pants. "But I'm feeling very inspired now." She tugs the fabric down around my thighs as she drops to her knees.

I bite my lip, balls dragging heavier between my legs as she wraps her fingers around my shaft, stroking me base to tip before guiding the already leaking head of my cock toward her mouth. Just as my burning skin is about to brush her lips, she pauses and looks up. "Any notes so far?" she asks, a teasing glitter in her blue eyes.

Deciding to give as good as I get, I hum thoughtfully, drawing out the moment for both of us. "You know, now that you mention it, why don't you take your bra off? So I can see your pretty tits while your mouth is wrapped around me?"

"All right." Holding my gaze, she releases my cock, setting it to bobbing between us as she sits back on her heels. She reaches behind her back, popping the clasp on her bra and drawing it slowly down her arms.

I suck in a breath as she bares her flushed nipples. "So beautiful."

"You like me on my knees for you?" she asks, the husky note in her voice destroying me nearly as much as the way she grips my shaft again, with more confidence this time.

"I like you close to me," I say honestly. "In any and every capacity. But yes, I like you on your knees, butterfly. Now suck me into your mouth like a good girl and show me how much you need me inside you."

Her eyes take on that glassy, slightly intoxicated sheen they always do when we play this game, but it's different this time. As she slips me between her lips, her gaze doesn't waver from mine. She looks up at me, *into* me, all her walls down, and every piece of her beautiful heart on display.

The heart that's clearly mine for the taking...

"Sydney," I murmur as I thread my fingers into her silky hair and cup her jaw gently in my palm. "You destroy me."

She suckles me deeper, her hands braced against my thighs. She pulls back and glides forward again, mimicking the slow, easy rhythm of our first time. It hits me all over again, how fucking grateful I am that I got to be her first, and how desperately I want to be her last.

She pauses at the tip of me this time, continuing to stroke my cock with one hand as she asks, "Is this okay? Any notes, sir?"

"Do you want notes, baby?" I brush my thumb gently over her soft cheek.

Her lips part. "Yes, I do. Tell me how you like it. Tell me how to be the best you've ever had."

Chest aching at her pure fucking sweetness, I tell her, "Play with my balls while you suck me. And you don't have to take me so deep if it's uncomfortable. You can wrap your fist around the base of my cock and just take me down to there, maybe give a little squeeze as you drag your lips back."

"I can do that," she says, curling her fingers around my shaft as she takes me into the warm, wet heat of her mouth again. Her other hand cradles my balls, rolling them gently in my swollen sac as she finds her rhythm. In just a few minutes, my breath is coming faster, and I can't stop my hips from jerking forward as her mouth sinks over me.

She moans and sucks me deeper, making me grip the back of the couch for balance. "Fuck, Sydney, you're so good. You make me feel so fucking good, but if you don't stop soon, I'm going to come in your mouth."

She hums around me and continues to destroy me with her lips and tongue, making it clear she's up for whatever comes next—pun intended. But as hot as that is, I need to be inside her. I've been dreaming about burying myself between her legs all day. Not even the best blow job can compare to being joined with her, watching her face as I fill her and fuck her and make her come for me.

I fist my hand at the base of her neck, gripping the silky strands hard enough to stop her when her head bobs back the next time. Her gaze jerks up to mine, her lips parting, letting the tip of my furiously swollen length slip from her mouth. "Something wrong?"

"No, I just need your pussy, baby," I say, my voice shaking with how much I need her. "I need you so fucking bad. Go get in bed. I'll be there in five seconds with a condom."

"Make it four," she says, before my feisty girl rises and jogs toward my bedroom in nothing but her lace panties.

"Those panties better be on the floor by the time I get in there," I call after her. "And your hands should be behind your knees, legs spread. I want to see every inch of your pussy, butterfly."

I hurry to grab the condoms I bought today from my briefcase, my gaze catching on the flowers and their butterfly decorations for a beat. The realization that it's ironic that Angela sent butterflies—my pet name for Sydney—in the arrangement zips through my head, but I don't linger on the idea for more than a second or two.

I'm too eager to get to the bedroom.

Later, I'll remember that moment and wish I'd done

a better job of connecting the dots, but right now my focus is all on my girl.

And when I get to the bedroom to see Sydney naked with her legs spread for me, baring her slick, swollen sex, all I'm thinking about is how fast I can be balls deep in her gorgeous body.

"Is this how you wanted me?" she asks as I join her on the bed, rolling the condom on as I move.

"Yes. Perfect." I lengthen myself on top of her. "Now wrap your legs around my waist, baby." She obeys and I whisper, "Good girl," into her ear, making her moan even before I fit my cock to her entrance and glide inside.

I make her come twice before I lose myself in her heat and end up having her again in the shower when she decides to join me halfway through. I'm taking her against the slick shower wall, in fact, when the first message comes through.

And the second and the third.

But my phone is in the other room. I won't realize what's going on for another fifteen minutes.

I have no idea that our lives are in the process of imploding or that our time in the shower is the last peace either of us will know for a while.

After our shower, I wrap up in one of Gideon's cozy robes, borrow a pair of his socks—I'm not about to wiggle into hose right now—and head out to the kitchen to fetch a glass of water while he gets dressed.

On my way to the cabinet, my gaze lands on the flower arrangement again and my nose wrinkles.

It's a beautiful gift, but it gives me an icky feeling for some reason, and not just because it's from Gideon's ex-wife. There's something ominous about the almost obscenely large roses and the bulbous eyes of the butterflies on their wiry stalks. And this is coming from a woman who loves butterflies enough to spend her summers counting them in a swamp.

Deciding to ask Gideon if he would mind moving the flowers to the entry table, so they aren't looming so large while we have dinner, I fill my water glass and go looking for my phone. I'm fairly certain I dropped my purse somewhere between the door and the couch and, sure enough, I find it a few feet from the hall closet.

I pluck it from the marble tile and wander back into the living room, smiling as I spot my dress and sweater puddled on the floor. I tidy up, folding my things and draping them over the back of the couch, then set my glass down on the coffee table and pull out my phone. I settle onto the overstuffed cushions to check food delivery times, but before I can open the delivery app, I see a series of missed calls and texts from Noelle.

My stomach twisting with guilt—hopefully the woman I sent to help is doing a good job and Noelle isn't upset with me for bailing—I tap on her messages.

By the time I get to the second line, my stomach is in free fall.

Oh my God, Sydney, text me right now! Right now! Or pick up the phone. I'll try calling again.

Shit, honey! Is your phone on silent? Please, you have to hear me. I'm willing you to hear me texting you.

I'm manifesting it.

Right now! Harder than I've ever manifested before.

Please, for the love of God, pick up your phone!

I scowl and shake my head, muttering, "What the hell?" as I scroll to the next message, sent almost fifteen minutes later.

Okay, so the cat is totally and completely out of the bag about you and Gideon. The cat jumped out of the bag, discovered a love for drama, workshopped a play, found backers, booked a theater, and put on a Broadway show.

Adrian knows, Syd.

He found out in a way that was um...VERY upsetting for

him and is going to be even more upsetting for you and Gideon. It would be upsetting for anyone, but especially for you because you're such a private person. I mean, you've never even sent a sext, have you?

Ugh, his mother is a monster, Syd, For real. I can't believe I ever thought she was nice and cool and had fabulous hair. I mean, her hair is still fabulous, but she's insane. And cruel.

This wasn't what anyone needed right now, least of all her son.

Anyway, that's all I should say right now. This isn't the kind of thing that should be explained in a text. Please, please, please call me as soon as you get this message. Before you call anyone else, okay? And don't let Gideon check his phone! I'm pretty sure Adrian texted him, and I don't want either of you to find out from Adrian. He's not in a good head space right now. Apparently, Gigi cancelled the amnio and is engaged to the drummer she cheated with in June.

Everything is such a hot mess. I have no idea how I'm going to focus on sewing tonight. But the lady you sent to help is amazing. She kept her head down in my room, packing up hamster clothes, while we all had a meltdown in the living room. So...there's that?

I love you. Everything will be okay, I promise. We'll get through this.

Call me!

By the time I'm done reading, my throat is so tight that when Gideon asks what's wrong, I can barely croak out, "I'm not exactly sure." I reach for my water, gulping a drink before muttering, "I have to call Noelle." I stand, starting toward the balcony, only to spin back to him with a hand raised, "Don't look at your phone, okay?

Something's happened, something bad, and she doesn't want you to find out about it from Adrian. She's pretty sure he texted you."

Gideon's brows snatch together. "What?" He moves toward the entryway, where he always drops his wallet and phone on the table by the door.

"Please, Gideon, don't," I say, my heart surging into my throat. "Noelle's been my friend since we were kids. She's not the kind of person to exaggerate in a crisis. If she thinks we'd be better off hearing about what happened from her, I'm sure she's right."

He hesitates. "He's not hurt?"

"No, not physically, anyway," I say. Gideon pulls in a breath, clearly about to ask a follow-up question, but I cut him off, "I'm not sure what's happened, only that it has something to do with your ex and Adrian. And us. And…Adrian finding out about us."

Gideon's face falls as he curses.

"I know. This sucks." I extend a hand. "Want to come outside with me? We can put Noelle on speakerphone? A little fresh air makes everything better, right?"

He hesitates only a beat more before crossing the room and wrapping his big palm around mine. "I'm so sorry. But I'm not sorry about you. Or us."

"Me, either," I say, wanting to tell him I'm pretty sure I'm in love with him, in fact. But this isn't the time. I don't want the memory of the first time I say those words to be tangled up in this mess. Instead, I squeeze his hand, and promise, "We'll handle this. Whatever it is. We're tougher than we look."

His lips hook up on one side. "You, maybe. I look

super tough. It's one of the first things people notice about me."

"Especially in pajama pants with tiny cows all over them," I say.

He shrugs. "They were a prank gift from a friend at the Vermont office. I need to do laundry."

"I love them," I whisper, letting him draw me against him. I rest my face against his chest, still warm from our shower beneath his white cotton shirt and draw his strength into my soul.

I'm about to pull back to head outside when my phone dings again.

I look down to see another text from Noelle—*Please call me, Syd! I just took a sewing break to check in with the boys, and Ben said Adrian's on his way to his dad's place right now. He could be there any second!*

I jerk my gaze up to Gideon, who's reading over my shoulder.

"Call her while I get dressed," he says, backing toward the bedroom. "You should get dressed, too."

I hurry toward the couch, snatching my dress and sweater off the cushions, my heart racing nearly as fast as my thoughts. But before I can dash into the bedroom or call Noelle or remember if I have mascara in my purse—I always feel more confident with a fresh coat of mascara—there's a sharp thud on the door.

A beat later, Adrian calls out, "I'm coming in. In case the two of you want to put on some clothes."

thirty
GIDEON

I hear Adrian's voice and curse again, my upper lip breaking out in a sweat as I jerk my jeans up around my hips. I scan the closet floor for shoes, but I've left them all by the door. If Adrian wants to get physical, I guess I'll be fighting my son in my socked feet.

Fuck! I don't want to fight my son.

I don't want to hurt Adrian in any way. That's why I wanted to find the perfect moment, the perfect words to explain how I came to be dating his ex-girlfriend and why I can't stop.

But Angela took that away from me. I'm not sure how, but she obviously got to our son, a fact that's underlined in glaring red ink as I head out to the living room to see Adrian pick up the flower arrangement Angela sent and hurl it across the room.

Sydney cries out in surprise, her hands instinctively flying up to shield her face as the vase explodes against the thicker glass of the windows, sending shards of glass, flowers, and water flying into the air. Thankfully, the explosion happened far enough away from her that she's in no danger, but the way her arms tremble as they drop to her sides makes my stomach roil.

"That's enough," I say in a firm voice, positioning myself between Syd and my red-faced son. "Go into the bedroom, Sydney, and lock the door."

"Stop it, I'm not going to hurt her," Adrian says, turning his puffy gaze my way. "Or you."

He's obviously been crying, a fact that intensifies the pain in my gut. But as much as I want to comfort him, Sydney's well-being is my top priority. She did absolutely nothing wrong here. She's innocent and doesn't deserve to be caught in the middle of a situation that makes her feel unsafe.

"All right," I say, casting a pointed glance toward the mess on the floor. "When I'm sure of that, Sydney can come out of the bedroom. If she wants to."

"I'm fine," she says, moving around my outstretched arm to stand beside me. "I don't need protection from Adrian. Or...whatever's going on. I didn't get a chance to talk to Noelle, Adrian. We don't know what happened with your mom and all that, but we're sorry. We weren't trying to be sneaky or cruel. We were just worried about you having too much on your plate. We planned to tell you we were dating as soon as the mess with Gigi was over."

Adrian winces. "Yeah, well, that won't be any time soon. She cancelled the DNA test and is engaged to Brett Lauder. Fucking Brett. She'd rather be with a guy named *Brett*, with a coke habit, a weak chin, and a bad bleach job, than with me." He swallows, his throat visibly working before he adds, "And that's after I told her I didn't care about the results. Yes, I wanted the test, so we could know who the father is for sure, but I told her I didn't care if the baby was mine. I still wanted to be with her, to try to be a family."

"I'm so sorry, son," I say, aching for him.

His chin snaps up, his eyes narrowing. "Don't call me son, okay? Not right now. I'm not pissed at you—well, not as pissed as I am at Mom, anyway—but we're not going to do any father-son bonding right now. It's too weird." He glances at Sydney, his voice softening, "But I get it. You two." His mouth curves into a sad smile. "I told you that you'd like my dad, right?" He exhales, shaking his head. "You must have laughed your ass off."

"That's not who I am, Adrian," Sydney says gently. "You know that. I didn't laugh. I felt uncomfortable. You're my friend. I don't like lying to my friends. It just felt like too big a secret to blurt out in the heat of the moment without talking to Gideon first."

"We didn't know, Adrian," I add. "When we first met and started to have feelings for each other, I had no idea the two of you used to date. Neither did Sydney. We didn't find out until the night of your fundraising party."

He nods, his gaze dropping to the floor with a sigh. "Yeah, well, it doesn't matter, I guess. You two clearly like each other. I wish I'd never seen...*anything* I saw tonight, but it's obvious it's more than fucking with you guys. Or more than blow jobs or...whatever."

I suck in a shocked breath and Sydney's hand comes to hover in front of her mouth, her face going pale.

Adrian motions toward the flowers now scattered across the marble. "There's a camera in one of the butterflies. Mom was coming to bug you about the apartment again one morning earlier this week and saw you and Sydney leaving your place together. She remembered Syd from my graduation party and put two and two together, but she didn't think I'd believe you were dating my ex unless I saw it with my own eyes. That's why she sent you flowers and sent *me* a link to the feed from the hidden camera."

"That's fucking insane," I grit out through a clenched jaw, planning on calling my lawyer as soon as Adrian leaves. Angela truly *is* insane if she thinks she's going to get away with spying on me in my own home.

Adrian nods. "I agree. Though, in her defense, I don't think she ever expected me to see what I saw. When I called her on the way over, she seemed shocked and swore you're not the kind to do anything provocative outside the bedroom."

"Your mother doesn't know me, not even close," I say. "But she's going to, once I file criminal charges."

"Please, don't," Adrian says, his gaze softening. "She knows how pissed I am. At *her*, not at the two of you. This is backfiring on her harder than any scheme has backfired before. I'll make sure she knows that if she so much as sends you a text message again, she won't have a son anymore. That'll scare Mom more than any criminal charge. I'm the only family she has left. Her parents haven't spoken to her since she got pregnant, and the rest of the family is always trying to make her join their weird cult." Glancing at Sydney, he adds, "They're part of some fundamentalist church that thinks women should stay home raising kids and putting up canned goods for the apocalypse while men do firearms training to combat the incoming forces of demonic zombies or whatever. She never had a chance of turning out normal. And she seemed sorry. I think she realizes now that what she did was wrong."

"Or she's just sorry it didn't work out the way she hoped it would," Sydney says, as astute as ever. "But I'm okay with not pressing charges if Gideon is." She points a firm finger at the remnants of the flower arrangement. "As long as any and all records of the footage are destroyed. If there's a chance in hell it's going to end up on the internet, then I'll want justice for that, Adrian. Like Noelle said to me earlier, I've never even sent a sexy text. I've been so careful not to do anything that might damage my reputation or my ability to fill my father's shoes. It isn't right for that to be undone by someone illegally filming me without my knowledge."

"I'll make sure of it, I promise," Adrian says. "I'll get with Mom tonight and take care of it. I'll destroy all the footage on the app, the cloud, check her devices, the whole nine yards. I'll wipe it all. You have my word."

Sydney glances up at me. "Is that okay with you?"

A part of me still wants to call the police and escalate this in a way that will make damned sure Angela doesn't think about interfering in my life again, but... she's the mother of my only child. And Adrian's right, he's the most important person in her life. It's why she went to these lengths in the first place, and why I'm confident she'll take his threats seriously and back off.

I nod at Sydney before turning back to Adrian. "All right. But she leaves town tomorrow and doesn't come back for a long, long time. And when she does, she makes no attempt to contact me. I'm done. I never want to see her again unless it's at your wedding, and we're on opposite sides of the church."

Adrian's shoulders slump a little, but I stand firm. Angela's put us both through too much. If he still wants a relationship with his mother, I can't blame him, but she's pushed me too far.

"All right," he says. "I'll let her know. Thanks for keeping this between us. She crossed way too many lines tonight but...she's still my mother."

"I understand," I say. "And I'm sorry you had to find out about Sydney and me this way. I hope this won't set us back in *our* relationship. I've really enjoyed spending time with you lately. I love you, Adrian. All I've ever wanted was to be close to you, to be a real part of your life."

He swallows again. "Nah, we're good, old man. I'll see you for lunch on Friday." He arches a brow Sydney's way. "But if you become my stepmom someday, I'm never calling you mommy. That's not anywhere on the table."

Sydney makes a gagging sound. "God, no. Ew. I feel sick just thinking about it."

Adrian grins. "Good. And let me know if you get tired of dating an old guy. I have loads of interesting friends I could set you up with. All of them closer to thirty than forty."

"Or not," I grumble, scowling.

Adrian laughs and Sydney crosses her arms. "You're a mess," she mutters. "Speaking of messes, you should get out of here before we put you to work cleaning up shattered glass."

Adrian's smile fades. "I can help. Sorry, I was just so fucking angry. I saw them and...snapped."

"I get it, don't worry about it," I tell him. "It's more important you get to your mother and take care of the footage. I'll clean up the mess. And I'll set aside those butterflies somewhere safe in case I need evidence that I was being filmed without my knowledge or consent. Be sure to mention *that* to your mother."

"Will do," Adrian says soberly. "I'll make sure she gets how serious this is, and...I'm sorry, too. You guys didn't deserve this. Not even close. You're actually both really good people." He holds my gaze. "Especially Sydney, so don't hurt her."

"Wouldn't even think about it," I promise. "I'd cut off my own hands first."

"I'm not worried," Sydney says, "but thank you, Adrian. I know this mess with Gigi has been so hard, but you've come a long way lately. You should be proud of who you're becoming."

He rolls his eyes good naturedly and mutters, "Yeah, yeah, stepmom."

"Call me that again and I'm putting ex-lax in your cocoa the next time you come over to my place with Ben," Sydney says, making him laugh.

"I'll walk you to the door." I cross around the opposite side of the couch to avoid the mess. When Adrian and I reach the hallway, I put a hand on his shoulder. Thankfully, he doesn't pull away. "Talk more about Gigi and the baby on Friday at lunch? I'd love to see if there's anything I can do to help."

"Yeah, sure," he says. "Sounds good." He pauses at the door, dropping his voice as he adds, "You should offer Sydney a job. She's miserable working for her father, but I know she'd fit in perfectly at G.P.G. Green. She's a big hippy, just like you and the rest of the Vermont office. And if things between you don't work out in the romance department, you're both grown-ups. You'd figure it out. Or she could transfer to the New York office if it was weird. I just hate to see her throwing her life away for a man who could give two shits about anything beyond his bottom line. Including his daughter's happiness."

"You're a good friend," I murmur.

"I'm getting there," he says. "And I'm serious. Think about it. She's fucking brilliant and the hardest worker I know. You'd be lucky to have her."

I know I would, and I absolutely intend to try to win Sydney around to the idea of working together eventually. But for now, we have other priorities.

"We should tell my dad," Sydney says when I return to the main room, proving we're on the same page. "Get all the hard things over at once and then we'll be free to wander around the city together all we want."

"Agreed," I say, fetching the dustpan from beneath

the kitchen sink. "Should we order food and make a plan?"

"Yes." She runs a hand through her hair with a sigh. "And open a bottle of wine. I know we already had an old-fashioned, but I need a glass of pinot after all that…excitement."

"I'm so sorry," I say, anger burning in my gut as I pluck the butterflies out of the scattered flowers first. I have no idea if they're still recording after being smashed against a wall and covered in water, but I'm not taking any chances.

"It's not your fault," Sydney says, appearing beside me, her palm extended. "I can take care of those."

I set them in her hand. "Just make sure to wrap them up in something before you put them away. Just in case they're still working."

Sydney smiles. "Don't worry. I have an idea."

She steps into the kitchen, collecting a plastic freezer bag before moving back into the bedroom. I hear her voice a moment later and can't resist following her.

When I reach the bathroom, Sydney's holding the butterflies up to the mirror as she says, "You hear me? Leave him alone. He's a good, kind man, who deserves a chance to be happy. And if you ever pull something like this again, I will bring the full power of my considerable fortune and connections to bear and sue you so deep into the ground, you'll never see sky again. I hope we're clear."

Then she slips the butterflies into the plastic bag and crosses to the toilet where she lifts the lid on the back of the tank and drops the package inside.

I grunt and she spins, a guilty expression on her face. "How long have you been there?"

"Long enough to hear you defending my honor."

Her cheeks flush as she pads across the room toward me. "I couldn't help it. If she's still listening, I needed her to know I mean business."

"Don't apologize. I loved it," I say, deciding I can't wait another second. I have to tell her. Now. "And I love you. I know it's probably too soon, but—"

She leans into my arms, cutting me off with a big hug. "No, it's not. It's perfect. I love you, too. And I want to move in." She pulls back, gazing up into my face. "I mean, if that's okay with you?"

"I wanted to ask you sooner."

Her smile widens. "Good. And sure, people might say we're rushing things, but what's the worst that could happen? I move in, we realize it's too soon, and I move out again, right? That's not so bad."

"Not bad at all," I say, my hands drifting down to squeeze her ass through her robe. "We should move your things this weekend. And if you can work remotely a few days next month, I'd love to show you my place in Burlington, introduce you to my friends there."

Her pretty face lights up. "I'd love that. And I can probably make it work." Her grin fades. "Assuming my dad doesn't freak out about us dating and try to make things difficult. He's never cared who my friends are, but dating is a different story. I was dating a guy he didn't like my senior year of high school, so Dad enrolled me in self-defense classes every Friday and

Saturday night. Seth broke up with me three weeks later for a girl who had at least part of her weekend free."

I hum low in my throat. "But you're not a child anymore. You don't have to put up with that kind of treatment. Even from your father."

"Who's also my boss," she says with a wry twist of her lips. "But you're right. Hopefully, once he realizes how I feel, he'll be supportive. And if not...I'll cross that bridge when I come to it. I'll see if he has time for dinner tomorrow night. We could meet at Benedict's uptown. It's his favorite. Very old-school, lots of grilled meat and dark booths where our family drama won't be observed."

"Maybe there won't be drama," I say. "Maybe all the drama is on my side and Silas will realize I only want the best for you."

She skims her nails up my neck to tangle my hair. "Maybe. But either way, I'm not giving you up, Mr. Gabaldon. I'm way too smitten." She kisses me, slowly, deeply, with so much sweetness that I start to think cleaning up and ordering dinner can wait...

We make love again, this time face to face, with so much heart, that by the time I come deep inside her, it feels like she's a part of me.

A part I never want to lose.

I don't think I've ever been this nervous, not even in my senior year of high school, when letters from colleges started arriving at our apartment, each one a chance to please (or to fail) my father.

I had to get in to at least *one* Ivy League school. I didn't have to go to Harvard or Yale—I already knew Boston University was the program I loved—but I had to get in. I had to turn *them* down, not vice versa, or my father would be so disappointed.

In the end I was waitlisted at Harvard but granted admission into both Yale and Princeton.

My papa was exceedingly proud.

He should be proud now, too, once he learns the identity of the mystery man, I'm bringing to dinner tonight. I've chosen an amazing guy to be my boyfriend, a kind, clever, successful, honorable person, who adores me. What more could any parent want for their child? If the only thing "wrong" with Gideon is our age gap, well, isn't that a minor factor compared to all the ways we're good together?

We are good, so, so good…

Walking hand in hand with him, through the city streets of my childhood neighborhood, my chest fills with a warm ache. Never in my wildest, most romantic dreams did I think I'd find a man who looks at me like this, like I'm a treasure he can't believe he's found and never wants to lose. I didn't see that on my father's face when he looked at my mother or reflected in any of my friends' parents' relationships. I never even saw it in my friend group until Ben and Noelle fell in love.

Love like this—fearless, shameless love—is rare. Precious.

As we wait for the crosswalk to turn green across the street from Benedict's red-and-gold-striped awning, I squeeze Gideon's hand.

He glances down at me and arches a brow. "Ready?"

"Ready. We've got this."

"*You've* got this," he counters. "I plan on letting you take the lead. I want Silas to know this is your call and what you believe will make you happy. If I had a daughter, that would be the most important thing to me."

If he had a daughter…

The words bring the only reservation I have about getting in deeper with Gideon bobbing to the surface. Is he open to having more children? Even after last night, I'm still hesitant to ask. Saying you love someone and want to move in with them is one thing. Asking them if they might want to knock you up one day and live happily ever after with three or four kids is quite another.

Babies are the ultimate escalation and Gideon's son is already grown. He might not want more children. Or he might want to wait until we're together for several years first, which raises concerns for me.

I'm in no big hurry to start a family, but I wouldn't want to wait *too* long. Gideon's already almost forty and I want my kids to have a father for as long as possible. Having lost a parent as a child myself, I know how hard that is.

But now isn't the time to have that discussion. Even if I wanted to, we're already stepping into the warm, comforting gloom of the restaurant, where my father is seated at his usual table in the back.

When he sees Gideon following me through the maze of tables, recognition animates his face. He surges to his feet, and my heart catapults into my throat. Panic dumps into my bloodstream and for a second, I'm positive I won't be able to speak. I'll just stand in front of my father, squeaking and hyperventilating until I manage to pull myself together.

But then, something unexpected happens.

My father's eyes light up. And then…he smiles.

Before I know what's happening, he's laughing as he grips Gideon's hand and claps him warmly on the shoulder. "Gabaldon, you sneaky son of a bitch. You should have told me, but you always did play your cards close to the vest."

"Silas," Gideon says, squeezing Dad's hand. "Thanks

for meeting us tonight. And thanks for raising such an incredible woman."

Dad's chest puffs up, but he only spares me a quick smile before turning back to Gideon. "She's a rare one, that's a fact. And even prettier than her mother. Come on, sit down. I'll order a bottle of champagne to celebrate."

Celebrate? He's acting like we're getting married, not announcing the fact that we're dating.

And what happened to his warning about staying away from the competition?

Dad clearly wasn't thrilled by the idea of me dating Adrian, but apparently his father is a different story?

"Sit, sit," Dad continues, shooing us into the large leather-cushioned seats. "I want to hear how you met, and all about that development in Coney Island. I hear there's been some trouble with the parking situation and your general contractor."

I slide into the empty seat on one side of my dad while Gideon settles into the other. My father has positioned himself between us, a strategic move to divide and conquer. But as the champagne is delivered, we order appetizers, and the conversation continues to flow, he doesn't seem interested in dividing, only…monopolizing.

Gideon keeps trying to include me—in the story of how we met and how we ran into each other again at Adrian's party—but my father redirects him every time. He doesn't seem interested in hearing from me at all.

I tell myself it's because he knows how *I* feel. I'm not

the kind of person to bring a man to meet my dad unless it's serious. That's why he's focused on Gideon.

Still, I can't help but feel excluded. I barely get a word in during appetizers and by the time our small plates are cleared, I've drunk so much water to occupy myself during my long silences that I need to hit the ladies' room.

"If you'll excuse me," I say, scooting my chair away from the table.

Gideon looks up with a smile, but before he can speak, Dad asks him about another project somewhere in South Asia and I'm shut out again.

"It's okay. It'll be over in an hour. Ninety minutes, tops," I tell my reflection as I'm washing my hands in the washroom. My dad's famous for dragging out a meal, but even if we linger over dessert, we'll be out of here by eight.

That leaves plenty of time to catch a cab back to Gideon's place and conduct an in-depth postmortem about why my father was being so weird. Maybe Gideon will have a clue. He's been to far more business dinners than I have.

Maybe this is how Dad is when they chat, and he's having a hard time transitioning from a professional mindset to a personal one?

I reapply a coat of lipstick and fluff my hair, bracing myself for another hour of trying to break into the shop talk, but when I reach the table, the vibe is very different from when I left for the ladies' room.

My dad sits in stony-faced silence, while Gideon...

Well, Gideon looks *pissed*.

I hesitate behind my chair, not certain it's safe to sit down. "Is something wrong?"

"Nothing you need to worry about, honey," Silas says. "Gideon and I seem to have a difference of opinion, but that's nothing new. We've always seen the world a little differently, but that's why we're such complimentary business partners."

Gideon mutters something beneath his breath before pushing his chair back. "I'm sorry, I can't do this, Sydney. I wanted to. For you. But I can't make nice with someone who doesn't see you the way I do. Or treat you the way you deserve to be treated."

I frown, my hands beginning to sweat on my small satin clutch. "What?"

"Ridiculous," Dad cuts in gruffly, his cheeks flushing. "You've always been dramatic, Gideon, but this is too much."

"He suggested our relationship would be great for the companies," Gideon says, ignoring my father, his gaze locked on mine. "He wants you out. He wants you home, having babies, while he and I build an empire for the son you'll hopefully have one day. A *son*, he specified, not a daughter."

"I didn't say that," my father says, his face even redder. "I said I'd rather see my daughter at home, raising children, where she'll be happy. The business world is hard on women. And the bigger the company, the harder it gets. Men are better suited to the ugly parts of what we do." He glances up at me. "You know how I feel about that, Sydney. I've never hidden that from you. I told you it was going to be harder for you to lead as a woman than it would be if you were a man."

He's right. He's never hidden the way he feels from me.

And even if he'd never said a word, his sexist side comes out loud and clear in a hundred unspoken ways. Like insisting on skirts in the office for women four days a week, though pants have been acceptable office wear for as long as he's been an adult. Or the way he defaults to promoting men and giving them all the juiciest leadership positions. There's only one female VP at Watson Global and she's as hard and competitive as the men, a product of the environment my father has created. And Martha didn't earn her position until she was in her early forties.

I'm the only woman who's been given a shot at advancement in her twenties and that's only because I'm Silas Perry-Watson's daughter.

I was the exception…one he's clearly ready to do away with now that he has a shot at passing the torch to a male heir.

It's disappointing, but far from shocking.

I knew this was a real possibility when I started at Watson Global, that I'd eventually be pushed out if Dad couldn't wrap his head around ceding control of his empire to a woman. I knew it in my bones, guts, and sinew. It's part of why I was dreading the move back to the city and why every Monday morning at my new job gets harder and harder.

Watson Global isn't where I belong.

Hell, this city isn't where I belong, not anymore. I'll

always love New York and treasure my friends here, but I ache for a quieter life, closer to nature.

That's the life I have to live, *my* life, not my father's.

It's suddenly so painfully obvious, but instead of feeling torn or terrified about disappointing him, I feel...free. It's like someone's ripped the blinders off my eyes and I can finally see clearly.

"I know, Dad." I pull in a deep breath, hesitating. I don't want to hurt him, but I'm done twisting myself in knots to fit in at a company that doesn't share my values. "I know you mean well and want what's best for me, but that's not for you to decide. That's my choice and it's become clear to me that I'm not a good fit for Watson Global."

His bushy brows shoot up. "What are you saying? You *are* Watson Global. This is your legacy as much as mine."

"But it's not, and I don't know if it ever could be, even if you gave me free rein to make all the changes I want to make." A sad smile curves my lips. "And you wouldn't let me, Dad. You'd fight me every step of the way because what you believe to be true and right and what I believe to be true and right are fundamentally at odds."

He shakes his head. "That isn't—"

"A Y chromosome doesn't make someone a superior leader or business mind," I cut in, interrupting my father for one of the first times in my life. "Not even close. And the reason so many corporate environments are callous and unwelcoming to women is because men made them that way. They were created without women in mind and without a place for us. But instead of pushing back against that, you think everything is as it should be. You think the fact that I'm a woman is the problem, but it's not, Dad. If I were just another recent graduate looking for a job, I would never work at a company like ours. I'd take one look at our stats on retaining and promoting female employees and skip the application altogether."

"Fine," my father snaps. "Two new female VPs and you can start a daycare on-site or whatever it is you wanted to do. I'm not so rigid I can't see the benefit in changing things up a bit."

"It would have to be so much more than that," I say. "It would have to be a systemic shift. You'd have to let me fire every dude bro who talks to his executive assistant like she's a lesser species. I'd need the freedom to expand parental leave for both mothers and fathers and allow more flexibility for people to work from home when they're sick or caring for relatives. I'd want to move toward projects that put worker and human well-being before the bottom line and investigate supply chains that will reduce or eliminate the chance we're using exploited workers. And that's just the tip of the iceberg."

"Sydney," he says, a pleading note in his voice I haven't heard before. "You'd ruin us. Profits have been down the last two quarters."

"Profits are still extraordinary," I counter. "That's your loss aversion bias talking, Dad. Just because we have *less*, doesn't mean we don't have more than *enough*. The company would absolutely survive these changes. In the long run, I think they'd even help it thrive."

He shakes his head slowly back and forth, the color draining from his face. "I can't. I can't risk my entire life's work on some progressive dream that might destroy everything I've built."

"And I can't abandon my dreams, no matter how much I want you to be proud of me," I say gently. "Please consider my resignation effective immediately. I'll tie up any loose ends and fetch my things from my office tomorrow morning."

Dad slumps in his chair. For a moment, I think he might tear up. Instead, he grunts, and his eyes narrow on Gideon. "This is your fault. You and your wild ideas, the same ideas that have kept G.P.G. Green a bit player on a stage Watson Global has dominated for the past fifteen years. Congratulations on dragging my daughter down to wallow with you in mediocrity."

I laugh at that. I can't help it. It's just so absurd. "Dad, stop, please. Gideon isn't mediocre and neither am I. Success means different things to different people. For me, success means having fulfilling work and close ties with the ones I love. I'm still your daughter and I love you. That's never going to change."

His cheeks sag. "I would threaten to disinherit you, but...I know you." He sighs, his lips curving slightly. "Better than you might think. I know that would only drive you farther away and I..." He sighs again. "Well, I don't want to lose you. I love you, daughter, as bad as I might be at showing it sometimes."

I circle around to his chair, leaning down to hug his

shoulders. "I love you, too, Dad. And we can get better at showing how we feel. I know we can." I pull back, smiling down at him. "That will probably be easier if we're just father and daughter, not co-workers. Now, tell Gideon you're sorry about calling him mediocre. I need all my favorite people to get along. That's very important to me."

He grunts again, but his smile widens, clearly pleased to hear he's still on my favorite list. It's unexpected and makes my heart swell as he grumbles, "Sorry, Gabaldon. Be good to my daughter or you'll get the same attitude adjustments as the rest of us. She's no pushover."

"No, she's not," Gideon says proudly, taking my hand as I come to stand beside him. "Thanks for the appetizers, Silas. Hopefully, I'll see you at Thanksgiving."

As we turn, starting toward the door, Gideon squeezes my hand and whispers, "How are you feeling?"

"Great," I whisper back, a smile stretching wide across my face. "I feel like I have my whole life in front of me." We exit the restaurant, pausing on the sidewalk outside. I pull in a deep breath of fall-tinged air and let it out in a rush. "And for the first time in a long time, that feels...exhilarating."

Gideon beams down at me. "Does this mean you're going to consider working for me? I hear your sexy boyfriend has a competitive compensation package and impressive benefits."

I smile as we start down the sleepy street, marveling again at how quiet the Upper East Side is compared to so many other places in the city. But I want even more quiet, the kind I only find in one place. "I'll be considering all my options, thank you, sir. But first, I'm going to need a week in Maine with my girls. It's almost October book club time and I don't want to miss seeing the cats at Elaina's café dressed in their costumes."

He nods. "Sounds good. I'll miss you, but I—"

"I hope you won't," I cut in. "I'd love for you to come along. I mean, I heard you're the big boss, Mr. Gabaldon. Surely you can take a week off…or work remotely every now and then."

"I certainly can, and I'd be honored," he says, drawing me to the side of the street near a white stone townhome and gathering me into his arms. "I want as much of your time as I can get."

"And what about kids?" I ask, deciding to take a chance and roll the dice. I've already made outrageous leaps of faith tonight. Might as well go for broke. "Would you maybe want a couple more someday? Assuming you met the right woman?"

He pulls me closer, his eyes locked on mine. "You told your dad you couldn't abandon your dreams."

I nod and murmur, "Yes."

"I've never abandoned mine, either. Except one. The dream where I get to spend the rest of my life with the woman who was meant for me. The dream where I get to have babies with her and be part of the kind of close, loving family I've always wanted. I thought I'd missed my shot at that. Forever. That it was too late for me." His eyes begin to shine as he adds, "And then I met you."

I cup his face, the back of my nose stinging. "I'm so

glad that storm brought you out of the sky and into my life."

"Me, too," he says. "Want to head home? Figure out what we'd like to dream up next?"

"More than anything," I whisper.

And so we do.

epilogue

Gideon

Two years later...

I t's the end of another summer in one of our favorite places on earth.

The sun is setting behind the softly rolling hills, the lobster pots are ready above the fire pits, and our nearest and dearest have joined us for one last beach party before we fly home to Vermont in the morning.

Everyone's chatting and drinking, enjoying the music from our portable speakers, and watching the waves roll in, as yet unaware that they've secretly been invited to our wedding.

The surprise was Sydney's idea. As soon as her dad confirmed he'd be able to make it up for the party—and that he didn't mind Adrian, Noelle, and Ben catching a ride with him on his private plane—she'd turned to me and asked, "You want to get married? Saturday night? I think I can pull it all together by then."

I'd said "hell, yes," of course.

The only thing better than living with Sydney, working with Sydney, and anticipating the birth of our daughter in just two months, is the chance to finally make her my wife. I tried to talk her into getting married after we learned we were pregnant, but she'd insisted she wanted to wait until the baby was born and she'd settled into being a mother before we planned a wedding.

But her father's heart attack earlier this summer changed things. It was only a minor cardiac event, and his prognosis is good as long as he makes some changes to his diet and lifestyle, but I could tell it spooked Syd. She only has one parent left and she wanted him at our wedding, even though she isn't having anyone give her away.

That custom didn't resonate with my independent better half. She's decided to give herself away, and she'll be walking down the narrow boardwalk leading from the lighthouse to the beach any second.

As soon as I have our guests in position...

"Hey, everyone, time for a group photo," I call out, lifting my camera into the air. "Adrian, find a place in the front row of seats, will you?"

"Will do," my son says, saluting me with his beer. The past two years have been an incredible time for us, as well. I finally have the close relationship with my son I've always hoped for. He even helped throw a surprise double birthday party for Sydney and me on New Year's Eve last year, spending the night in sleepy Vermont with us instead of in Paris with his friends.

Adrian makes time for me in his busy, art-world-dominating schedule and he's so excited for his little brother or sister (though equally grateful he doesn't have a child of his own to care for right now). It turns out Brett was the father of Gigi's baby. The poor kid emerged with Brett's blond hair, weak chin, and all.

"Let's have the book club, Mitch and Amy, Noelle and Ben, and Silas in the front, too," I add. "Everyone else can file into the second row?"

Our guests move into the seats I set up facing the lighthouse—everyone except Elaina, who comes to stand at the end of the boardwalk, right before it gives way to rocks and sand.

"Over here, Elaina," Maya says. "There's an empty seat next to mine."

"I'm okay here," Elaina says, her eyes glittering with excitement. She pulls out her phone and taps a button. A beat later, Pachelbel's Canon begins to play from the portable speakers, underscored by the soft shushing of the waves and the cries of the seabirds.

I shift to stand by Elaina just as Noelle gasps and bursts into tears.

"What's wrong?" I hear her fiancé, Ben, murmur.

"They're getting married!" Noelle says, sending a ripple of excitement through the assembled company.

The ripple transforms to cries of delight as Sydney appears at the top of the dunes.

Instantly, I forget how to breathe.

She looks like a goddess in her white lace wedding dress. Her strawberry blond curls fall around her face beneath a crown of wildflowers, her lips shine a deep pink, and her cheeks are flushed the way they have been all summer. No matter how much sunscreen she put on, she always got a little sun-kissed.

Maya's grandmother said it was the baby, that pregnancy can make women burn more easily than they did before. I said it was because even the sun couldn't stay away from her.

She teased me for being a hopeless romantic, but I'm not hopeless. I have so much hope now, and it's all because of this amazing woman walking down the boardwalk to meet me, the sea breeze in her hair. She's stunning, inside and out, and in just a few minutes, she'll be my wife.

By the time she comes to stand across from me in front of Elaina, there are tears in my eyes.

"Here, buddy, I've got you," Elaina says, pressing a tissue from the pocket of her sundress into my hands, triggering laughter from our friends and family. As I dab at my eyes and Sydney reaches out to squeeze my hand, Elaina continues, "Dearly beloved, as you may have guessed, we're not here simply to eat lots of yummy lobster and drink fantastic local beer. We're here to witness the marriage of two of our favorite people, Sydney and Gideon."

"About time," Sydney's dad calls out good-naturedly, summoning more laughter from the group.

He's come a long way in the past few years, too. He shows his love more freely than ever before and has already drawn up the paperwork leaving Sydney in control of Watson Global in the event of his death. When he passes, she'll be able to run the company the way she's always wanted, but neither of us are in any rush for that to happen.

We want Silas around for a long time, hopefully long enough to meet all the grandchildren we plan to give him.

"Indeed," Elaina agrees. "But never fear. Sydney and Gideon have requested a swift and efficient ceremony. Probably because they're worried the baby might be born at any minute."

"Two months," Sydney says peacefully, smiling up at me as she threads her fingers through mine. "We have two months. Just enough time for vows, lobster, and a really long honeymoon."

"Amen to that," Elaina says. "So, without further ado, I invite Gideon to start the ceremony with his vows."

I start to reach for the cheat sheet in my pocket but think better of it. I don't need my notes. I just need to look into the blue eyes of this woman who means the world to me and it's all going to come out just fine.

"Two years ago, I was a different man," I say. "If you'd asked me at the time, I would have said I was happy. I had rewarding work, time to volunteer and pursue my hobbies, and all the money I could ever need. To a lot of people, I'm sure it looked like I was living the dream."

I pull in a breath, swallowing past the lump in my throat as Sydney's eyes begin to shine. "But I wasn't. I wasn't living *my* dream. I wasn't even going after my dream. I thought what I wanted most from this life had passed me by. I didn't think a wife and family were in my future, but I knew that was partly my fault. Because I didn't want to compromise. I wanted that big, life-changing, heart-stopping, forever love or nothing at all. But never in my wildest dreams did I imagine a woman like Sydney existed."

Tightening my grip on her hand, I continue, "You're everything I hoped I'd find and so much more, butterfly. You're my best friend, my teammate, my encourager when times get tough and my biggest cheerleader on the victory laps. You are kind and funny and so damned smart. You bowl me over every day with the way you think, but it's nothing compared to the way you love."

Sydney sniffs and swipes at her eyes with her free hand.

"You have the biggest, sweetest heart," I say, fighting to maintain control. "You're a gift to your friends, your family, and to me, and I intend to spend the rest of our lives making sure you never doubt how special you are. I love you, baby, and I know you're going to be the best mother any kid ever had. Thanks for choosing me. I promise I'll never give you a reason to regret it."

"Beautiful, Gideon," Elaina says, passing Sydney a tissue. "It's your turn when you're ready, Syd."

She sniffs and wipes her nose, before standing frozen for a moment, clearly torn about where to put the tissue.

"Here," Elaina says, curling her fingers. "Give it to me. I'll put it in my pocket. We're basically sisters by this point. I'm not afraid of your snot."

The moment brings some much-needed levity, giving our guests a laugh and both of us the chance to compose ourselves before Sydney's vows.

"Gideon Gabaldon," she says, her voice wavering only the slightest bit. "You are so many things to me. My best friend, my protector, my champion, and always first in line to celebrate my successes. But more than all that, you always make me feel like I'm enough—*more* than enough—just the way I am. If there's a better gift in all the world than that, I can't name it. Thank you for loving me with all your big heart and letting me love you with all of mine. I can't wait to spend my life with you and to see all the things we dream up next." She smiles, her eyes shining again. "Starting with our baby. I couldn't ask for a better father for our son or daughter. They're going to be the luckiest person in the world, right after their mama."

We exchange rings, Elaina finishes the rest of the ceremony, and we kiss in the warm sunset light, applauded by the people we love.

Afterward, as we're finishing our feast at the picnic tables, Sydney leans over and whispers, "Ready for your wedding gift?"

I smile. "I am, but I have a confession to make."

She arches a brow. "What's that?"

"I already know what it is."

Her jaw drops. "What? Maya told me she'd keep it a secret."

"She did. But when she told me the lighthouse had already been sold a few weeks ago, I went snooping for records in town. It took about ten minutes to get the dirt from the listing agent."

Sydney curses. "I knew I should have reminded her it was a surprise. Helen is a doll, but her memory isn't the best these days."

"I doubt mine will be at eighty-one, either," I say, squeezing her thigh beneath the table. "But it didn't ruin the surprise, I promise. It made it better in a way, knowing we're still on the same page, as always."

"Always," she echoes, smiling as her lips drift closer to mine. "And now we can spend every summer in Maine with the baby, visit whenever we want, and bang in the same place we banged the first time for the rest of our lives."

I hum against her lips as we kiss before pulling back to whisper, "Speaking of banging…"

"Oh yeah, we're gonna," she says. "I can't wait until the party's over. I'll pretend I need to pee. Meet me in bed in five minutes for a quickie." She starts to rise from her chair, but turns back to add, "Actually, make it eight minutes. I really do need to pee. The baby's tapdancing on my bladder again."

I grin. "Got it."

Approximately seven and a half minutes later, I'm pushing Sydney up against the door in our bedroom as we kiss like we're starved for each other, even though we just made love this morning, after celebratory wedding day lemon souffle pancakes. I've learned to make the pancakes we loved on our first real date, as well as all Sydney's favorite dishes. I'm the cook in our family, heading home early from the office most days to prep dinner after my hike, while Sydney finishes up her work for the day.

She's become an irreplaceable asset at G.P.G. Green, the way I knew she would, and I've protected her time among the butterflies, the way I promised. Every summer, we spend a month or two in Maine with the butterflies and seabirds. Sydney donates her time to the conservancy she worked for in college while I make several day trips to transport animals to no-kill shelters up and down the eastern seaboard.

It's an incredible life, and it's only getting better, a fact brought home by the fact that very few positions are currently available to us at the moment.

"You're beautiful with this belly, but I'm excited for missionary position again someday soon," I say, as I guide Sydney's dress up around her hips and tug her panties down, preparing to take her from behind.

She giggles as she braces her hands against the door. "I bet that's something you never expected to say."

"I love missionary with you." I kiss her cheek, nipping at her neck before I add, "I love every position with you, wife."

"I love you, husband." She sighs. "You're my husband."

"Not yet," I say, positioning myself at her entrance. "Not until we consummate the union, Mrs. Gabaldon."

"Then we'd better get to consummating, Mr. Gabaldon," she says, moaning as I slide inside her slick, welcoming body, the one I know so well by now, but still cherish more with every passing day. "Yes, you feel so good. I love you so much."

"I love you too, butterfly," I say, taking her slow and as deep as the baby will allow. "Your vows were perfect."

"Yours, too," she says, pressing back against me as I glide forward. "They were so sweet and wonderful and made me wildly horny."

I laugh as I kiss her cheek again. "Everything makes you wildly horny. I *will* miss that part of being pregnant."

"I'll still be horny for you, baby. Always." She moans and presses back again, urging me to move faster. "I promise. Oh, yes, Gideon. There, just like that."

We come a few minutes later, first Sydney and then myself not long after, spiraling out into bliss that still feels so precious.

And I know it always will. I waited too long for this woman to take a single second with her for granted.

That's a promise I was made to keep, from this day until the last day I'm lucky enough to share my dream come true.

The End

about the author

Author of over forty novels, *USA Today* Bestseller **Lili Valente** writes everything from steamy suspense to laugh-out-loud romantic comedies. A die-hard romantic, she can't resist a story where love wins big. Because love should always win. She lives in Vermont with her two big-hearted boy children and a dog named Pippa Jane.

Find Lili at...
www.lilivalente.com

also by lili valente

The McGuire Brothers

Boss Without Benefits

Not Today Bossman

Boss Me Around

When It Pours (novella)

Kind of a Sexy Jerk

When it Shines (novella)

Kind of a Hot Mess

Kind of a Dirty Talker

The Virgin Playbook

Scored

Screwed

Seduced

Sparked

Scooped

Hot Royal Romance

The Playboy Prince

The Grumpy Prince

The Bossy Prince

Laugh-out-Loud Rocker Rom Coms

The Bangover

Bang Theory

Banging The Enemy

The Rock Star's Baby Bargain

The Bliss River Small Town Series

Falling for the Fling

Falling for the Ex

Falling for the Bad Boy

The Hunter Brothers

The Baby Maker

The Troublemaker

The Heartbreaker

The Panty Melter

Bad Motherpuckers Series

Hot as Puck

Sexy Motherpucker

Puck-Aholic

Puck me Baby

Pucked Up Love

Puck Buddies

Big O Dating Specialists
Romantic Comedies

Hot Revenge for Hire

Hot Knight for Hire

Hot Mess for Hire

Hot Ghosthunter for Hire

The Lonesome Point Series

(Sexy Cowboys)

Leather and Lace

Saddles and Sin

Diamonds and Dust

12 Dates of Christmas

Glitter and Grit

Sunny with a Chance of True Love

Chaps and Chance

Ropes and Revenge

8 Second Angel

The Good Love Series

(co-written with Lauren Blakely)

The V Card

Good with His Hands

Good to be Bad

Made in United States
Orlando, FL
14 November 2024

53898430R10205